WHITEOUT

R. S. Burnett grew up in the Falkland Islands and began his writing career on the local newspaper, *Penguin News*. He studied English at the University of Leicester and then worked as a journalist in London until he returned to the Falklands in 2021.

𝕏 @RobBurnett

WHITEOUT

R.S. BURNETT

HarperCollins*Publishers*

HarperCollins*Publishers* Ltd
1 London Bridge Street
London SE1 9GF

www.harpercollins.co.uk

HarperCollins*Publishers*
Macken House,
39/40 Mayor Street Upper,
Dublin 1
D01 C9W8
Ireland

First published by HarperCollins*Publishers* Ltd 2025
1

A catalogue record for this book is available from the British Library.

ISBN: 978-0-00-869643-6 (PB)
ISBN: 978-0-00-869644-3 (TPB)

This novel is entirely a work of fiction.
The names, characters and incidents portrayed in it are
the work of the author's imagination. Any resemblance to
actual persons, living or dead, events or localities is
entirely coincidental.

This book is set in Minion Pro by HarperCollins*Publishers* India

Printed and bound in Great Britain by Clays Ltd, Elcograf S.p.A.

This book contains FSC™ certified paper and other controlled
sources to ensure responsible forest management.

For more information visit: www.harpercollins.co.uk/green

1

This is the Wartime Broadcasting Service from the BBC in London. This country has been attacked with nuclear weapons. Communications have been severely disrupted, and the number of casualties and the extent of the damage are not yet known. We shall bring you further information as soon as possible. Meanwhile, stay tuned to this wavelength, stay calm and stay in your own homes.

Remember there is nothing to be gained by trying to get away. By leaving your homes you could be exposing yourselves to greater danger. If you leave, you may find yourself without food, without water, without accommodation and without protection. Radioactive fallout, which follows a nuclear explosion, is many times more dangerous if you are directly exposed to it in the open. Roofs and walls offer substantial protection. The safest place is indoors.

Make sure gas and other fuel supplies are turned off and that all fires are extinguished. If mains water is available, this can be used for fire-fighting. You should also refill all your containers for drinking water because the mains water supply may not be available for very long. Water must not be used for flushing lavatories. Use your water only for essential drinking and cooking purposes. Water means life. Don't waste it.

Make your food stocks last: ration your supply, because it may have to last for fourteen days or more. If you have fresh food in the house, use this first to avoid wasting it: food in tins will keep. If you live in an area where a fallout warning has been given, stay in your fallout room until you are told it is safe to come out. When the immediate danger has passed the sirens will sound a steady note. The 'all-clear' message will also be given on this wavelength.

Do not, in any circumstances, go outside the house. Radioactive fallout can kill. You cannot see it or feel it, but it is there. If you go outside, you will bring danger to your family and you may die. Stay in your fallout room until you are told it is safe to come out or you hear the 'all-clear' on the sirens.

We shall repeat this broadcast in two hours' time. Stay tuned to this wavelength, but switch your radios off now to save

2

```
your batteries until we come on the air
again. That is the end of this broadcast.
```

Rachael switched off the radio and checked the time on her watch. She set its alarm for just short of two hours, 1.58 p.m., then stepped towards the hatch and looked out of the tiny porthole into the pitch-black abyss that surrounded her. Not a hint of light. She knew it was far too early for that, but she couldn't help but hope it might come soon. Hope. What else did she have?

She tore her eyes away from the darkness, zipped up her purple fleece tighter around her neck to keep out the cold and sat down at the three-foot-by-two slab of lightweight plastic which functioned as her dinner table and desk. She flipped open her journal, picked up her pencil and began to write.

Date: 15 July
Mission day: 128
Temperature: −69 C
Windspeed: 63mph, gale force 10
I haven't cried yet.

I don't know why. I should be crying for you and for Izzy, but I haven't. Maybe because I'm worried that if I start, I won't be able to stop.

I don't feel anything. I'm just . . . numb. I can't believe you're both really gone. I don't feel it in my bones. This must all be some gigantic mistake.

It's now thirty-six days since last contact. I'm still receiving the BBC World Service message every two hours, but nothing more. The VHF radio still works, but because of my location I could only ever raise Station Z with that. And they're not answering. Maybe the rest of them succumbed to Guy's illness as well. Henriksen did say Zak was getting worse the last time I spoke to him. Or have they been caught up in all this somehow? But if they have, why haven't I?

One thing is clear: no one is coming for me.

But I won't linger on that thought – it's too horrifying.

I've tried raising McMurdo and Amundsen–Scott stations, but got nothing. Given my position this side of the mountain, I'm not likely to reach them even if they are listening, but I'll keep trying.

I've been trying the satphone as well, but that's getting no signal either. And that's the real kicker, Adam. That's the real smack in the face. Because there is nowhere on the planet that phone should not work. Nowhere. From the tiniest, most remote atoll in the Pacific, to the middle of the Sahara Desert, to the top of Mount Everest. Sure, if I can't reach Station Z on the radio that's one thing, but the satphone? The unit itself turns on, but it never finds a signal. It's as if the satellites just aren't there anymore. Maybe they've been destroyed too. Can a nuclear attack do that? It all sounds a bit Star Wars, but could they have been knocked out or something? It's not my area of expertise – and I suppose it doesn't matter either way. Not now.

I activated my emergency beacon after three days of no contact. Maybe I should have done it earlier, but – and this sounds a bit silly now I'm writing it down – I didn't want to overreact. Out here in deep field, in this perpetual darkness and cold, alone, you start to second-guess yourself. Question every thought. After arguing about it in my own head (and sometimes aloud – it's weird how much I've started talking to myself since I've been on my own), I activated the bloody thing. It flashed its little light, but I have no idea if it was able to connect with the satellite because flashing its little light was as far as it got. And obviously no one's turned up or contacted me, so either it didn't work, or there's no one out there to hear it.

It was the day after that I tried the old radio I found amongst the supplies I brought out with me. God knows who packed that – Zak, I guess – but the batteries were still good. I knew I was so far south here I was unlikely to pick anything up, but after playing with the dial I got *The Broadcast*. I think it must be being relayed from Station Z somehow.

But that's all I got. That's all I've heard for over a month now. The same announcement, every two hours. And nothing else.

Nowadays we're all used to being instantly contactable, wherever we are, twenty-four seven. We have our phones with us at all times, and next to the bed at night. And look at us – we can't bear to be away from them for more than two minutes. Communicating. Checking in, liking, tweeting, scrolling. Logged on. Plugged in.

I never liked that. Or rather, I never liked the idea of it. In reality of course I was just as addicted to the whole thing as everyone else. It was one of the reasons I loved coming down here so much. To get away from all that. And I never actually missed it when I was here. I loved the feeling of being disconnected for a while. Until now. Now I have nothing. No smart phone, no satphone, no people, no contact, nothing. Complete silence. Total isolation.

This all leads me to one conclusion. It's not one I'm keen to make, but as a scientist I know my personal feelings on the matter are neither here nor there. Evidence is what matters. Evidence is the only way to judge anything. That's why I'm here in the first place, isn't it, to gather evidence. And you *can't just decide to ignore evidence because you don't like what it tells you. In science, evidence is everything. And it's entirely, completely, 100 per cent dispassionate. It doesn't care about you, about your feelings, hopes or fears. It just is. And in this case, it is increasingly pointing to only one logical conclusion: that I may very well be one of the last people alive on earth.*

2

It was time to go outside. She couldn't tell what time it was from the natural light – there was none – but her watch told her she must. Routine. Rachael knew routine was vital if she stood any chance of keeping her sanity. It was a mantra that had been drummed into her over the course of her career. Routine would keep you safe, keep you sane, and keep you alive.

She glanced out of the porthole above her desk into the endless sea of black that surrounded her. She felt like she was drowning in it, as if the darkness was leaking into her little hut, ready to overwhelm her at any moment. The void was so vast, and her hut so tiny, like a little rowing boat on a mighty ocean. She wondered how long she could stay afloat like this – utterly alone, trapped and abandoned. She wanted to cry, to surrender herself to her dread, her heartbreak, her terror. But still the tears would not come, not even when she allowed herself to think what must have happened to Adam and her beloved Izzy.

She closed her eyes and forced herself to look away from the darkness. She took a deep breath and tried to root herself back in the present. After downing the last few drops of her instant coffee, she rinsed out her mug in the plastic tub she was using as a sink, and began the long process of getting dressed for deep field outdoor work in the middle of the austral winter. To the thermals and polar fleece she was already wearing she added a pair of waterproof trousers. Then she pulled on her fleece-lined boots, tied the laces and tightened the strap of the snow spikes on the bottom. A warm goose-down jacket came next, followed by a neck warmer, a face mask that made her look like a very colourful and well-insulated bank robber, goggles to keep the snow out of her eyes, and a woolly hat. Next came her red, windproof, high-vis overcoat – a garment issued to every person who set foot on this unique continent and known universally as 'Big Red'. For her hands she had a pair of finger gloves that fitted her tightly to allow her to work, and a big pair of mittens to go over those for when she was moving around. They had big fluffy tops which were essential for wiping the snot off your face before it could freeze in place and bring on frostbite. Next, she slipped the elasticated strap of her torch over her head, then pulled it down and adjusted the position of the light on her forehead so it pointed wherever she was looking. Lastly, she pulled up the hood of her Big Red. Every inch of her skin was covered.

She pulled out a plastic storage bin from underneath her bunk and snapped the lid open. Inside it was a rectangular box with a black bottom and orange top. It was about the size and shape of a small, carry-on suitcase and had a single wheel run off two arms that extended from the rear. A three-metre-long strap was hooked on at the front. A clasp around the top of the device held down a secondary part: a small screen, a little like an iPad, but much thicker and chunkier, and with a strap of its own. She unclasped this and pressed the button hidden in the top to start it up. A few moments later the screen flickered into life. A warning flashed, indicating the battery was running low. She would have to recharge it tonight, but she knew she'd have enough power left to complete today's work. She waited a few moments for the device to boot up, then looped the strap around her neck so the screen rested on her chest, allowing her to see it and keep her hands free.

She turned towards the door of her pod, twisted the handle upwards and prepared herself for the rush of extreme cold she knew would follow like a punch in the face. 'Here we go,' she said aloud as she pushed the hatch open and was hit with the same icy blast as she had been on every single day since the start of this expedition. This cold was truly extreme. Despite being a seasoned Antarctic veteran, she had never experienced cold like this: cold that snaked its way inside you in seconds and seemed to freeze over your very bones. Cold that overwhelmed you, stopped your hands from working properly and even slowed down the functions of your brain. Opening the door was, she imagined, what it would be like to be hit with a wall of liquid nitrogen on a daily basis. Every time she opened the hatch it reminded her of that scene in the *Terminator* film when the bad guy was covered with the stuff and was instantly frozen in place, before being shattered into a thousand fragments by a bullet from Arnie's shotgun.

She picked up the black and orange device and stepped outside, setting it down on the ice before pushing the hatch shut behind her to keep as much warmth as possible inside her little round hut.

The intense and debilitating cold wasn't her only enemy outside in the open: she also had to fight against the relentless wind that had been blowing without respite for well over a month now. It roared at her as she tried to move around, and howled and screamed with a ferocity she'd never encountered before. Although little fresh snow fell this far inland, it didn't feel that way in the blizzard as the wind snatched up the loose snow on the surface of the ice and used it to attack Rachael from all sides. In the worst moments her visibility reduced to less than a metre – in these whiteout conditions every direction looked the same: left, right, up, down, forwards and back: it was all just a blank wall of nothing. It was another way the conditions messed with her mind, making it difficult even to know if she was hiking up or downhill, let alone in the right direction. More than once she'd felt a surge of panic rising within her when she'd lost sight of her hut, despite being only a few hundred feet away. She'd taken the precaution of laying down an orange rope between the Apple and her survey site. She always tried to keep one hand on it while she was outside, knowing she could follow it back to the cabin even if the storm and the snow overwhelmed her senses.

She hooked the long strap from the black and orange device onto the carabiners attached to the loops sewn into the back of her Big Red, then pulled her goggles down and began to walk. As she felt her way along the rope, the wind picked up even more, forcing her to lean into it at almost a forty-five-degree angle. After half an hour of battling through the elements, she reached her survey site, a location predetermined by a combination of satellite and seismic data gathered by the team in Cambridge before she had even left the UK, and marked by a series of flag-topped poles she had planted herself some seven weeks earlier. The relentless wind had bent and bowed them all, but she'd hammered them deep into the ice and so far, they all remained in position. She checked the device was live, and then began walking slowly between the marker poles, a route that criss-crossed a section of the ice just over a kilometre wide and three kilometres long. As she did so she watched the screen as it recorded the measurements being taken from the machine she was dragging along behind her. The suitcase-shaped instrument was a ground-penetrating radar transmitter and antenna that emitted high-frequency electromagnetic energy waves down into the ice below it. Once the waves encountered a buried object or a material of a different density to the ice, they bounced back and were picked up by the antenna. This method allowed Rachael to measure the thickness of the ice beneath her survey site with incredible precision, without having to drill a single borehole. As she walked, the computer inside the device registered the figures on the screen, though it was almost impossible to read them clearly in the dark and the snow.

Once she reached the final marker, she paused for a moment to catch her breath – even walking slowly was exhausting in these conditions while wearing the layers of clothes required to avoid catching hypothermia – then turned and began the gruelling journey back to her hut. She walked with purpose through the gale and the blizzard, the cold slithering its way inside her many layers, finding the weak points in her polar armour and attacking them with icy precision as the wind buffeted her like a kite in a frozen tornado. She wanted to stop, to rest and get her breath back, but she was getting far too cold for that – already her hands and feet were going numb – so she pressed on, dreaming of the warmth of the cabin.

When she finally reached it she climbed inside and wrestled the hatch shut behind her, muffling the roar of the bitter and unrelenting wind. *Safety*. She closed her eyes in the relative quiet of the cabin as she leaned back against the door and caught her breath, then called out, 'Honey, I'm home!'

For a moment she was back in the hallway of their house in London. She could hear Adam calling to her from the kitchen, and the sound of Izzy giggling at something he was doing to make her laugh. She walked down the hall with the shopping bags and there they were: Izzy in her highchair at the table, Adam bouncing her cuddly Tigger doll in front of her.

Rachael dropped the bags on the table, kissed Izzy on the back of her head, then draped her arms around Adam, resting her head next to his, her chin on his shoulder.

'Hey you,' she said quietly into his ear. She could feel him relax into her embrace.

'Hey you,' he replied, reaching up with his arm and placing it over hers. He was still bouncing Tigger in front of a delighted Izzy with the other. 'She loves this thing.'

'I know – I tried to put her down without it last night and she cried bloody murder. Poor thing must be filthy but I don't know how I'm ever going to wash it if she won't sleep without it.'

Rachael stood up and began unpacking the shopping bags on the table. 'Huge queue, and only one poor girl on the checkout again.'

'I told you I would have gone.'

'No, no. It's fine. I fancied a walk – get out of the house, you know,' she said as she stacked up some tins of chopped tomatoes in the cupboard.

'Well how about we all go out this afternoon? Walk around the park. Feed the ducks. Izzy loves the ducks, don't you, Izzy,' he said, his voice going up in pitch as he addressed his daughter.

Rachael opened the fridge to put away the milk and yogurt. 'That would be nice – although I don't think we're supposed to feed the ducks anymore. They've put a sign up.'

'You're joking?'

'Or maybe you're just not supposed to feed them bread. I can't remember now.'

'Oh well, a walk then. Be nice to get Izzy out in the fresh air at least.'

Rachael nodded. 'She'll need to eat first. Let's try her on some of that parsnip. She loved the mashed potato yesterday.'

'I'll do it.' Adam brought his face down to Izzy's. 'Are you hungry, Isabella Mozzarella?'

She was reaching out for the Tigger doll that Adam was still

12

bouncing up and down in front of her. He bounced it up her arm and on top of her head, Izzy giggling in response.

Rachael stuffed the empty shopping bags into the cotton bag holder hanging on a hook on the back door, then walked back to the fridge and pulled out a bowl of mashed parsnip, grabbed a small plastic spoon from the drawer and put it down in front of Adam.

'Come on, baby girl, time for your lunch,' Adam said as he set the Tigger down on the table and picked up the spoon.

'That thing really is filthy,' Rachael said, nodding at the doll.

'We'll have to get another one and alternate them for washing,' Adam replied as he removed the wax paper covering from the bowl, scooped up some parsnip and opened his mouth wide to encourage Izzy to copy him.

Rachael smiled. 'Good idea,' she said as she watched him aeroplane a spoonful of beige puree into Izzy's waiting mouth.

She wanted so badly to stay here, to stay with her family, but she knew she had to face reality. She had to leave them again. She opened her eyes and looked around the tiny space of the hut. Everything was exactly as she had left it. The portholes were black and cold. The wind roared and howled outside the cabin.

Alone again.

3

Rachael busied herself to try to shake off her melancholy. She unhooked the GPR machine from her Big Red, then fired up her gas heater and began stripping out of her outdoor clothes. Despite the ferocious cold outside, the tiny cabin was well insulated and warmed up remarkably quickly once the heater was running. Within a few minutes she was wearing an old pair of jogging bottoms and a King's College hoodie, and was melting some fresh ice on the single-ring hob to make coffee. She noticed with alarm the flame flickering in and out as she waited for the ice first to melt, then boil. The gas canister must be nearly empty. She made a mental note to switch it over to the spare when she went out to the survey site tomorrow. It was her last bottle. She'd have to be frugal with it from now on, she thought ruefully. As soon as that canister was done, so was she. It was another dark thought she dare not linger on, so she poured the steaming hot water over the instant coffee granules in her mug and sat down at her workbench.

She opened her laptop, waited for it to boot up, then fired up the music player software and selected the only album she ever listened to anymore: Pink Floyd's *The Wall*. She'd been a fan since Adam introduced her to the band when they first began dating, but since her period of isolation had begun, something about the record resonated even more with her. Every track, every lyric, every strum of Dave Gilmour's guitar or Roger Waters' bass seemed to take on an intense new meaning when she listened to it all alone inside her tiny hut at the end of the world.

As the first track, 'In the Flesh?', began playing on the tinny laptop speakers, she began her work. She plugged the mobile GPR screen into the computer and downloaded the data she had collected, then began manually inputting the ice thickness numbers into a spreadsheet. The figures were alarming. The crack was widening. The data she was adding each day was proving that, and it was happening at a much faster rate than either she or Guy had predicted.

She pushed the laptop to one side, took out her journal, and began to write as the Floyd played on.

> *Date: 16 July*
> *Mission day: 129*
> *Temperature: –72C*
> *Windspeed: 67mph, gale force 10+*
> *Days since last contact: 37*
> *I'm back in from today's fieldwork. I think the storm's getting worse – it's getting harder and harder to walk, let alone work out there. I don't even really know why I'm still going out to record the data, but I need something to do. I can't just sit here ... waiting. It keeps my mind on something other than the pain of thinking too much about you and Izzy. When I'm not out there in the cold or working inside, I find myself lying on my bunk staring at the picture you slipped into my notepad – the one of you, me and Izzy on the day we brought her home from the hospital. God, I look a state! I'd hardly had any sleep for three days. She didn't come without a fight, did she?*
> *I lie in my sleeping bag, staring and staring at that picture*

for hours, looking at every detail: the wisps of white hair on her tiny head, the bags under my eyes, the sheer love radiating from yours. I drink it in greedily.

It's my last connection to you both. I look at the picture and pretend you're still out there, waiting for me. And I keep working. It's a reason to keep going, to stay alive.

I guess it's also that bloody sense of duty. I wonder where that comes from. It's what got me into this – at least partly. I was sent to do a job, and if nothing else I want to finish it. Even if no one will ever know.

There's no doubt about it now – the data proves Guy's theory. The crack is growing. The ice is getting thinner, the shelf is weakening. I knew that a month ago. I was even able to confirm it to Station Z on the radio. I think that was the last time I spoke to them. The last time I spoke to anyone.

God help us if it continues at this rate – or speeds up. The consequences don't bear thinking about. Well, they didn't before all this happened. Maybe it doesn't matter now. Either way, Guy was right. I know you might not want to hear that, but he was. And anyway, you really need to get over that. You always had that wrong. Me and him. That wasn't what our relationship was about.

It's still dark. I mean, of course it is, but I guess I didn't realize how unrelentingly dark it could be down here. There's nothing. The only light visible for hundreds of miles in any direction is from my own tiny cocoon. My little hut must look like a single bulb in a great black ocean – like a solitary Christmas tree light in the middle of the Atlantic.

And it <u>never</u> lets up. There's no respite. Not a single second. I haven't seen daylight since 22 May. Can you imagine that? No light, no sun, just perpetual darkness for months. Of course you tried to warn me. And of course I wouldn't listen *(classic you, classic me!). But I didn't realize how . . . what's the word? Oppressive? Yes, how oppressive it would be.*

And the cold! I've never seen temperatures like this. I know they've recorded lower at the pole, but I'm a long way from there. It's extraordinary. The blizzard blows and blows for weeks on end, and never seems to get tired. I've started to wonder if this extreme cold and these never-ending winds are the effects of the nuclear winter. Would it be happening this fast?

Still I suppose I shouldn't complain. It's bizarre to think, but in this situation, I'm actually the lucky one. Well, depending on how you look at it.

I've thought a lot about how it actually happened. Did you get warning? Did you try to run? Did you have any time to do anything? To prepare? Or was it a complete shock?

I mean, I know the potential was always there, lurking in the background of our lives, but everything was normal when I left – well, as normal as it has been for the past few years, anyway. I just can't understand how it could have come to this. Why didn't somebody see sense?

It's a bit like cancer, I guess. You never think it'll happen to you until it does. We've all been living in a world where nuclear war has been a possibility for so long, yet for some reason we can't imagine it actually happening in real life. It's like something out of a film.

I remember when we were learning about the Cuban Missile Crisis in school, I asked Mum what it was like living through it. She said she couldn't even remember it, so I asked Grandad Ray. He said all that stuff about people going mad, not turning up for work, thinking the world was about to be blown up was, in his considered words, 'a load of old bollocks'. He even dug out his old diary for me and we looked up the dates. On the day Kennedy went on TV and called out Khrushchev, Grandad's journal entry was just one line. It said: 'Got in a new line of so-called healthy cereal bars at the shop today. Don't think they'll catch on.'

I thought it was weird at first. But then, that's what people do, isn't it? They carry on. Whether there's an imminent nuclear war or not doesn't change the fact the baby is crying, or the bins need putting out, or the shop needs opening, or the tax return needs filling in. People carry on.

And who started it? Was it the Russians? North Korea? I keep wondering if you knew it was going to happen, or whether it was all a secret until it was too late.

I can't decide what would have been better – that you had some warning, some time to make your peace, make sure you were with Izzy, or that it came out of nowhere.

But even as I write that, I still can't believe you're both gone. Already it hurts so much, I can't imagine it getting worse. The pain feels like a black poison trying to creep into my heart, but I won't let it. <u>I won't.</u>

She set down her pencil, stopped the music with a click of her trackpad, stood up from her plastic desk and pressed the tiny side button on her digital watch to silence the alarm. Then she picked up the little black transistor radio from the shelf built into the curved wall of the capsule, and slid the switch to the 'on' position.

Silence.

She waited the usual two minutes, but still it didn't start. Where was it? She frowned and turned the volume wheel up, but there was still nothing. Where was it? Her heart rate quickened. Where was it?

She shook the radio as if she might jolt it into life. 'Please,' she said out loud. 'I'm not ready for this.'

18

Then there was a burst of static, and the familiar, comforting voice began speaking to her again.

```
This is the Wartime Broadcasting Service
from the BBC in London . . .
```

She let out a breath of relief and clung tightly to the radio, staring at it, as if she might somehow convey her presence through the airwaves. She mouthed along with the words as they were spoken: '. . . the number of casualties and the extent of the damage are not yet known. We shall bring you further information as soon as possible. Meanwhile, stay tuned to this wavelength, stay calm and stay in your own homes . . .'

Once it was finished, she clicked the radio off and repeated the ritual with her watch, setting the alarm for just shy of two hours from now.

'Stay in your own homes,' she said aloud, looking around her tiny cabin. Nicknamed an 'Apple hut' because it was red and spherical, it was a lightweight shelter used for deep field research work where something sturdier than a tent was required but building a full-sized station wasn't necessary or possible. Described by the manufacturer as being akin to a 'rigid tent', the insulated, fibreglass structures could be transported by helicopter or overland, and were designed as short-term accommodation for two people. They were really little more than survival shelters but this one had been Rachael's living quarters for almost two months now. Four square metres in floor space and two metres high at the top of the dome, it had two bunks, a workbench that doubled as a desk and a dinner table, what seemed like dozens of little cupboards for storage, and a single-ring gas stove for cooking next to the makeshift sink. A small heater powered by the same gas canister that ran the stove provided her warmth. Including the one set into the door, she had four portholes, though none, of course, was currently letting in any light.

She closed her eyes and was instantly back in her house in London, staring out the window into the dark of the night. Too tired to be awake, but unable to sleep. She remembered this specific night vividly. It was the night when nothing happened, but everything changed. Izzy's first birthday. They'd had a little party: cake, bubbles, her parents and Adam's. Everyone around the table singing 'Happy Birthday' to the bewildered child.

Rachael knew she should have been happy. She knew what she was meant to be feeling: the proud mother with a healthy daughter, a loving husband, a beautiful home, surrounded by her loved ones. And she was, on a logical, intellectual level. But something was missing. And she'd felt so ashamed. Why wasn't she satisfied?

For a time she'd wondered if she was suffering from postnatal depression, but she had no problem bonding with Izzy, and her feelings didn't seem to fit the list of symptoms she'd read about. And while she couldn't quite pin down the cause of her dissatisfaction, she didn't feel depressed. Just . . . what? Bored? Lonely? Tired?

And then when the parents had all left and they were clearing up the plates and the glasses, Adam had put his arm around her as she stood rinsing dishes in the sink, the way he had a thousand times before. Only this time it was different. And it terrified her. She couldn't tell whether he noticed or not, but she felt it. She felt herself flinch at his touch. And that was that. A tiny movement, but one that meant so much. Later she'd looked down at him sleeping soundly in their bed and felt a confusing mixture of guilt, fear and love, then looked back into the black of the long dark night.

The sound of the ferocious polar wind howling outside in

the darkness brought her back to the present. She could hear it whipping up the loose snow and hurling it at her little cocoon, like a pack of baying wolves at the door trying to claw their way in. The storm was definitely getting worse. She sat down at the desk and picked up her pencil, before clicking the music back on. She almost laughed out loud when David Gilmour began singing 'Goodbye Blue Sky' as she gazed out of the perfectly black porthole above her desk.

Have you ever had one of those dreams where you wake up, get out of bed, have a shower, get dressed, eat your breakfast and go to work? All very boring and normal stuff, but then it turns out to be a dream when you do wake up. Someone once told me that was a classic sign of stress: your brain is so keen to get on and solve the problems you have, it's already preparing for the day to start before it actually does.

Well, I have those every night. In my dreams I still have contact with Station Z. I speak to them twice a day on the radio, as per the regs, and Guy is here with me. You and Izzy are waiting for me back home. Everything is normal. The trip is going fine. Although there is one strange thing I've noticed: whenever I dream about being here it's always daylight. And not just daylight, but bright, midday sun daylight. I guess I must be missing it.

Maybe I'm starting to go a little bit mad. That can happen, when you're on your own for a long time. Probably doesn't even really take that long. Have you ever spent two months completely alone? Two weeks? Two days even? They say isolation is the purest form of torture. They use it as a punishment in prison. 'The hole'. I never saw the point in that, the cruelty of it. I do now.

I did an inventory last night. Obviously I have nothing fresh. God, what I would do for a banana or an orange right now. But I have plenty of cereal protein bars (looks like you were wrong about that, Grandad Ray!), six full boxes of porridge packets, loads of 9 Bars, four boxes of Green and Black's dark chocolate, plenty of coffee and powdered cream, and twelve boxes of freeze-dried dinner packets. By my reckoning I have enough food to last for at least another six weeks, maybe two months if I start rationing. After that – well, after that, I'm in deep shit, to put it bluntly.

Of course, I have all the water I'll ever need. As long as I have the means to melt it. I've also got plenty of diesel for the generator, so I'll still have power.

So I'm going to stick to the plan: stay here in the Apple.

Stay calm and stay in your own homes.

That's what surviving in the Antarctic is all about. You have a plan and you stick to it. It's when people start going off half cock that things go wrong. That's what you always say. So that's what I'm going to do. I have shelter, warmth, food and water. I'll sit tight.

If you go outside, you will bring danger to your family and you may die.

I don't have much choice. Leaving the hut now would be suicide, especially in this storm. I'm ninety-odd miles away from the nearest station, and between me and the base is a crevasse field. And I have no transport. My Snowcat vehicle broke down on my way here. I had to do the last eight miles to the Apple on foot. Thank God it wasn't any further or I never would have made it.

I've done plenty of deep field work over the years, but trying to reach Station Z on my own, on foot, in these conditions – in this darkness . . . I wouldn't get ten miles. The choice is really no choice at all: stay here and survive, or go out into the unknown and die. So I'll stay where I am. This tiny hut is at once my prison and my cocoon.

Remember there is nothing to be gained by trying to get away. By leaving your homes you could be exposing yourselves to greater danger.

That's what I should have done. I should have stayed at home. You asked me to but I wouldn't listen. I could have been there with you and Izzy. I could have been there at the end, if that's what it came to. I should never have left.

If you go outside, you will bring danger to your family and you may die.

I should have been there. We could have been toget—

She couldn't finish the word because at that moment the cabin lights went out, plunging her into total darkness.

4

Izzy was crying again. Rachael put her coffee mug down next to the squawking baby monitor on the perfectly gnarled bespoke kitchen table and made her way down the tastefully decorated hallway of her Victorian terrace, then up the stairs and down the landing to Izzy's room at the back of the house. She was standing up in her cot, fingers clutched tightly onto the rails as she wailed.

'What's all this shouting about, then?' Rachael said in a soothing voice.

'Mama, up,' Izzy managed through her tears.

Rachael leaned in and picked her up, gently bouncing Izzy up and down on her chest. She felt her nappy, but it was dry. She glanced at the big clock on the wall with the rubber duck background: just gone three o'clock. She shouldn't be hungry yet.

'What is it, sweetheart?' Rachael asked.

'Mama,' was the only reply she got.

Rachael sighed and held her daughter close as she walked with her back down the stairs and into the kitchen. Izzy had been active and restless in the womb, and not much had changed since birth. Rachael knew she wanted nothing, except not to be left alone. She had a clean nappy and wasn't hungry, but she wouldn't fall asleep on her own now. She was already showing signs of her personality – and she didn't like being alone. She liked company. Voices. People.

Rachael checked her coffee. Cold. She flicked the radio on with one hand and poured the coffee down the sink.

'Tensions rose today in the ongoing trade war between the United States and China as the president's new tariff on Chinese steel imports provoked anger in Beijing, with the promise of reprisals that the Chinese government insisted would "damage" the US economy.'

Rachael refilled the kettle and set it back on its stand as she continued to try to calm Izzy. The voice from the radio seemed to be helping.

'But as our US correspondent Nikita Duggan reports, the stand-off with China is just the latest in a long line of controversial trade policies from the president which have been branded "protectionist" and "short-sighted" by critics, though White House officials insist the president is simply delivering on his election promises to put American workers first.'

As the kettle boiled, Rachael poured the hot water into the mug, added a splash of milk, and began to stir. She glanced at the expensive, almost professional-level coffee machine that stood gleaming on the kitchen counter and felt mildly guilty that she was making instant instead of using it, like she was driving an old banger when she had a brand-new Ferrari on the driveway. But it seemed such a waste to use the real coffee and the fancy machine when she hardly ever got to finish a cup these days anyway. And the truth was, after years of habit, she actually preferred the instant. Though she didn't have the heart to admit that to Adam – not after he had so proudly bought her the machine and all the related bits and pieces to go with it.

'That's right, Owen. Not content with a failing relationship with the EU, a positively hostile one with the OPEC nations and now deepening worries about his dealings with the Chinese, the president is facing another crisis tonight after a coalition of Central and South American countries reacted to his latest tariffs on their imports by threatening to cut off their oil supply to the US if he does not reconsider.'

Izzy was finally beginning to settle, but Rachael daren't put her down, even for a moment, as she knew the crying would resume and the arms would be outstretched, desperate for her mother's touch. If anything, she was starting to get even more clingy – though all Rachael's parenting books said that was normal for her age.

'The US currently relies on Mexico and Venezuela for almost twenty per cent of its oil, but after the president pushed ahead with his policy of building a wall along the US/Mexican border, along with his mass-deportation programme for Mexican immigrants and his high tariffs on manufacturing imports, the two countries have said they will divert their oil exports elsewhere if his administration does not think again.'

Rachael took a sip of her coffee and glanced down to see if Izzy had drifted off to sleep. Her heavy eyelids were starting to droop, but as ever, she was fighting to stay awake.

'Combined with the OPEC blockade that's been in place since May, it means the US is at risk of losing a massive thirty-five per cent of its oil supply. And a national energy crisis like that is something that perhaps even this president cannot survive. Join us at six this evening when we'll be hosting a panel discussion on the latest crisis, live. In other news, there are reports of more skirmishes today on the Indian/Pakistan border—'

The doorbell rang with a loud and invasive trill. Izzy opened her eyes wide in response as she sensed activity. Rachael sighed at the thought of another ruined nap for her daughter and made her way down the hall to the front door. She swung it open to find Guy Barnard standing on the front step. It was early

February and the wind was icy but as usual, he was wearing just a pair of shorts, an old Wales rugby shirt and flip-flops, with a tatty rucksack slung over one shoulder. His beard was perhaps slightly more unkempt than usual – and a little greyer than the last time she'd seen him – but other than that Rachael thought he was looking as fit and lean as ever, despite the fact he was approaching sixty.

'You busy?' he asked, as the crying returned and Izzy kicked her lungs into top gear.

'Well, she's awake now, so you might as well come in.'

'Top banana.' He smiled as he rubbed his hands together and closed the door behind him. 'Is there a coffee on the go?'

She led him through to the kitchen at the back of the house.

'Nice place,' he said, taking in his surroundings.

'Don't patronize me,' she said wearily. 'You hate it.'

He laughed, a big throaty laugh that shook all six foot two of his big frame. 'I just never pictured you in a place like this: three beds, two baths and a Volvo out the front.'

'It's a Prius, actually.'

'Of course.'

'It's called a normal life,' she said as she flicked the kettle on, once again ignoring the fancy coffee machine. 'You should try it,' she smiled.

'Not on your nelly,' he said as he dropped his rucksack down next to the table. 'How's, umm . . . Aaron?'

'Adam.'

'Yeah, Adam. How's Adam?'

'He's fine, Guy.'

She spotted a flash of silver hung round his neck on a chain. His St Christopher pendant. Rachael knew it had been a gift from his first wife, Nancy. She hadn't seen him wear it in years. It could only mean one thing. 'What about you – how's Barbara?'

He looked away. 'She's fine. Hunky-dory. Tickety-boo.'

'Don't lie to me.'

He met her gaze. 'She's moved out. We're taking a break. It's, uh, complicated. Isn't that what people say?'

'Oh Guy, I'm so sorry.'

'It's not her fault. I know I'm hard to live with.'

'It might help if you were ever there, you know.'

'That's the secret, is it?'

'There is no secret, you should know that by now.'

'I suppose so. But never mind all that. This must be little . . .'

'Izzy.'

'Hello, Izzy,' Guy said hesitantly as he leaned in towards her in the way people do to try to register their presence with babies and small children.

'Thanks for waking her up, by the way.' Rachael handed her to him. 'You got her going, so you can have a go at getting her to stop,' she said.

He took her uncertainly as he sat down at the table. 'I don't really . . . I mean, I never had children.'

'She won't bite, but fair warning: she might slobber on you. Or possibly worse.'

Guy frowned as he tried bouncing her on his knee in an attempt to stop her crying. Rachael smiled inwardly. The fearless Guy Barnard rendered helpless by a tiny child. She enjoyed his awkwardness – a small measure of revenge for his having woken Izzy up.

She busied herself at the counter making his coffee. 'Still milk and three, I take it?'

He nodded. He was still gently bouncing Izzy on his knee and, to Rachael's great surprise, it seemed to be working. *Damn him*. Damn him for taking to this as naturally as he did everything else.

28

'So what do you want? Or did you come round to offer yourself as a babysitter?'

He was making a funny face by raising his eyebrows and pursing his lips as he looked at Izzy. She was smiling in response. And she'd stopped crying altogether. *God, he's infuriating,* she thought.

'Nope.' He looked up at her. 'I need you to help me save the world, Rach.'

She rolled her eyes. 'I don't have time for this.'

'Just listen, will you? It's the US. They're going to drill for oil in Antarctica.'

Rachael put down her mug. 'Where?'

'The Ross Shelf – McMurdo. Where they've been doing the testing. Only this time it's not exploration – it's extraction. The whole works.'

'They can't! What about the treaty?'

'You think this president cares about treaties? He's already withdrawn from the Paris Climate Agreement, the Trans-Pacific Partnership, a load of trade deals – he doesn't give a toss.'

'But they can't!' she repeated. 'The treaty will be ripped up. The Russians will follow, Argentina will be next – it'll be a gold rush. The whole place will be torn up and ruined.'

'It could be worse than that. We've continued the research you started. The latest figures show the pace of ice loss has tripled since 2012.'

She came back to the table with two steaming mugs of coffee. 'Tripled? That's even worse than we forecast.'

'Two hundred billion tons lost every single year.'

'I know the sums.'

'I know you do, that's why I need you.'

She sighed. 'Not this again.'

'This is important, Rachael.'

'I know it is. But so is my family. We made a decision. I promised Adam. Izzy only turned one two months ago. And you've got plenty of good people. Simon knows his stuff, so does Alexi – and Sasha.'

'Yeah, they're all good, but you lived and breathed all this for years, Rach. No one knows more about this than you do.'

'I've told you already, I'm not coming back to work, Guy. I can't.'

He smiled at Izzy and took a sip of his coffee. 'I thought you'd say that.'

'Well it's true.'

'You know what else is true? Every minute we sit and debate this, the melting continues. It's happening. It's really happening – and it's about to get a lot worse. In a couple of days it'll be announced. Joint release from us, the Argentinians, New Zealand, Australia, Russia and the Koreans.'

'What will?'

He opened and closed his mouth like a fish as he continued to hold Izzy's attention. 'The Ross Shelf.' He looked up at Rachael. 'A big one is about to calve off.'

'How big?'

'About four trillion tons. Twenty-three thousand square kilometres – or, if you prefer, about the size of Wales.'

Rachael's eyes widened. 'Jesus,' she said quietly. 'That's the biggest yet. What are the Americans saying?'

'The usual bullshit. "Not linked to climate change, natural evolution, blah, blah, blah."'

She rolled her eyes. 'Fake news.'

'Exactly,' he laughed. 'Thing is, this time they may be right.'

'What do you mean?'

'Well, they may be *half* right. I don't think this is just an effect of climate change. I think this is related to their other recent activities.'

'The drilling?'

He nodded. 'The drilling.'

Guy's distraction techniques were wearing off. Izzy's face creased up in a way Rachael had seen a thousand times before. Seconds later she began crying again.

'She's probably hungry.' Rachael took her from Guy and sat her down in the highchair next to the table, then fetched a small yogurt pot from the fridge and began feeding the contents to Izzy, who did indeed stop crying the moment food was available.

'So what's going on?' Rachael said as she scooped a stray bit of yogurt from Izzy's cheek.

Guy undid the toggle from his rucksack and pulled out an A4 manilla envelope, then slipped the contents out onto the table. 'Have a look at these,' he said as he fanned them out for her.

She looked from one to the other as she waited for Izzy to swallow. 'Satellite thermal images of . . . the Ross Shelf?'

He pointed her to one specific sheet. 'Look at this. What do you see?'

Rachael studied it closely. 'Wait,' she said, 'what's this?' She pointed to a red line that snaked its way along the edge of the shelf at the point where it joined the land mass.

'That's a weak spot in the ice, where it's thinning.' He pulled out another sheet of paper. 'This is a satellite photograph of the same area. And here are some close-ups.'

'When were these taken?'

'Last week.'

'Before or after the thermal images?'

'After.'

Rachael frowned. 'But that doesn't make any sense,' she said. 'The photographs don't show any sign of cracking at all. Not even any crevasses opening up along there.' She looked up at Guy. 'How can that be?'

He pulled out two more sheets. 'This thermal image is from three months ago, and this one' – he tapped one of the pages – 'is from two weeks ago.'

Rachael could see instantly the second had a much thicker red line than the first. 'So it's getting worse?' she said as she continued to feed Izzy.

'Much worse. And quickly.'

'But how come the satellite pictures aren't showing anything?'

Guy said nothing for a moment and took another sip of his coffee.

'Unless,' Rachael said, her mind spinning into action. 'Unless it's . . . happening from the *bottom up*?' she said, frowning in confusion even as she said it, holding the little plastic yogurt spoon in mid-air. She looked at Guy, who slowly nodded.

'The bottom up? You're serious?' She searched her memory. 'We've never seen that before.'

'That's what we thought, until I talked to Bob Shafer over at Ohio. You remember when that berg calved off from the Pine Island Glacier back in 2015?'

'Yeah, what was it, two hundred and fifty square miles? The one that caught us all out – no one saw it coming.'

'Bob's team went back and checked the thermal imagery, trying to see how no one spotted it,' Guy said. 'And guess what?'

'The crack formed from the bottom up?'

'Bingo.' Guy pulled out another folder of photographs from his bag and spread them out on the table.

'It looks exactly like the Ross Shelf ones,' Rachael said.

'Precisely – only this is on a much, *much* larger scale.'

'So what the hell's going on here?'

'I have a theory.'

'I thought you might.'

'So we've been recording the melting ice on Ross for years, right? You did a lot of it yourself.'

She nodded, and scooped out another spoonful of yogurt.

'And it's been getting particularly bad where the ice shelf meets the land mass itself, this side of the Transatlantic Mountain range.' He pointed to a spot on the photograph. 'It's precisely on that line that they did the exploratory drilling last year – well, one end of it, at McMurdo Sound. Up and down, hole after hole, trying to locate the biggest wells they can then drill commercially.'

Rachael quickly connected the dots. 'And the seismic activity of the drilling is exacerbating the structural weaknesses where the ice is already melting.'

'Exactly.'

'But that means – if you're right – that means . . . Jesus . . . the whole thing could go.' She looked up at him.

He stared back at her as he let the realization sink in.

'Christ, we've never even modelled that, have we?'

'We have now,' he said grimly.

'What would the sea level rise be?'

Guy took a pencil from his bag and turned over one of the satellite printouts. Starting at the bottom left corner of the paper, he drew a diagonal line at a forty-degree angle to the bottom, about ten centimetres long. 'So this is the rise over the last thirty years,' he said. 'With the X axis time, and the Y axis the mean sea level rise.'

She nodded. 'About eight centimetres since, what, 1990?'

'Right.'

Then he took the pencil and continued the line almost straight up, until he ran out of paper.

Rachael looked at the paper, then at Guy, a look of shock on her face.

'Exactly,' he said.

'But that must be, what, four, five metres?'

'We could be looking at a rise in sea levels of up to six metres,' Guy said.

'In how long?'

'Could be five years. Could be two. Could be even less. Remember Larsen-B? Once it started, that went in less than a month. If the Ross Shelf goes, all bets are off – there will be nothing stopping all the billions and billions of tons of ice that it's currently holding back from slipping into the sea.'

'The fallout would be catastrophic,' Rachael said quietly as she thought through the implications. 'Flooding, migrant crises, famine, disease . . . war.' She shook her head. 'Can it be stopped?'

Guy winced. 'Our modelling shows that it can be – but only if there's no further drilling. If there is, then we're buggered.'

'When are they due to drill again?'

'Soon. They were thrilled with the exploratory work they've been doing. Positively gleeful. There's oceans of it down there, so they want to start as soon as they can. Next summer, if possible.'

'How can we stop it?' Rachael scraped the last of the yogurt from the pot and offered it up to Izzy.

'Well, they have to get a vote past the Senate first.'

'Why?'

'Because drilling with commercial rather than research intent means breaking the Antarctic Treaty, and the president can't break an international binding agreement unilaterally – he needs Congress to sign off on it.'

'So what does that mean for us?'

'We've got a friendly senator who's leading the opposition charge. The Democrats will oppose, but there aren't enough of them to win. But I have a few contacts in Washington, and the word is we might be able to persuade a few Republicans to come over. We'd only need three to win the vote.'

'And how are you going to do that?'

He put his coffee mug down, took her hand, and looked right into her eyes. 'That's what I need you for.'

5

Rachael knew the generator had failed. It was the only explanation for the blackout. And in that instant she felt a surge of panic shoot its way up her spine – she knew her chances of survival had just dropped dramatically. Was this it – the beginning of the end? 'No,' she said aloud. 'Not now. Not yet. I'm not ready,' she shouted. 'I'm not ready!'

She tried to work out why it had stopped running: it was surely too early for it to have run out of diesel, which meant it must have suffered some kind of mechanical failure, and the chances of her having either the expertise, the tools or the parts to fix it were somewhere between slim and none. Nonetheless, she had to try.

She felt her way to her bunk, then reached down and pulled out the head torch she kept stowed beneath it. She flicked it on, bringing light back to the confines of the cabin, then slipped it over her head. She then began the lengthy process of getting dressed for going outside as her battery-powered laptop continued playing Pink Floyd. The foreboding beat of 'Empty Spaces' pumped out from the speakers as she pulled on her fleece and Gore-Tex trousers, laced up her boots and zipped up her goose-down jacket by torchlight. Once dressed and ready for battle, she pulled out one of the storage boxes underneath her bunk and took out a pair of pliers which she tucked into the pocket of her Big Red. She was ready. She took a deep breath, and pushed open the hatch.

A wall of icy cold slammed into her face, and the howling wind pushed and pulled at her as she battled to shut the door behind her. She bent forward and forced her way through the blizzard to the generator shed: a converted, twenty-foot-long shipping container, which stood just ten yards from the Apple hut. Once she'd cleared enough of the accumulated snow from around the door to be able to move it, she yanked down the handle, dragged it wide open, stepped inside, then hauled it closed behind her. She examined the generator for signs of any obvious problem but, finding nothing, she began the process of re-starting it. She talked herself through the procedure as she went. 'Check fuel pump. Turn the choke tap to "full". Watch the pressure gauge, and then hit the starter button.' She held her breath, said a short, silent prayer, and pressed the orange button on the side of the machine.

Nothing.

She turned the fuel pump back and forth once, and tried the starter button again. 'Come on,' she hissed as it made a weak effort at turning over. She held the button down but soon it was silent again. Dead.

'Why won't you work!' she shouted. She kicked the machine twice in succession as if it might suddenly roar back to life, but it sat, silent and maddeningly motionless.

She tried not to panic. Panic was how you made mistakes. Panic was how people died in situations like this. 'Think,' she told herself. She knew it couldn't be out of fuel already, she had only topped it up a few days ago. Or was it last week – or the week before? She was finding it difficult to nail down details like that in her own mind, and without going back to check her journal she couldn't be sure. Using the light from her head torch she found a jerry can of diesel in the far corner of the shed. She unscrewed the fuel filler cap on the generator and lifted the can up to begin pouring the liquid in. She knew she had to be extremely careful – the specialist fuel that had to be used in these extreme temperatures was so toxic it would burn you as soon as it touched your skin. She had seen it happen once, to a young first-timer at Rothera. The burns were so bad he had to be medevacked out on the first available flight and ended up needing a skin graft. She could still hear his screams if she closed her eyes.

But Rachael didn't have any such safety net, so she acted with extreme caution as she hoisted the can up onto her shoulder. Despite the cold, the combination of lifting up the heavy diesel can and the terror of the liquid burning her skin meant she was sweating inside her Big Red and she was breathing in quick, short breaths. She took a moment to steady herself – one slip and she would be covered in the corrosive fuel – and then slowly tipped the can up to the filler pipe. 'Easy does it,' she said as she tilted the can at a greater angle. 'Easy . . .' Nothing came out. She frowned in confusion. That couldn't be right – it was too heavy to be empty. She tipped it up further. Still nothing. She shook the can gently, but heard nothing. As the wind whipped under the door where she had cleared the snow and gave her a momentary blast of cold air, she realized with a rising sense of disbelief that the diesel in the can and the generator itself must have frozen. 'It can't be,' she whispered.

She carefully lowered the can and sat it down on the metal floor. An old crowbar was propped up against the wall next to the generator. She picked it up and inserted it inside the jerry can, then pulled it back out. It was now coated in a thick gel. 'Jesus,' she said as she examined it in the torchlight. She knew this diesel had been specially treated with anti-gelling and anti-microbial agents which would normally keep it in liquid form, even in the extreme cold of the Antarctic winter. But apparently this was no normal Antarctic winter. She checked two more cans and got the same result.

There was no way she would be getting the generator started again until the temperature rose enough for the diesel to liquefy, so she stowed the fuel cans, pulled her goggles back down over her eyes, and walked out into the cold, heaving the container door shut behind her.

When she got to the Apple, she walked around to the back and took out the pliers from her pocket. She turned the gas supply to the 'off' position, and then used the pliers to unscrew the metal fixing on the hose from the tank. Within just a few seconds her fingers were so cold she couldn't feel them at all. As she fumbled with the pliers her hands felt like two inanimate blocks of ice on the end of her arms, completely disconnected from her brain.

With great difficulty she removed the hose and then began screwing it into the valve on the second tank. Her fingers burned with the cold but she knew she had to complete the job or she would freeze to death within hours, even inside the Apple. With her reluctant fingers slowing her down it took an age to finish but eventually she was satisfied it was on tight, and she slipped the pliers back into her pocket, turned the supply tap on, and hurried back inside the hut. She pulled the hatch back into place to shut out the wind and was breathing hard as she leaned against the door for a moment while she waited for her heart rate to slow down. She shoved her hands underneath her armpits to try to warm them up, and assessed her situation. She was back inside her cocoon for now. Her fuel supply was now unusable – at least until it got a little warmer, so she'd be without electricity until that happened. Even then, she had no idea if the generator would fire back up, or whether the frozen fuel had clogged it up for all eternity. Only time and rising temperatures would tell. Without power, she had only the light of her torch – for as long as the battery lasted – and no way of charging her laptop, the GPR device, her VHF radio or satphone. She tried to remember where her emergency stash of candles were, as in the darkness of the hut Pink Floyd continued, belting out 'Don't Leave Me Now' from her laptop.

Without knowing when, or even if, she might get the generator back up and running, Rachael knew she had to act quickly. She took out two USB pen drives from a plastic storage tub and downloaded all her research, all her data, the 3D animations and the spreadsheets onto both of them. She slipped one into her rucksack, and the second into an internal zip-up pocket in her fleece. Then she cut the music and powered down the laptop to save the battery. She stowed the GPR machine under her bunk to get it out of the way, and as she was snapping the lid back on the storage case the beeping from her watch reminded her it was time to turn on the radio.

She began her now familiar routine; the routine that was so important to her solitary existence, where day was as dark as night and the only external stimuli were the ceaseless wind and that single, repetitive broadcast. She had come to cling to the radio message like a drowning person would cling to a lifebelt in a storm. It was her last connection with the world and now her entire life revolved around it. She planned her work, her eating, her sleeping, her essential maintenance, and her journal writing around it. It was human. It was contact. It was *something*.

She clicked on the little radio – relieved that it ran on batteries and not mains power – and set it back down on the shelf. She was always careful to turn it on at least a minute before it started, lest she miss a single second of the BBC voice. And yet for every second she waited for it to start, she fretted that today might be the day it never came. She wasn't ready to deal with that.

The man reading out the message sounded familiar. He was clearly a well-used BBC radio presenter, though he didn't identify himself in the recording. One of the newsreaders probably, but she couldn't tell which one. His familiarity was a comfort. His authoritative voice and perfect diction had an air of 'everything will be all right' to it. She imagined him sitting in a recording booth with a nice cup of tea as he delivered his devastating news.

```
This is the Wartime Broadcasting Service
from the BBC in London. This country has
been attacked with nuclear weapons . . .
```

She turned off her head torch and lay down on her bunk to listen in the darkness, as had become her custom. She mouthed along with the words, trapped in her own tiny, dark, frozen world. She knew each one of them by now. She knew each pause, each tiny crackle of the recording, the timbre of his voice over each vowel sound.

When it finished, she stood up, turned her head torch back on, clicked the radio off and set her alarm for one hour and fifty-eight minutes.

Then she picked up the portable VHF radio set from the shelf next to her desk, switched on the power and found the correct wavelength.

'This is Graphite Peak calling Station Z. Graphite Peak calling Station Z. Come in, over.'

She paused for a good thirty seconds as she allowed time for a response, then she repeated her call.

Again a pause. She depressed the transmit button again. 'This is Graphite Peak calling Station Z. Daily radio check number two, daily radio check number two from Graphite Peak. Come in Station Z.'

This time she allowed a full minute to elapse before repeating the message.

There was no reply. The airwaves were as empty as the black nothingness outside her porthole. She turned the VHF radio off and stowed it back on the shelf, then picked up the satellite phone that was placed next to it. She turned it on and the small green screen came to life. She held it close to her face as she studied it intently, watching the tiny aerial graphic and the spinning electronic wheel next to it, as the words 'SEARCHING FOR SIGNAL' flashed on and off. Maybe today would be the day. Maybe today it would work. Maybe she would be speaking to someone in a matter of seconds. Maybe this whole thing was a mistake and she would be rescued any day now. The wheel stopped. The flashing stopped. The words changed. 'NO SIGNAL.'

Her heart dropped. She'd carried out the routine thirty-seven times already with the same result, but every time she did, a tiny nugget of hope was born, deep within her. And every time she found nothing, the nugget died, only to somehow regrow again by the following day.

She put the satphone back on the shelf and turned her attention to food. She selected a silver packet of freeze-dried chicken dhansak with rice from the box she kept next to the hob. All she had to do was boil some water, pour it in, and then eat directly from the packet. She took her saucepan from the hook, set it down on the hob, then turned on the gas supply and pressed down on the button that emitted an electric spark to ignite the gas.

The moment she did she saw a flash of orange and felt an incredible, scorching heat before she was thrown violently backwards against the opposite wall of the hut. She cried out in pain as her head snapped back against something – a shelf, a handle, a cupboard – then it all went black.

6

'What's for dinner?' Adam asked as he gave her a perfunctory peck on the cheek and hung his jacket on the back of a kitchen chair. Tall, with a naturally pale complexion and light brown hair that he had kept in the same short, spiky style for as long as Rachael had known him, Adam was slender to the point where he found it difficult to buy trousers long enough to fit him without being loose at the waist, and somehow his jackets always looked half a size too big for his frame.

Rachael stood at the sink rinsing out jars and bottles ready for recycling. 'There's some leftover chicken.'

He loosened his tie and pulled open the fridge. 'Where's Izzy?'

'She's upstairs. I finally got her to sleep.'

He grabbed a bottle of orange juice from the door of the fridge and began gulping it down. 'I'll go and kiss her goodnight.'

'No, Adam.' She turned to face him. 'Please don't. It took me hours to get her off. I can't deal with her waking up again.'

He looked deflated, but said nothing. He drained the last of the juice from the bottle and tossed it into the bin near the back door. She sighed, walked over to retrieve it, then began rinsing it out to go with the others.

He spotted two coffee cups left on the kitchen table. 'You had visitors?'

'Just one,' she said. 'Guy popped round.'

'Guy?'

Rachael could see Adam trying not to let his displeasure show. 'What did he want?'

'Things are bad, Adam.'

'What do you mean?'

'Down south. The Americans are going to drill for oil. Guy thinks the whole Ross Shelf could go. There's a massive fault line developing – where they did the exploration drilling.'

'Christ, the whole thing?'

She nodded.

'How big is Ross?'

'Almost two hundred thousand square miles. About the size of France.'

'Jesus. What happens if it goes?'

'Disaster. Sea levels will rise by something like five or six metres.'

'Bloody hell. So what's Guy going to do?'

She paused for half a beat. 'He's leading a team down there. Collect the data, try to stop them drilling. He needs a ground team to corroborate the satellite data.'

Adam sighed. 'And he wants you.'

It was half question, half statement, and Rachael's silence merely confirmed it.

'And you want to go?'

'He says they need me.'

'He would say that.'

Rachael tried to ignore his tone. 'Adam, this is massive. And we've only got one shot at stopping this, we need to get it right first time.'

'But there are others. There are plenty of researchers he could take. Look, Rach, don't get me wrong: you're great at what you do. There's no one better. But that doesn't mean there isn't someone else who can go on the trip. Won't they need someone back here, analysing or something?'

'I'd need to be there, on the ground.' She dried her hands on a tea towel and leaned against the sink, as if for support. She knew this was going to be a difficult conversation, for all sorts of reasons, and she didn't want to be having it. But there was no choice now.

'Why?'

'You know what it's like down there: one of a thousand different things could go wrong. I'd need to be there when it did. If we're going to get the data we need, I'll have to make decisions on the fly – adapt, react. I can't do that from twelve thousand miles away.'

'When's he going?'

'Next month.'

'Next month?! Not much notice, is it?'

'It's then or never. Next summer will be too late.'

'And for how long?'

'Four or five months.'

'Five *months*?' His face contorted with shock and disbelief. 'What about Izzy? You want to leave her? For five *months*?'

'She's almost fifteen months old now. Plenty of mothers go back to work sooner than that.'

'Yes, but they don't abandon their children and go halfway round the world for five months.'

'I'm sorry – *abandon*?' She tried to sound defiant, but could already feel the guilt rising up inside her at the thought of leaving Izzy behind for so long.

'You heard me,' he said evenly.

'Plenty of fathers go away for work,' she replied.

'Yes, but not mothers. She needs *you*.'

'Jesus, Adam.' She could feel the guilt giving way to anger. She couldn't believe the man she'd married was actually saying this to her. 'Why does it always have to be the mother who stays at home with the kids? You're Izzy's parent just as much as I am.'

Adam stood up and went back to the fridge in search of something to eat. 'I can't believe you're seriously considering leaving our little girl for five months. I really can't.' He shook his head as he pulled out a plate of chicken offcuts.

Her anger intensified. She felt it being stoked with every word he said now. He was using Izzy, using the guilt he knew she would be feeling to try to stop her going. How fucking *dare* he? She closed her eyes tightly and clenched her jaw. She knew right then that *this* – this dynamic, this reality she'd somehow found herself in which saw her playing the part of stay-at-home mum with no career and no focus other than her husband and child – was exactly why she needed to go. She suddenly saw with perfect clarity the resentment that had been building up inside her. Resentment at her situation. She didn't resent Izzy – she loved her more than she'd thought it was possible to love anyone or anything, but she *did* resent letting herself lose other parts of her life – of her identity – which had always been so important to her. And though the guilt about being away from Izzy was as strong as ever, any guilt she felt about leaving Adam behind had just evaporated.

She had to go because Guy needed her – the *world* needed her. But she also needed to go for herself. She loved Izzy, she loved being a mother, but that didn't stop her feeling trapped. A big part of her yearned to get back to her old child-free existence. To get away. To get out. This was her chance, and she wanted to take it. 'I would miss Izzy every single second I was away, but she'll have you,' she said. 'She'll be absolutely fine.'

'It's not the same. And who's going to look after her? I can't just take five months off work.' He sat down at the table and began picking at a chicken leg.

Even the fact that he continued to eat while they argued annoyed her now. How could he eat while they were discussing this? 'My mother will help. So will yours – they're always offering,' she said. 'And we can afford to pay for some childcare. We can work it out – plenty of other people do.'

'She needs her mother, Rachael.'

So he was sticking to his sexist guns. 'I'll be back before she even notices,' she shot back.

He looked up from the plate. 'You said going south next month?'

She nodded.

'So you'd be over-wintering? It'll be dangerous.'

'I've been south plenty of times.'

'But you've never over-wintered. That's a whole different story to the trips you've done.'

'It can't be that bad – you've done it.'

'Yes, I did it once, and I swore I'd never do it again. It's nothing like the summers: the cold is unlike anything you've ever experienced.'

'I know cold, Adam. I've been down there plenty of times.'

'Not like this.' He shook his head. 'It gets in your bones, Rach. It gets into your *mind*. So does the darkness, the constant darkness. Have you any idea what it's like to have no daylight for months at a time? It's like living your life underground in a cave. It fucks with you. Some people can't cope with it.'

She stared back at him defiantly. 'I will,' she snapped. With each new objection he threw in her way she found herself becoming more and more determined to go.

'No one ever thinks they won't be able to cope.'

'Hundreds of people do it every year.'

'It's not a judgement on you, Rach. It's just . . . I've seen it happen.'

'Seen what?'

'I've seen people . . .' He paused as he searched for the correct word. 'Crack.'

She resented his implication that it would be too difficult for her. She'd done five times as many trips south as he had – and considered herself as good as anyone she knew at coping with the conditions. It felt like he was trying to take away her professional experience and skills, reducing her somehow, when she knew how capable she was and what she had to offer. 'What are you talking about?' she asked with an impatient shake of the head.

'Rothera – that winter I did. I never told you what happened.'

'Yes you did. We met the year after that, remember?' She thought back to their first meeting, at the British Antarctic Survey base at Halley. He was on his second tour as a field guide – someone to look after the travel, safety, logistics and any other support needed for a scientific expedition – and had been assigned to her for a deep field trip to gather some data on the Brunt Ice Shelf. There'd been an instant spark between them. Both had done their level best to ignore it while out in the field – Rachael knew the isolation could have a warping effect on feelings. Out there, just the two of them, working away and huddled in a tent together at night – it was easy to think something was more than it really was. So she tried to ignore it, worried the feelings wouldn't survive contact with the wider world. But that proved impossible. She treasured the fact that their first kiss had been out on the ice, the two of them the only people for hundreds of miles around. They'd been trekking for three days to a drill site and had reached the spot shortly before midnight. The wind had been roaring all day but once they reached their site it seemed to rest just as they did. They set up camp, ate a hot meal and then sat at the entrance to the tent looking out over the ice as the sun got low – but never set

49

entirely. She'd known his hand was resting on the canvas floor next to hers. Slowly, she'd moved her hand to his and they locked fingers. Neither said a word. Nothing needed to be said. When the kiss came, it felt like just the perfect thing to do.

It was all impossibly romantic and Rachael was always worried the magic would disappear when they left the ice. He'd picked up on that though, and once they'd both got back to the UK at the end of the season he assumed nothing and instead asked her to go for a drink – a first 'proper date', he'd called it. She'd loved that he understood and she soon found her feelings were as strong as they'd been out on the glacier.

That had turned out to be his last trip south – an itch he'd successfully scratched before settling down with an IT job in the City, like a gap-year adventure before he became a real grown-up. Antarctica didn't have the same hold over him as it did Rachael. But did he have the same hold over her as he'd had down there? Was this only ever supposed to be a fling – had she still been in the after-glow of that first burst of attraction when they got back to England? Or did she need to go back out onto the ice just to feel alive again?

'Of course I remember.' He discarded the chicken bone on the side of the plate and looked up at her. 'But I never told you what really happened. I couldn't. I wasn't allowed to. None of us were.'

'You weren't *allowed* to? What are you talking about?'

He pushed the plate away. 'They made us sign an NDA. If you tell anyone about this I could be sued. It could cost us thousands – end both our careers.'

'Jesus, Adam, just tell me.'

'Sit down.'

She did as he asked. *Where's he going with this?* she wondered.

'There were twelve of us there for the duration that season: eight support staff, including me, and four scientists. It was my first winter down there, and afterwards I swore it would be the last.'

'Why?'

'Two things happened that year: one of the scientists, Brian Collins, a biologist, was taken seriously ill with appendicitis and was medevacked out on the first flight of the summer; and second, the main lab building, the Bonner Lab, burned down.'

'I remember that,' Rachael said, searching her memory. 'Electrical fire, wasn't it?'

'No.' Adam shook his head. 'It wasn't.'

'I'm sure I remember someone telling me that – I was at Rothera two summers after that when they were rebuilding it.' She wondered if he was lying to her – coming up with some scare story to try to stop her going.

'I'm sure that's what you were told. That was the story. The story we were given. The story we've all stuck to. But that's not what happened.'

She frowned. 'What was it then?'

'That scientist, Collins – he didn't really have appendicitis.'

'No?'

He shook his head. 'No. He snapped. Flipped out. Lost his marbles, whatever you want to call it. He became paranoid. Thought two of the others were trying to kill him, so he set fire to the lab while they were inside working.'

Rachael raised her hand to her mouth.

'Luckily we managed to get them out, but it was too late to save the lab. Whole thing went up.'

'And what about Collins?'

'We had to physically restrain him – two of the guys sat on him, the medical officer gave him an injection to calm him down.' He looked up at her. 'We actually had to put him in a straitjacket.'

51

'A straitjacket? Jesus.' This was no story. She knew him well enough to know he was telling the truth.

'Every base has one. You must have known that?'

She shrugged. 'I'd heard rumours. I always thought it was a joke.'

'It isn't,' he said.

'So what did you do with him after that?'

'This was the middle of winter. We were almost two months away from the first flight of the season. The first ship wasn't due for another week after that. We asked for an early evac but Cambridge refused, said it was too dangerous. So we had to watch him. The base commander drew up a rota, and we kept watch on him, round the clock, until they took him away on the first flight of the spring.'

'That's terrible.' She thought back to her many trips south, the times she had been alone, miles from anywhere with only one other person for company. She knew it was not a situation that everyone was suited for. Antarctica was a place that could bend minds, even break them.

'It can happen. The cold. The dark. The isolation. He just couldn't handle it. As I said, he snapped.'

'And there were no warning signs?' Rachael found herself so absorbed in Adam's story she'd momentarily forgotten how angry she was with him.

'Looking back, there were. He'd started to become moody, quiet. Spent more and more time on his own. Started eating meals alone, that kind of thing. But none of that is unusual. Everyone goes a little bit funny at some point. Two months in the dark is a long time. At Rothera you do at least get a couple of hours of twilight in the middle of the day, but it's not much – and you never actually see the sun.'

'Were you scared?' She suddenly felt bad for having doubted him.

'What me? Scared? Stuck on an Antarctic base in the middle of winter with a crazed scientist setting fire to the buildings? Nah. All in a day's work.'

She cocked her head to the side. 'Adam . . .'

'Well, watching that lab go up was pretty scary – last thing you want out there with no help for a thousand miles is a fire you can't put out – but by then we'd got Collins under control. Mind you, it took four of us to do it.'

'What happened to him afterwards?'

'Collins? Got brought back to UK, given treatment, I guess. I think he's still doing research – he's just not allowed on field trips anymore.'

'But how come we never heard about this?'

'It was all hushed up. Brushed under the carpet. They came up with that electrical fault story for the fire, made us all sign NDAs.'

'But why? Why hush it up?'

'I dunno.' Adam shrugged. 'Doesn't look great, I suppose, your researchers losing it and burning down labs. I think they were in the middle of negotiating a new round of funding. There was fifty-odd million quid in the balance. They didn't want difficult questions asked in the middle of all that.'

That made sense, she thought.

'It was arse-covering, Rach. That's all it ever is.'

'Why are you telling me this now, Adam? After all this time? You think I can't handle it? You think I'll crack up like that guy?' She felt herself naturally kicking against his lack of faith, his every word of warning only reinforcing her determination to go, to prove him wrong and reclaim that part of her identity she now realized had been slipping away, bit by bit, day by day, for months.

'No of course not. But it doesn't have to be you cracking to put you in danger.'

'Antarctica *is* dangerous. It's all about managing the risk.'

'Don't talk to me like I'm a civilian,' he said. 'It's different in the winter. Any tiny thing can develop into a crisis in minutes. You trip down a crevasse in a snow storm – no one will know in that darkness. You slice open your hand on a knife and it gets infected? You better hope you've got the right antibiotics. And the worst thing? There's no rescue. You'll be alone. In winter they can't fly down there. No planes at all. That means you're stuck there until the spring – whatever happens. You're trapped. And believe me, it feels like a long time in that cold, that dark – especially when you know you can't get out.'

It's not the only way a person can be trapped, she thought. 'I know about the dangers,' she said quietly.

He shook his head. 'You've read about them. You don't *know*. Not in winter.'

'They need me, Adam.'

'Now who's talking bullshit?' he said, raising his eyebrows, his blue eyes locked on hers as if he were conducting a police interrogation. 'Don't give me that crap,' he sniffed dismissively. 'You *want* to go. I know you, Rachael, so don't try to sell me the reluctant hero story. You *want* to go. This life's never been enough for you, has it?' His eyes locked onto hers again, ready to sniff out her reaction like a lie detector machine.

She opened her mouth to reply, and then paused. He'd said it. She'd never admitted anything like that to him – she'd been too scared to puncture his bubble of apparent domestic bliss, but he was right. And she was momentarily knocked off balance as she realized he'd seen through her. She felt naked, exposed. He'd cut through the facade she'd built up so carefully, its walls now lying in rubble at her feet. She was ashamed too – ashamed that somehow this perfect life wasn't enough for her. And now he could see it. 'It's not that. But all this' – she gestured around her – 'the house, the car, the suburbs, the bloody coffee machine – ultimately it's all meaningless, Adam. This is a chance for me to actually help.'

'What about *me*?'

'What about you?'

'Don't I get a say in this? Would you even miss me?'

'Of course.' She hesitated. 'It's not about that.'

'Really?' he said sceptically.

'Adam—'

'Come on, Rach. Don't just run away from this.'

'I'm not. From what?' Rachael turned away. She knew where he was heading with this and she didn't want to go there – because she was at a loss as to what to say.

'You know what. You can't solve this by running off to the Antarctic.'

'I don't know what you mean.'

'I mean us! You and me! Our marriage!'

There it was. The elephant in the room that had been growing larger and larger by the day had finally been mentioned by name. 'Don't raise your voice. Izzy's asleep.'

'Rach, I'm right here. Talk to me,' he pleaded.

'I do talk to you,' she said in a small, unconvincing voice. But she knew she wasn't being truthful. She knew they hadn't really talked in weeks – months. She felt so distant from him. They both knew it, though neither had plucked up the courage to talk about it until now – perhaps both of them scared that to vocalize it would be to somehow make it even more real.

'Why do you always do this? Why do you always put up these walls between us when things are difficult?' he asked.

'I don't,' she said defensively.

'Yes you do. And no one can get in. Least of all me.'

'You're being ridiculous.' She was saying the words, but she knew he wasn't. She just didn't know what to say to make it any better, and she didn't want to say anything to make it worse.

'Am I? We never talk anymore, not really. I've tried, but you always bat me away. It feels like you're not really here anymore. Christ, we haven't even shared a bed in months.'

'It's just easier, with Izzy, you know, in the night, if I go in the spare room.' That was the story she'd been telling herself, though she knew it was only an excuse. She thought back to the last time they'd slept in the same bed – though she hadn't got much sleep. She remembered looking at him in the darkness, watching his chest rise and fall as he slept. There was a vast space separating them and she had no idea how to bridge it. He'd felt almost like a stranger in her bed. It was unbearable. After that, it was easier for her to sleep in the spare room than face the gulf between them every night.

'Is that the reason?'

'No point both of us losing sleep.'

'But I *am* losing sleep, Rachael. I'm losing sleep about us. Why won't you let me in? Why won't you tell me what's wrong? Why are you running away?'

She said nothing. She couldn't think of anything meaningful to say.

'Is this about him?' Adam asked after a pause.

'Who?' she replied, though she knew perfectly well who he meant.

'Guy,' he spat. He grimaced, as if even just saying the word caused him pain.

Jesus Christ. She was so tired of his hang-up about Guy. 'Of course not. I wish you'd get over that. It's not what you think.'

'I wish *you'd* get over him!'

'Look, he's my friend. My boss. That's all.'

'That's all? Really? You're telling me there was never anything more between you?'

'We've been through this, Adam. There was a time, yes, when I thought I wanted more. But that was a long time ago, and nothing ever happened between us. I promise you that.' She looked him in the eye. 'And I married you, didn't I?'

'Yes, you did, and now the minute Guy turns up here, completely out of the blue, you agree to run off to the other side of the world with him for five months!' he shouted. Then he took a breath, and the anger in his eyes made way for sadness. Helplessness. 'Can't you see how that makes me feel?'

'Look, I told you: that's not what this is about,' she said, though for a second she wondered who she was trying to convince. Was he right – was Guy a factor here? It was true, she'd had a crush on him years ago, but that had been a silly, short-lived infatuation. He was old enough to be her father, for God's sake. They were still close, he would always be her mentor, and she did love him, in a way, but not like *that*. Not now. Why could Adam never understand that?

'So what is it about?'

'It's about this being a chance for me to help. To change things.' This was the truth, or part of it at least. Her work had been her passion, and this was an emergency she was uniquely qualified to respond to. He had to see that.

'So you admit it?' he said, his voice rising. 'You do want to go?'

'And what if I do?' she hit back. 'Everything's going to shit, Adam. The planet is dying around us. Someone's got to *do* something. This is my something that will actually make a difference.'

'Yes, but—'

She cut him off. 'Global warming, climate change – it's the biggest threat humanity has ever faced. And no one seems to care. No one's doing anything about it. We're killing the planet, and every day we put it off till tomorrow. *Killing it*, Adam. And no one cares.' She shook her head. 'Do you want Izzy to have to grow up in a world that we've destroyed?'

He raised his hands in surrender. 'Look, I'm not saying this isn't serious. I'm only saying there are plenty of people who can do something. It doesn't have to be you.' He took a deep breath. He was at the end of his rope. He'd made his pitch, and used everything he could think of to keep her close. And nothing he'd said had worked. 'Listen: I can't stop you. But I don't want you to go.'

It was the most heartfelt and honest thing he'd said all night, and for a moment it took the sting out of their row. 'I know,' she said softly. She took his hand and looked him in the eye. 'But I have to, Adam. Can't you understand that?'

He pulled away, walked to the door, then stopped and looked over his shoulder. 'If you do this, people will think you're a bad mother.'

She narrowed her eyes and felt the anger bubbling back up inside her. After the moment they'd just shared – the closest she'd felt to him in months – he'd ruined it all over again. 'Is that what you'll think?' she asked, her eyes now boring into his.

The question went unanswered as he refused to meet her gaze.

She felt a buzzing coming from her pocket. She pulled her phone out and saw Guy's name illuminated on the screen. 'It's Guy.'

Adam sighed heavily and crossed his arms.

'Hello?'

'Turn on your TV. BBC News.'

'Why?' She reached for the remote for their wall-mounted TV. 'What's going on?'

'BBC News,' Guy repeated. 'Now.'

The screen came to life and above the rolling ticker at the bottom was a shot of miles and miles of white, snow-covered ice. Rachael caught the end of the newsreader's sentence. '. . . and at over five trillion tons, is the biggest iceberg to break off the shelf in recorded history. Dr Jeremy Houghton is a researcher from Oxford University and joins us now. Dr Houghton, was this expected?'

'Well, there had been some indication that a calving event might occur, but not on this scale . . .'

'Five trillion tons, Rachael,' Guy said.

She turned down the volume on the TV. 'Oh my God, Guy. It's even bigger than you said it would be.'

'It's five times bigger than the one off Larsen last year. *Five times*. And it's only the first, Rachael. We've just got the new sat imagery. There are going to be more in the next few months – some twice as big as this. It's happening, Rach. It's happening now. If we don't act, it won't be long before this could happen to the whole Ross Shelf. We're out of time.'

Rachael watched the screen in horrified silence as the coverage showed footage taken from a British Antarctic Survey plane of a crack running down the ice that snaked off into the horizon. She turned to look at Adam, who stood in the kitchen doorway staring at her, his jaw clenched tight. She held his gaze as she brought the phone back to her lips. 'When do we leave?'

Adam shook his head, turned on his heels and walked out of the house, slamming the painstakingly restored Victorian front door behind him. A moment passed after the bang, then the baby monitor crackled into life as Izzy woke and began to cry.

7

Rachael was woken by her own violent coughing fit as her lungs revolted against an invasion of toxic fumes. In the moment she came to, she struggled to remember where she was. But it only took a split second once she opened her eyes: she was in the Apple hut – and it was on fire.

A surge of panic rushed up from the bottom of her stomach and through her chest like a wave of molten lava.

Smoke was rapidly filling her tiny cabin and stinging her eyes. Her head throbbed. She reached up and gingerly touched the source of the pain. When she brought her hand back to her face she glimpsed the deep red of blood. But the pain would have to wait. She had much bigger problems: her little hob was now at the centre of a raging fire that was spreading rapidly. It was a steady, even flame, pouring out of . . . somewhere. And she had to put it out. Now.

Every atom in her body was screaming to simply run: get away from the blaze, get out into the open and run. Back to Izzy and Adam. Run, run, run. But she knew she had to resist that feeling. She had to stay and fight the fire.

In her many journeys to, from and around the Antarctic, Rachael had spent plenty of time on ships. On a ship, the biggest enemy wasn't sinking or taking on water. It was fire. From the deep recesses of her brain her marine fire training kicked in. It had been drilled into her a thousand times that, unlike a fire in a house or a normal building, you should not simply run and try to get out. On a ship, you had to fight it. You had to save the ship. Even in its worst state, a ship is always a better life raft than a life raft. And if your life raft itself was on fire, you really had no option.

The panic was translating into adrenaline, and Rachael knew she had to use it and act now if she had any chance of stopping the blaze and staying alive.

She jumped to her feet and snatched the fire extinguisher from its clasp on the wall. It only took her another few seconds to realize what was fuelling the inferno: the gas tank. *Shit*. Had she failed to fit it correctly when she changed it earlier? Maybe the extreme cold had somehow cracked the pipe? It didn't matter now. But it did mean it would be almost impossible to put it out. *Shit, shit, shit.*

She threw down the extinguisher. It would be useless against the gas. Instead she grabbed a towel. Through the smoke she managed to find one of the big, three-litre bottles of water she had already melted from the fresh snow outside. Her breaths came short and shallow as she poured the water all over the towel until it was soaked through, then threw it on the source of the fire. The towel sizzled on the roasting hot surface of the stove and the flames disappeared under it – but only for a few seconds before the fire fought back and began devouring the towel with what seemed like an even greater ferocity, as if Rachael's attempts to kill it had only served to anger the blaze. More and more choking black smoke was filling up the cabin as the fire continued to spread. *What now?*

Rachael's eyes were streaming and stinging in pain but she had to keep them open if she had any chance of putting out the fire and saving her cocoon. In desperation, she picked up the extinguisher she'd discarded moments earlier, pulled out the pin and attacked the flames. But the only result was a further intensifying of the smoke that was scratching at her lungs and filling her eyes. The fire reached her bunk and began devouring her sleeping bag with alarming speed. Through the smoke she could see the flames were licking up the length of the cabin wall to the ceiling behind the stove. The fibreglass wall was beginning to melt. The panic raced through her veins once again as she realized she was fighting a losing battle. Her lifeboat was about to sink.

She sprayed the fire extinguisher at the wall behind the stove, desperately trying to cool it down and prevent it from cracking open but within seconds the canister was completely empty and the fire was getting ever more intense.

In that second Rachael made the only decision she could. She grabbed the few items she could see and stuffed them into her backpack – a water bottle, her journal, radio, head torch, and as much of her outdoor gear as she could reach – and made for the hatch. It was time to abandon ship.

But she was too late. Through the smoke and her stinging eyes she could see the fire had already begun to take hold of the door, warping and melting the plastic and fibreglass. The handle was metal, but was now too hot to touch. Her eyes darted left to a hook above her bunk where a second towel hung. She grabbed it and doused it in water from one of the big bottles, then wrapped it around the handle and tried to yank it upwards. The handle itself moved and she had a brief moment of elation, but it was quickly dashed when she realized that although the handle had moved, the door itself had already begun to melt into the frame. *Shit*. Using the towel as a fire guard, she heaved her shoulder against it again and again, but it wouldn't budge. She was trapped.

A new wave of panic overwhelmed her and she screamed at

the top of her voice. Izzy's tiny face flashed across her mind as the fire raged and smoke continued to fill the cabin. This was it. Her brain was pulling up memories of Izzy because she knew her time was up. *No, no, no.*

Then she realized what she had to do. *The escape hatch.*

The smoke was causing tears to stream down her face as she grabbed the plastic stool from under her desk and set it on the floor, right in the middle of the pod. Then she stepped up onto it and, using the towel again to shield her hands, she reached up and yanked at the wheel lock that was right at the apex of the domed roof of the Apple. It was stuck fast. She steadied herself and yanked it again, but it still wouldn't yield. 'Move!' she shouted through her tears and the smoke and the terror.

She could feel the flames licking up at her legs and as she glanced down she saw the plastic chair she was standing on was now beginning to melt under her feet. She reached up again and with as much strength as she could muster she heaved the wheel hard left, and finally felt it come loose. *Yes!* She felt a burst of elation and lifted one foot from the now-sticky melting stool as she turned the wheel again and again. After seven turns she felt the hatch come loose and she reached up to push it out of its frame.

The instant she did so, fresh air rushed into the tiny, smoke-filled cabin and fuelled the fire anew. With a huge bang the hungry inferno was replenished by the fresh air and a giant ball of flame was created in an instant, knocking Rachael off the stool and onto her back in the process. She landed hard on the unforgiving floor but pulled herself up, grabbed her backpack and threw it out of the hole above. She eyed the melting plastic stool sceptically for a split second but glancing around the hut realized she had no other option so stood up on it, then heaved her head and shoulders up and out into the darkness and the cold, and sucked in a deep lungful of the cold fresh air. She hauled herself through the hatch, yanked her feet from the melting stool and was out in the open.

She slid down the outside of the Apple and landed on the snow, before grabbing her backpack and stumbling a few metres away to a safe distance. She turned just in time to see a second explosion rip the Apple apart. Now being fed by all the fresh air it could ever want, the fire licked up around every part of the little hut.

She began coughing: deep, bottom-of-the-chest coughs that shook her whole body as she tried to expel the smoke from her lungs. Then she fell back into the snow, exhausted from her escape and the retching fit. Her throat burned like she had been swallowing acid laced with razor blades, and as she sat up to try to control the coughing and regulate her breathing, she was suddenly overcome with nausea. She leaned forward and vomited in the snow.

She managed a few sips of water from her canteen and then sat and tried to catch her breath as the furious gale kicked up loose snow around her, like she was in her own enormous snow globe. Trapped forever in a picture-perfect world of snow, ice and fire.

She looked back at the bonfire that her Apple hut had become. Her prison, her cocoon, her life raft, and almost her coffin. It was now virtually unrecognizable – the fire had claimed it as its own, the fibreglass hull melting and cracking and emitting a foul stench. She sat in the dark and watched it burn.

8

The sun was shining brightly but there was frost on the tiny patch of grass that separated the house from the pavement. The taxi driver honked twice when he'd pulled up, causing Rachael to wince. It was too early for that – the neighbours wouldn't be impressed. She checked that her passport was safely tucked into the pocket of her rucksack for the fifth time, then set it down in the hallway underneath the mirror and walked back up to Izzy's room. Her little girl was already awake – she'd clearly sensed there was activity in the house. Rachael looked down at her daughter in her cot, cuddly Tigger doll by her side as always.

'Hello my little Isabella Mozzarella,' she said quietly. 'Are you awake already?'

'Mama, up,' she replied. Her new morning refrain.

Rachael reached down and picked her up, wanting one last long hug before she left. She shut her eyes and held her as close as she could, savouring her feel, her smell, as she gently bobbed up and down. In that moment as she cuddled Izzy tightly to her, she was seized with a flood of guilt and doubt. Right then she never ever wanted to leave Izzy, never wanted to let go of her, never let her out of her sight. The whole idea was unthinkable. Should she simply call Guy and tell him she couldn't come?

'I think the driver's about to wake up the whole street.' Adam was in the doorway, wearing his blue dressing gown and slippers, his bed hair spiking out in all sorts of bizarre directions.

Rachael nodded and took a deep breath. Torturous though it was to leave her daughter, she knew she had to go. She had to go for all the reasons Guy had explained to her, for all the reasons she'd fought for with Adam over dinners gone cold and television shows left playing to no one. And she had to go to get some space, to think clearly, to shake off this heavy blanket of doubt and confusion she was being suffocated with every moment she stayed in this house. She had to go because she couldn't face detonating a bomb right in the middle of her marriage. She just had to go.

The three of them walked downstairs, Izzy in Rachael's arms as they went, Adam carrying Tigger. That was good, Rachael thought. They would need the distraction when the moment came for her to leave.

'I'll get your bag,' Adam said.

They walked out into the crisp March morning, Rachael clutching on for as long as she could to Izzy, who was wriggling in her arms and chatting away merrily with her half-formed words. She seemed so content. She didn't know what was about to happen. She didn't know her mother was about to leave her.

Adam pulled open the boot and stowed her rucksack, then stood and waited, hands in the pockets of his robe.

Rachael hugged Izzy closer and could feel the tears coming. 'You look after Daddy, OK?' she said as she kissed her cheek. 'Give Mummy a kiss.'

Izzy leaned her head forward clumsily and gave Rachael her slobbery version of a kiss.

Rachael squeezed her once last time, and then, in what felt like the act of giving up a limb, she passed her to Adam.

The three of them stood on the pavement outside their house, the silence broken only by the taxi's idling engine, the muffled voices of the talk radio station the driver was listening to and Izzy's half-talk. Rachael's eyes were glassy with tears and she couldn't resist reaching out to caress her daughter's cheek. One last touch. She glanced up at Adam. He looked defeated, crushed even, though she could tell he was trying not to show it.

'I'll call you when I get there,' was all she could think to say. Such a pointless platitude. It seemed so inadequate, but she couldn't bring herself to say anything bigger. Not now. Not with the plane to catch and the taxi waiting and the driver tapping his fingers on the steering wheel. Not with Adam standing out in the cold in his dressing gown, and Izzy in her pyjamas. And even if she'd wanted to, what could she say? There had already been countless resigned conversations and tearful fights over the past few weeks since Guy's visit. There was nothing left to say at this point. There he was, standing there trying to love her, and she just wouldn't let him. And she wished she knew how to fix it.

'Safe journey,' he said, offering his own pointless platitude. There was no kiss between them. 'Say bye-bye to Mummy,' he said to Izzy.

Rachael leaned in and waved to her daughter. 'Bye-bye, Izzy,' she said as the tears began falling down her face. 'Bye-bye.'

Izzy flapped her arm in her version of a wave. 'Ba ba,' she said.

Unable to take it anymore, Rachael climbed into the back of the taxi and pulled the door shut behind her.

'Heathrow?' the driver asked.

She nodded. 'Terminal Two,' she replied as she pulled the seat belt across her. She looked through the window at Adam and Izzy, kissed her hand and waved it at them as the tears rolled down her face and the driver pulled away.

9

Rachael stood as close to her destroyed Apple hut as she dared, sucking up all the warmth she could from the fire. She felt a momentary surge of panic rise up inside her chest as a thought occurred to her. She bent down, pulled open her rucksack and rifled frantically through the contents. The wave of panic only subsided when she felt the glossy surface of the photograph in her hands. She tugged it out of the bag and held it to her heart for a relief-filled moment, before pulling it back and gazing down at Izzy and Adam in the picture, their faces illuminated by the orange glow of the fire.

Her mind suddenly conjured up a horrifying image of the two of them, trapped in their house in London as fire and chaos and fear raged all around them: a terrified Adam clinging onto Izzy in their darkened kitchen as explosions rattled the windows and sirens wailed in the distance and competed with Izzy's crying. The power out, the phone lines dead. Was that what it was like? Was that what had happened to them? It was simply too awful to contemplate. She dared not let her mind go down that road any further.

She slipped the picture back inside her rucksack and stood in silence for a moment as she watched the fire burn; crackling and popping and hissing and hungrily devouring what had been her sanctuary.

Then she turned her attention to staying alive. She now had no shelter, no food, no stove – which meant no drinking water once she had emptied her canteen – and no transport. But she was alive, and she was quickly forming a plan. She took one last look at the red embers of what was once her little home, swung her bag onto her back, pulled her hood up and her goggles down, and began to march.

She knew in the summer she could average seventeen miles a day if she pushed hard. But this wasn't summer. She had no light by which to see – other than her head torch – but even if she did, the constant wind whipped up the loose snow so she could hardly see where she was going anyway. She also knew she would be slowed by the wind blowing against her. But as she pushed on, she soon discovered that the strength of it was not the worst thing about the wind: it was its unpredictability. It was so strong she had to lean forward into it to avoid toppling backwards. But then, without warning it would drop to nothing for half a second, and she would find herself face-planting into the snow. Each time it happened, she immediately pulled herself up to her feet. She didn't allow herself a moment's rest. She knew if she stopped, even for a moment, she might not be able to start again. So on she marched.

Her mind marched along with her, and she was unable to stop it returning to Izzy. She could see her on the carpet in the living room, playing with her blocks and the red plastic racing car Adam's parents had given her, pushing it across the floor and hitting the blocks with it again and again. Her little face a picture of concentration as she pushed it along. Rachael found it fascinating to watch her learn and adjust to the world around her; she seemed to discover a new skill or sensation every day. She remembered the day she'd taken her first steps – a week after her first birthday – wobbling unsteadily along while holding onto the side of the sofa in the living room, before she lost her balance and sat back down with a bump and giggled.

Such a happy memory, but one that was now wrapped up in so much pain. She brought her gloved hand up to her chest for a moment as the sadness and grief threatened to overwhelm her entirely. Every thought of her family, every memory, every vision of their faces – each one brought a stabbing pain to her chest that burned her insides hotter than even the flames she'd just escaped.

The wind abated for a moment and she fell face first into the snow again. She didn't pause, even for a second, and pulled herself up to continue her march. Adam's face was the next to flash across her mind. She felt a pang of guilt come with it, at how she'd left things with him. He'd accused her of running away. Running away from him. From them.

'The thing is,' she said out loud as she yomped through the snow and ice, 'you were right, Adam: I did want to come here. And now I'm stuck here. And the question I keep asking myself is: did I come out here because I was bored? Because I was running away from us like you said?' She took in a breath of the cold, fresh air. 'But now you're gone – both of you. And I should have been there. I am a bad mother. I should have been there to hold your hands when the end came. Instead I'm here. Alone. And I'm probably going to die alone too.' She felt so overwhelmed with grief and emptiness she wanted to cry, but still the tears wouldn't come.

So on she marched. Through the snow and the wind and the dark, for mile after exhausting, gruelling mile, fighting a never-ending battle between thinking of Izzy and Adam, and trying not to when it became too painful.

But the pain wasn't just emotional: her lungs still felt scratchy and raw from the smoke she had inhaled in the fire, causing sporadic bouts of deep coughing so severe she had to stop walking until they had passed. Her head still throbbed from the blow that had knocked her unconscious, and her legs were beginning to ache from the long trek. But on she marched.

And then she saw it – only glimpses at first through the blizzard when her head torch caught a reflective surface for a moment. She thought she might be dreaming, hallucinating. But no, it was definitely there. And as she got within the last few hundred metres, there was no doubt. The Snowcat.

The red truck mounted on tracks that had brought her from Station Z to within eight miles of the Apple hut before it had broken down. Back then she'd cursed it, kicked it and screamed as it refused to come back to life, but right now she couldn't have been more pleased to see it if it was a five-star hotel with room service, a twenty-four-hour concierge and lifts to all floors. Because now, it was going to save her life.

She yanked the door of the front cab open and hauled herself inside before pulling the door shut tight behind her. It brought her immediate relief from the incessant wind and for a minute or so she sat in silence, trying to slow her breathing. She looked around the cab: it was exactly as she had left it almost two months earlier. The vehicle – which was just over twenty feet in length – was divided into two: the front cab which had two seats, the driver controls and a high, wide windscreen; and the rear cargo cab, which was self-contained and accessed through a door at the back. At the front of the vehicle there was a six-foot-long boom that hung out over the snow ahead, with a ground-penetrating radar device on the end, designed so the driver or passenger could detect if they were about to drive over a crevasse that had become covered with a thin layer of ice.

Once she'd got her breathing under control, she took a few swigs of water as the wind rocked the vehicle. Then with a shaking hand, she reached across to the ignition key which was mounted in the middle of the dashboard, and held it for a moment. If, by some miracle, whatever fault that had caused the engine to die on her two months ago had somehow worked itself out, she could simply fire it up and drive back to Station Z. She could be back within twenty-four hours. It was a long shot, but there was no reason not to try. She held her breath, and turned the key.

10

Rachael was the only passenger on the United States Air Force C-17 transport plane. She was already eight days into her journey, having first flown from the UK to New Zealand with a stopover in Singapore, before five frustrating days sitting in a hotel near Christchurch airport, waiting for a break in the polar weather that would allow her flight into McMurdo Station to get through. They'd made one abortive attempt two days earlier, but after four hours in the air, the weather closed in again and forced them to return to Christchurch.

She sat up against the bulkhead with her back to the hull, a row of empty seats stretching away from her down the side of the aircraft. Primarily a transport and cargo flight, the interior of the plane was stripped out completely – there were none of the internal fixtures and fittings found on a passenger airliner which usually dulled the roar of the engines.

As she sat, facing the middle of the plane wearing a pair of red ear defenders to counter the deafening noise, she was reminded of those old war movies. She half expected to turn and see a commando with a rifle sitting next to her, saying a prayer and daubing his face in camouflage paint.

But she was alone – the only person on the aircraft other than the flight crew. This time of year – when the temperatures were starting to plummet and the nights were drawing in – was for getting out of Antarctica, not in.

She unclipped the top of her rucksack and felt around inside it for her book. As she pulled it out, a brown, padded envelope came with it, with the words: 'Rachael – to be opened when you arrive' written on the front. She glanced at her watch, noted the flying time and reasoned that by now she was close enough. She ripped it open and found a red A5 notepad inside. She opened it to the first page and as she did so a photograph fell out and onto her lap. It was a picture of herself, Adam and Izzy, in the kitchen at home. She remembered her mother taking the photo the day they'd brought the baby home from the hospital. Little Izzy was so tiny. Barely even a day old. Rachael stared at the picture. Adam held Izzy. She was wearing a Tigger babygrow and had her eyes wide open, as if taking in her new surroundings. Rachael and Adam were smiling down at her, both exhausted but utterly in love with the new member of the family. Smiles. Happiness. Love. It seemed a lifetime ago.

She looked back at the notepad. Inside the cover was a note. *Good luck on your trip. Write everything down so you can tell us about it when you get back. Come back safe to us. We'll miss you. Love, Adam and Izzy.*

She looked back at the photo. 'I miss you, too,' she mouthed. She felt a rush of guilt about leaving them behind, and a stabbing pain at the thought she wouldn't get to see Izzy again for a whole five months. She knew how much she would grow in that time, how different she would be by then. She'd be walking properly for one thing. A new and awful thought crossed her mind: *will she even remember me?* She could suddenly see five months into the future, arriving home and picking Izzy up, showering her with kisses, only for her to squirm and cry and pull away, with only Adam now able to pacify her.

God, would that be how it was – would she be a stranger to her own child?

She thought about the expedition, about how Guy had persuaded her. Yes, it was important – as important as it could get – but was it worth losing so much time with her only daughter? Did it *really* need to be her that came on this trip? All of a sudden she wasn't so sure.

A part of her knew she'd done it simply to get away. Away from the pressure of her and Adam. Just to give herself some time and space. She'd felt herself pulling further and further away from him over the past few months, and she'd used his anger at her agreeing to come on the trip as a pretext to put more distance between them. But truthfully, it had started long before that. Though she hated to make the connection, in retrospect it probably started after Izzy was born. She loved that girl with all her heart, but suddenly Rachael found herself at home all day. As a professional, she'd been a leading voice in her field – she'd been making a real difference, was respected, and went to work each day filled with purpose. After Izzy came she'd given all that up. Stayed at home to nurture her child. She loved that part of it, but she knew there was something missing. Meanwhile Adam's hours got longer, his commitment to his own work seemed to strengthen, while she felt she'd been forced to give hers up. She'd tried to hint she was finding it hard but Adam was such an infuriating optimist. A positive thinker. 'You'll get used to it,' he'd say. 'It was always going to be strange at first.' 'I'd love to be able to be at home all day with Izzy.' That one had really pissed her off. Why couldn't he see she was struggling? Why wouldn't he listen to her? He just didn't want to hear it and she began to resent him for it.

Was it over, and she simply didn't want to see it? Or was she doing what she always did: pulling away and putting up barriers when things got tough? Had the stresses and strains of becoming a mother changed her feelings for him? Or were they simply hidden from her somehow? Did she still love him? Her thoughts felt cloudy, muddled. She wished she could see things clearly.

She knew he was angry with her for leaving, and she was angry with him, too, though she couldn't fathom exactly why. But despite all that he'd still made the effort – the notepad, the photograph, the little note. He was still trying. But was she? She wondered if this trip was her way of giving them the space they needed to end it. She tried hard to work out if it already had ended for her, but she just couldn't see the answer. What would she do? Take Izzy to her parents', she supposed. Or maybe Adam would leave them in the house. It was all such a mess. How had it come to this?

The dull grey plane banked as it began its descent into Phoenix Airfield, the compressed snow runway that served McMurdo Station. Rachael turned to look out the window over her left shoulder – and that's when she saw it. She involuntarily brought her hand up to her mouth as she got a full view of the huge iceberg that had sheared off the Ross Shelf. She'd known the size of it by the numbers, but that hadn't prepared her for her first sight of it with her own eyes. Miles and miles and miles of ice, it stretched on and on for further than her view afforded her – even at this height. The scale was almost incomprehensible, yet she knew it was nothing – barely an ice cube in an Olympic-sized swimming pool compared to the Ross Shelf itself. She was overwhelmed by a sense of duty and urgency. At that moment, and despite the painful heartache of leaving Izzy behind, she knew she had to be here to try and stop this from happening again on an even larger scale.

Rachael usually loved the final approach into Antarctica. It meant she was nearly there. She had never been able to explain her attraction to the ice continent, but from the moment she'd first set foot on it, it had felt . . . right. Not like home exactly, that wouldn't be correct, but like she was *meant* to be there. Her whole body relaxed whenever she arrived. But this time was different. This time she was coming in an emergency. Her pristine paradise was under threat. It was dying. And as the plane banked again to line up for the airstrip, Rachael felt like a vet, called to aid a stricken elephant in the savannah. She only hoped she wasn't already too late.

As the C-17 continued its final approach she caught her first glimpse of the station itself: a collection of low-slung timber and metal-clad buildings, with shipping containers and water and fuel towers dotted about between them. Despite her nine previous Antarctic visits, it was her first sighting of McMurdo. On all her other trips she'd arrived at Rothera, the British Antarctic Survey's, or BAS's, main base of operations at Adelaide Island just off the Antarctic Peninsula. That journey was usually conducted by an RAF transport flight from the UK to the Falkland Islands, before boarding either a BAS Dash-7 plane for the final leg, or hopping aboard one of the distinctive red and white BAS research ships.

But Rothera was more than a thousand miles away from their survey site. It made far more sense to arrive here. Situated on the southern tip of Ross Island and in the shadow of nearby Observation Hill, McMurdo was the biggest station on the entire continent. First established by legendary British explorer Robert Falcon Scott – whose original hut still stood a mere three hundred metres to the west of the modern facility – McMurdo was now operated by the United States Antarctic Programme. It was their gateway to the south – all US personnel and equipment came in and out through it before heading off to work out in deep field, or at the US's other main facility, the Amundsen–Scott South Pole Station. A busy, bustling mini-city, it was home to more than twelve hundred people during the summer months, and less than a quarter of that over the winter.

Rachael felt the clunk of the landing gear being deployed beneath her and just a few moments later the aircraft touched down on the ice. She heard the engines roar as the captain engaged full reverse power and as the C-17 taxied to a stop she could already see Guy standing and waiting for her next to a blue jeep, his Big Red Antarctic jacket flapping in the wind as he stood on the apron cut into the snow. Her heart lifted a little at the sight of his familiar face. For a moment she wondered if Adam had been right about her rushing off the moment Guy asked her to. Had she been too quick to leave for the familiar comfort of Guy's company?

She was brought back to the present when the plane stopped on its marks and the loadmaster came back from the cockpit and motioned for her to grab her rucksack and disembark.

Stepping off the plane and onto the ice for the first time was always an emotional, even spiritual, experience for Rachael. As her boots hit the compacted snow she sucked in a deep breath: the cold, dry air filled her lungs and she felt instantly more alive. She blinked as her eyes fought to adjust to the incredible brilliance of the sunlight reflecting off the pure white snow. She squinted as she took in her surroundings: the base nestled down in the bay, the endless white of the McMurdo Ice Shelf stretching towards the Ross Shelf to the south, with Mount Discovery at the head of McMurdo Sound, the Transatlantic Mountains running along the western horizon, and the enormous Mount Erebus towering over everything. Even for a seasoned polar visitor like Rachael, it was a breathtaking sight.

'Not a bad spot, is it?' Guy said as he embraced her warmly.

'It's beautiful,' she said as she hugged him back.

'Let's hope we can keep it that way.'

Guy hauled Rachael's rucksack into the back of the jeep before the two of them set off for the base itself as the ground crew began unloading the aircraft behind them. As they drove along the snow-covered gravel track that led down to the station from the airfield, Guy pointed out the cargo ship tied up at the dock. 'They used to have to send an ice-breaker in first to clear a path through the pack ice before the ship could get in,' he said. 'They haven't had to bother in the past two seasons.'

'Where's the rig?'

'They towed it away three weeks ago. On its way to Venezuela for a few months, I think.'

As they neared the base, Rachael could see it was a hive of activity: people packing up containers, forklift trucks stowing loads, and windows being boarded up. The station was shutting down, preparing for the long, dark, winter months when only the most essential of maintenance crews would remain, there to keep the base barely alive until the next summer when the scientists would return and the work could begin again.

'Never seems like a good idea to hang around when the locals are packing up to leave,' she said, as Guy pulled over to allow a forklift truck with huge wheels to pass on the narrow track.

'That's why we're not gonna hang around,' Guy replied with a smile as he pulled back onto the track.

He stopped the jeep in front of a beige, two-storey building. It was clad in corrugated iron and would have looked like a warehouse, except for the eight matching windows set into its sides. A tatty American flag flapped from a pole outside the front door. 'We're in here for now,' he said as he killed the jeep's engine.

He led her through the main entrance and into the building. 'It's transit accommodation, for people coming in and out for Amendsen-Scott and the other deep field stations,' he explained. 'The others will be in the mess. Presume you'll want to call home and check in first, so use my office, then come and say hello to the others when you're ready.'

She nodded.

They walked down a corridor with chipped floor tiles and fading paint. 'We leave tomorrow,' he said, 'so don't make yourself too comfy.'

'Don't think that will be a problem,' she said as Guy kicked open the reluctant door to his office.

'Mess is down there, door at the far end of the hall,' he said, before leaving her to it.

She dropped her bag and sat down behind Guy's desk, which was covered in maps and data printouts. She checked the time, coming up on 10 a.m. That meant it would be almost 11 p.m. in London. She dialled the number, unsure whether she was hoping Adam was still up or not.

He answered after five rings, his voice low and sleepy as he said hello.

'Hey, it's me. Just calling to let you know I've arrived.'

'Oh, oh good. How was the flight?'

'The usual. You know.' She hesitated for a moment, hating the way their communications had become so stilted and awkward. 'Thank you for the picture, and the notepad. It was really thoughtful.'

'You're welcome. Just wanted to remind you that we're here, waiting for you.'

She didn't know what to say to that, so she moved on. 'How's Izzy?'

'She misses her mother.'

Rachael shook her head, hearing the edge of coldness in his voice. He was doing it on purpose. Laying on the guilt. And it was working. But it also made her angry at him. She hated him using Izzy like that, like a weapon to hurt her with. She tried to ignore it. 'Is your mum there?'

'Yes, she's here until Friday, then I have the weekend on my own, then your mum is coming over for a few days next week.'

'They must be loving it – so much time with their grand-daughter.'

'I guess so.'

Rachael heard a muffled cry in the background.

'That's her awake again,' Adam said. 'She hasn't been sleeping.' More guilt.

'I'd better go and check on her.'

'OK. I'll call again when I get a chance.' Rachael could feel tears beginning to form in her eyes as she thought of her daughter, all those thousands of miles away.

'OK. Love you.'

She paused. She wanted to say it back, but it felt somehow dishonest.

'Give Izzy a kiss from me,' she said.

The line went dead.

Rachael took a deep breath and fought back the tears. She had to keep it together. Now was not the time. She needed the distraction of other people so she stood up and made her way down the corridor and pushed open the door at the very end.

She found herself in a room containing a kitchen area and dining tables at one end, a pool table at the other, and an old TV and DVD player on a trolley in the middle. A pair of faded chintz sofas sat facing the screen at an angle. Two men stood around the pool table, cues in hand.

'Bloody hell, Beckett, what time do you call this?' The lanky figure of Mikael Henriksen dropped his cue on the green baize, came lumbering towards her and pulled her into a slightly awkward hug. Henriksen, a Norwegian mechanic and maintenance technician, was a fellow old hand at Antarctic visits and Rachael had known him for almost ten years, their paths crossing on several previous research trips. He was a little too blokeish for her tastes – the constant dirty jokes and football references, and the topless calendar he always seemed to insist on pinning up in his dorm made him a hard man for her to actively like – but he was a good field guide who knew his job inside out and was, as far as she could tell, entirely unflappable. And for some reason he always called her by her surname.

'About time we had some females around here,' he added.

The hug brought her nose into contact with the stained woolly hat on top of his head. Red with a white stripe, it had a Manchester United Football Club crest on the front.

'Jesus, Mik, you still wearing that ratty old hat?'

'Gotta wear this – it's my lucky hat. Never had a bad scrape in all the years I've been wearing this beaut. Never leaves my head – not even when I'm, you know, *busy*,' he said with a wink that almost made Rachael shudder.

She frowned. 'You could at least give it a wash once in a while.'

He looked genuinely puzzled. 'What, and wash off all the luck? You must be mad.'

Guy stepped forward to introduce her to the other man. 'Rachael, this is Lieutenant Zachariah Connelly, RN.'

'Zak,' he said warmly as he offered her his hand.

He was tall – almost as tall as Henriksen, but much broader in the chest, with wide shoulders and strong, muscular arms that filled out his T-shirt.

'Zak is our medical and safety expert for the trip,' Guy added.

'Oh – what happened to Rowan?'

Rachael tried not to make her displeasure obvious. Working in a dangerous environment like the Antarctic meant you needed to completely trust your colleagues. One of the reasons she'd agreed to come was that she would be working with people she knew. She didn't like the sound of this late change.

'Had to pull out at the last minute. He was taken sick – some stomach thing – so he had to stay home. Zak came highly recommended.'

'You'll have to make do with me, I'm afraid,' Zak said, smiling at Rachael.

'How many trips down here have you done?' she asked sceptically.

'Seven, including this one.'

'And what made you want to join ours?'

'Heard Guy here needed a safety officer last minute. I've just come out the other side of a divorce, fancied some time away. And you can't get any further than this.'

'That's true,' she said. She hadn't allowed the 'd word' to enter her thinking yet, but at Zak's mention of it she couldn't help but wonder if that's where she and Adam were heading. She tried to put it out of her mind. 'So, you're in charge of our safety and physical well-being, correct?'

Zak nodded. 'Uh huh. And your mental well-being. I offer a complete service.' He flashed her another smile. There was something about him – probably that disarming smile – that put her instantly at ease and she felt her qualms about his last-minute addition to the team already melting away.

'Well in that case, can you order Henriksen to give that bloody hat a good wash? Or get him to soak it in bleach for a week? It's got to be a health hazard.'

Zak laughed.

'No one touches this hat,' Henriksen said in a deadly serious tone. 'It's done me right on nine expeditions.' He pointed to it. 'This hat was given to me personally by Ole Gunnar Solskjær, and it stays on.'

'Oh come on, Mik,' Rachael said, 'let me take it down to the laundry facility. I'll get it back good as new – luck still included.'

'Over my dead body,' he replied.

'All right you lot,' Guy said, raising one of his big, paw-like hands. 'We fly out tomorrow and we haven't much time, so let's go through the plan, shall we?' He made for the pool table and pushed the balls out of his way before unfurling a large paper map of the Ross Ice Shelf.

'Shouldn't we wait for the others?' Rachael said.

Guy glanced nervously at Zak and Henriksen. 'Let's run through the gist.'

'Wouldn't it make more sense to do it with everyone here? Where are they?' She knew they'd need a team at least two or three times this size to safely carry out this expedition.

'It's just us here, Rach,' Guy said.

'So everyone else is coming in on the next flight?'

Guy cleared his throat. 'Not exactly.'

'Oh, there's another ship coming in? Bit late for that, isn't it? I would've thought they'd be sailing north by now.'

'No, there are no more ships this season.'

'So . . . what then?' She frowned. Guy was being cagey. Something was wrong here.

There was a moment of silence. 'Can you give us a minute please, chaps?' Guy said quietly.

Zak and Henriksen shuffled out the door, studiously avoiding eye contact with Rachael.

'What's going on, Guy?' she said once the door was closed. 'Where's the rest of the crew?'

Guy walked across to one of the dining tables, pulled out a chair and sat down. He nodded at the chair opposite him.

'No thank you,' she replied firmly. 'You said we'd have a full team for this expedition. Researchers, assistants, field guides, medical, safety, maintenance. Where are they all?'

'We do have a full crew,' he said quietly.

'So where are they?'

'They're here. You, me, Zak, Henriksen. That's all we need.'

She took two steps towards him. 'Four?! Four of us? Are you serious?'

'Perfectly.'

'Four people? To go on a five-month Antarctic expedition. In winter. Out in deep field?' She couldn't believe what she was hearing. A team of four people to complete this job was woefully inadequate – and Guy knew that. There must be more to this than he was letting on.

'Yes.'

'Have you lost it? That's impossible!' She tried to think through the work that lay ahead of them, the research, the travel – the everyday stuff they would need to do just to stay alive. It was too much, far too much, especially in winter.

'Why? We've done similar expeditions dozens of times with a team of four.'

He was twisting things. 'Yes, in the summer. With support staff nearby, air support if necessary – and on the coast. You're talking about a thousand miles inland, on our own, with no support, in winter.'

'The principles are the same. The work is the same.'

'Yes, but Guy, for an expedition of this size, this length, in winter – you're looking at eight people, minimum, just to cope with the travel, the supplies, the base maintenance, not to mention the research. It can't be done with four people, and you know it.'

'It can, and it will.'

She shook her head in disbelief. 'There's no way Cambridge would ever have signed off on this. How did you get this through—' She stopped, and took another step towards him as she began to connect the dots. 'Wait a minute. The tiny crew, these crap digs, me hitching a ride on that USAF C-17 . . . my God, Guy.'

He looked up at her from underneath his bushy eyebrows.

'This isn't an official BAS expedition, is it?'

11

Rachael realized she was holding her breath as she prepared to turn the key in the ignition of the Snowcat. If it started, she could be back at Station Z in a day. If it didn't, she had a long and treacherous march ahead of her that truthfully she didn't know if she could survive.

She forced herself to exhale, then turned the key. The instant she did, she jumped. The engine didn't kick in but the battery did, and with it, the stereo system came to life and began blasting Pink Floyd out of the cabin speakers. She glanced down at the centre console and saw one of her USB sticks plugged into the stereo, left there when she'd driven out to the survey site before the vehicle had died on her. She turned the volume down, then her hand went back to the key in the centre of the dashboard and she turned it all the way to the right. She heard the engine trying to turn over as the starter motor battled to coax the sleeping machine into life, but after a couple of attempts she could hear it struggling more and more until eventually it stopped even trying. Her heart sank. It was as dead as it had been when she left it. It hadn't miraculously fixed itself in the last two months. She sat and stared out of the big windscreen at the pitch-black nothingness for a moment, as the Floyd played 'Is There Anybody Out There?' on the stereo.

'Just a little help?' she said, before she clenched her jaw, shut her eyes and turned the key one last time. Nothing.

She let the music play on as she gazed out into the endless night, until the last few plucks of classical guitar brought the track to an end. Then she reached out and turned the ignition off.

Alone again.

She took a deep breath as she battled the emotions of despair and anger that threatened to overwhelm her. She was also overcome with a strong urge to sleep. She looked around the cab and briefly considered sleeping where she was, or in the rear cabin, but she quickly dismissed that thought. Easy though it would be to let herself fall asleep where she sat, she knew she'd be dead from the cold within a few hours if she did. And she knew she'd burned a lot of calories on her trek – calories she needed to replace soon.

She pulled down her hood, took off her hat and removed her right glove, then felt the back of her head gingerly, wincing at the pain as her fingers touched the wound. She could feel the stickiness of drying blood in her hair. She leaned across and opened the storage unit built into the dashboard, and pulled out the green first aid kit. She swallowed two aspirin and looped a roll of bandage around her head. It was a bodge job, but it would have to do for now.

Then she pulled her hat back on, replaced her gloves, zipped up her Big Red, and nodded to herself in the reflection looking back at her in the windscreen. 'Come on, Rach, no time for feeling sorry for yourself,' she said, before she opened the door and climbed down from the cab, using the tracks as a step. She walked to the rear compartment and swung open the hatch. A tiny ceiling light illuminated her treasure: a sled, walking poles, a shovel, a pyramid-shaped Scott tent, two sleeping bags, a stove, a pair of ice axes, cups, cutlery, pans, and several boxes of freeze-dried food. She paused for a moment and allowed a smile to cross her lips as she surveyed the equipment. Her hut now may be just a pile of ashes, her head might be throbbing with pain and her body aching all over from her long march through the snow, but she had made it – and now she had everything she needed to stay alive.

She pulled the tent out and prepared for battle with the gale. Exhausted as she was, she knew her efforts to get this far would all be for nothing if she didn't get it erected quickly. Had she had more time, she would have cut out ice blocks and built a wall to shelter the tent from the wind, but instead she decided to simply use the Snowcat as a windbreak.

Her position decided, she battled the freezing temperatures and the relentless wind to build her new shelter. The cold took hold of her fingers, causing her to fumble and slip as she tried to piece together the poles, and the wind snatched and grabbed at the canvas, threatening to rip it away from her entirely and carry it off into the darkness at every turn as she fought to hold on. But once she had the pegs hammered into the ice and hooked on securely she painstakingly threaded each pole, stood her new home upright, then pegged and tightened the upwind guys, and with her reserves of strength and energy depleting rapidly, packed the valances with snow.

She stood back and admired her work, breathing hard, heart pumping fast. It had been a fight with the gale – and was for this reason usually a two-person job – but the pyramid-shaped tent was ready. Based on the very design that Scott himself had used over a century ago, the modern version had been improved upon both in terms of design and materials, and could withstand winds of up to sixty miles an hour. Which was a good job, Rachael thought, given the current blizzard conditions. By erecting the tent, she'd scored a tiny victory in her battle to stay alive.

She went back to the Snowcat and retrieved one of the sleeping bags, the stove and two packets of instant food, plus a pan, a cup, and a small pouch of instant coffee. She stowed all this in the tent, scooped up some fresh ice, then crawled inside and zipped herself in. Then she fired up the stove.

Only once she had eaten a packet of freeze-dried risotto and drunk a litre of water, did she allow herself to climb inside her sleeping bag. She was asleep within seconds.

12

Rachael held Guy's gaze. 'Tell me the truth,' she said evenly. 'Did Cambridge sign off on this?'

He cleared his throat. 'Not um . . . not . . . officially, no.'

She brought her hand to her mouth. The implications began to race through her mind. 'Oh my God, Guy. How *could* you?'

'How could I what?'

'Bring me here, for this . . . I mean, what is this?' She frowned in confusion. 'How have you even done this?'

'It's complicated.'

'Explain it to me,' she said firmly.

'There are only four of us, because four is all I could afford.'

She'd asked and he was answering, but she was hardly listening. She could feel the fury rising up inside her chest as she realized what he'd done. She'd left her daughter and her marriage to follow him out here – and she'd been in so much of a hurry to get away from home she'd blindly trusted him. Now it turned out it was all a house of cards, and it was about to come tumbling down. 'How . . . I mean why . . . how . . .' She couldn't find the words as the scale of his deceit became clear to her. 'You *lied* to me.'

He looked up at her. 'I never lied.'

'Well maybe not an outright lie, but you knew what I would think. You knew I thought this was all official. You knew that, and you *never* said anything.'

'I couldn't, could I?' he shouted as he stood up. 'You were on the fence about coming anyway.' He sucked in a big deep breath and let it out again. 'And I needed you.'

'And your plan was . . . what? Get me out here so it's too late to say no?'

He shook his head.

'Fly me halfway around the world, away from my Izzy, away from Adam.' The volume of her voice was rising with each word as she paced back and forth in front of him.

'No, no, no.'

'Away from everyone I love, to come to the most dangerous place on the planet, and all based on your lies?' She thought of Adam. How on earth was she going to tell him? She could already hear the barbed comments about Guy he was bound to come out with. And right now, she was inclined to agree with them. She couldn't believe Guy had duped her like this, not after all these years – and that she'd been so blinded by her need to escape her life that she hadn't picked up on it before now.

'NO!' he shouted. He slapped his hand down on the Formica tabletop with a bang that stopped her dead. 'No,' he repeated quietly as he sank back down into the chair.

She stared at him, shocked that he'd raised his voice. He never did that. In fifteen years she couldn't recall one occasion when he had lost his temper with her – he was always so calm, so measured, like he'd thought five chess moves ahead of you and knew exactly how things were going to play out so he had no need to get angry. 'What, then?' she asked, her tone hard. Cold.

'I didn't lie to you about the data. I didn't lie to you about the ice shelf. I didn't lie to you about the drilling. I didn't lie to you about the Senate vote. About all this. You've seen the sat imagery. You've seen the analysis. I never lied to you about any of that.'

That was self-evident – but was not a sufficient answer. 'So why isn't this an official trip?' She sat down opposite him at the little table.

'Politics.'

'Politics? BAS is a non-political organization. How is that possible?'

'Come on, Rachael. There's no such thing as a non-political organization. Not anymore. Look, you and I know what the data means, what it will mean for the world if this continues. You and I know that the response should be a worldwide joint effort from the scientific community to gather more information, to prove it beyond doubt and stop what they're doing.'

She nodded.

'And perhaps, in normal times, that is what would've happened. But these' – he looked up at her – 'are not normal times.'

She placed her hands flat on the surface of the table, as if for balance. She was still reeling from his confession and felt light-headed as she tried to take it all in. 'So what happened?'

'I submitted my proposal for a fully funded, official expedition. Joint with the Australians, the Kiwis, the Argentines and the US.'

'And?'

'The US killed it.'

'How?'

'The US Antarctic Program is pretty much fully funded by the federal government. The same federal government that's pushing the drilling programme. All it took was a word in the right ear. "Do this expedition and you can kiss goodbye to your funding . . ."'

'But the Aussies, the Argentines, the Kiwis?'

'The Argentines can't go if the US says no – the Americans threatened to call in their loans. Their economy would have collapsed overnight.'

'And us?'

'The "special relationship".' He raised his bushy eyebrows. 'You know, it's funny – the Americans only ever seem to use that phrase when they want something.'

'What about the others?'

'When it became clear the Yanks weren't into it, I redrafted the plan as a British/Aussie/Kiwi thing. Scaled down, but still doable. Then one day Bridgewater summons me into the office with a face as white as a Beardmore blizzard.'

Rachael pictured the stern, angular face of Professor Helen Bridgewater, the Director of BAS, and Guy's boss. A formidable woman who Rachael had always found more than slightly intimidating.

'Why?'

'She'd been called into Whitehall and given a right old going-over by the permanent secretary.'

'But why? What do they care?'

'Trade, among other things.'

'What's that got to do with this?' She was getting irritated by his long-winded and circuitous explanation. None of it changed what he had done to get her here.

'The UK/US trade deal. The civil service has been putting in months of work to convince the Americans to sign a new deal. Without it, we're sunk, apparently: guaranteed recession, back to austerity, unemployment, the whole thing. It'll be like the thirties only worse. So the Yanks lean on the foreign secretary, insinuate ever so tactfully that they won't look too kindly on an expedition that's setting out to discredit the president's entire energy strategy for the next decade. And just like that, it's gone. Bridgewater told me BAS can't have anything to do with it.'

'But that's crazy! How can they be so short-sighted?'

'They're politicians,' he shrugged. 'They care about the now. They don't care about ten years from now when they won't be in power anymore. Ask yourself: what's more frightening to a minister: the *certainty* of a huge recession, massive unemployment and billions of pounds of cuts – that they will get the blame for – or the potential that some Antarctic sea ice *might* melt?'

'Not *might*.' She pulled out the data sheets from her backpack that she had been studying on the flight. '*Will*. According to the data we've already got, *will*.'

'They don't see it that way.'

'They're wrong,' she said firmly.

'I know that,' he said. 'That's why we're here.'

Damn him, he was trying to shift her anger away from him and onto the faceless bureaucrats who'd tried to stop the mission. And it was starting to work. *Damn him*. 'But, without BAS, how did you even do this?' Despite her anger, she could already feel herself starting to soften – he was right about the data, about the ice shelf, about the mission. She cared about that cause every bit as much as he did. And he knew it.

'I've been coming down here for over thirty years. You get to know people. People who owe you favours. People who don't want to see this drilling happen any more than we do. People who understand – even the Yanks here at Mac Town.'

'How are they getting away with it?'

'The base commander's an old mate of mine. He's organized logistical support – all at local level, all off the books. The Aussies are lending us the use of one of their Apple huts for the deep field work, the Kiwis are letting us use Station Z, and a BAS Twin Otter will fly us out there. And I managed to raise some money to pay for you, Zak and Henriksen.'

'How?'

'I sold a few things.'

'Like what?' She could already feel her initial rage subsiding.

She wasn't sold yet, but she couldn't stop her brain from moving on to the details.

'Nothing that can't be replaced.'

'Like what, Guy?'

'My Cessna.'

'But you love that plane.' She knew that outside of his work flying was his only hobby.

He cleared his throat and looked away. 'And my house.'

'Jesus! Your *house?!*' She was shocked, and yet not shocked at the same time. He was a man of conviction, a man untroubled by the need for material possessions and utterly uninterested in worrying about practicalities like where he lived or whether he had a pension – not when there were far more pressing things to focus on. He had owned the same car for as long as she'd known him, yet she knew he wouldn't even be able to tell her what make it was. For him it was simply a necessary tool, not an object of pride. His utter devotion to his cause, and his complete lack of interest in such trivialities was one of the things she loved about him, and part of what made him so inspiring to work with.

'It's only bricks and mortar.'

His silver St Christopher pendant caught the light for a split second, and Rachael made the connection instantly. 'That's why Barbara left, isn't it? Jesus, Guy.'

'Well, let's just say she was not all that impressed.'

She shook her head. 'I'm not surprised. Where are you going to live?'

'You've got a spare room, haven't you?' he smiled.

'Guy, I'm serious.'

'So am I. I had to do this.'

'But you can't go around selling your house – what about your future?'

'Listen, I didn't do this on the spur of the moment. I thought about it. I thought about it a lot. I could've stayed at home. Written reports, made speeches, published articles. But I asked myself: was that enough?'

He pushed his chair back and stood up. 'People talk about the meaning of life. What are we here for? What's the point of it all? I always thought that was a load of old cobblers. We're here – does there have to be a reason for it? I always thought it was about making the best of it.'

He turned and walked to the window. 'Some people are able to make a real difference in their lives. A real difference for others, to make the world better – in however small a way. People like doctors and teachers. But we can't all do that. That's not the path for all of us. I, like you, was drawn to science. And because of plenty of twists and turns along the way that probably didn't seem significant at the time, I ended up in this field. Climate change, glaciology. And as these past few months have played out, it dawned on me that I was one of a handful of people in the world – *in the world* – with the knowledge, ability and opportunity to actually do something.' He pulled a strand of the Venetian blind down so he could see out over the base. 'Not just writing articles and arguing with politicians from the comfort of my office, but actually *do* something. Something to really make a difference.' He let the blind snap back into place. 'Before it's too late.'

He turned to look at her once more. She stared right back at him. Everything he was saying was true. She couldn't deny that.

'This has been my life's work for thirty years, but it would have all been for nothing if, when the time came, when the chips were down, when it was all on the line, I didn't do everything in my power to stop it. And I mean everything. How could I have carried on, knowing I could have done more?' He walked back over to the table. 'I'm damn serious about this. And whether we change anyone's mind or not, whether we stop this or not, I knew I had to try. I knew I had to come. Whatever it took.' He sat down and looked directly into her eyes. 'And I knew I needed you, too.'

She said nothing. He had her in a bind now, and they both knew it. He'd gone all in on this trip: sacrificed his home, his job – even his own marriage – to make it happen. And if she quit on him now, it would all have been for nothing – there was absolutely no way he could do it without her. They'd all have to go home. And that would be it. She resented him for putting her in this position, but at the same time she was just as committed to the cause as he was.

'We only need four of us,' he said softly.

She narrowed her eyes sceptically, though she couldn't help but start to think through how they could pull it off.

'But even if we did . . . Henriksen? Really?'

'What about him?'

'He never shuts up about football!'

Guy smiled.

'And who's this Zak? I've never heard of him.'

'He comes very highly recommended. Ex-Navy. Very capable. Knows what he's doing.'

She thought for a moment. 'You really think we can do it with only the four of us?'

'You know we can.'

She took a deep breath. He was getting to her. He could be bloody persuasive, and at that moment she hated and admired that fact in equal measure. It was remarkable he'd even got this far without any official help. She couldn't think of a single other person in the world who could have pulled it off.

'And I'm sorry I got you here under slightly false pretences. When this is over, you're free to never speak to me again. Report me to whoever you like. Have them take away my Polar bloody

Medal for all I care. But this was too important for me not to get you here. And I'm sorry but that's the way it is.'

She looked up at him, at his round face, his big eyes under those big eyebrows. He really had risked everything. Put all his chips on this one throw of the dice. And he needed her.

'But I'm not forcing you into anything. There's a C-17 transport leaving for Christchurch in three hours. You can be on it. And I won't hold it against you. Go home to your husband and child. It's completely up to you.'

Rachael's mind flashed back to Izzy. The plaintive cry she'd heard down the phone line when she called Adam. She felt sick just thinking about it. She knew she was going to miss her but she hadn't expected it to be this hard – and she was barely a week into the trip. And now Guy was giving her an out. She could go home, she could be back cuddling Izzy within a few days. And no one would blame her – especially given the fast one Guy had pulled. But deep down, she knew he was right. He may have broken the rules to get this far, but he was still right.

'But what about you? What about the expedition? If I go home, you can't do it without me,' she said. Though he was much older than her, she felt an almost maternal responsibility towards him. He was so focused on his work he needed someone looking out for him.

'I'll figure something out. I always do.'

She stared at him for a full minute while she thought it all through. He had, at the very least, lied by omission to get her out here. But that didn't change what was happening on the ice. It didn't change the fact that this was their last chance to try to stop what would undoubtedly be the biggest environmental disaster in modern history. His actions had been rash and dishonest . . . but his motive was pure. And in the end, the mission mattered more. As angry as she was with him, she knew she had to stay and do the job. 'You and me could do the data sampling and the analysis between us,' she began, cautiously. 'Henriksen and Zak for support . . . I suppose it could be done.'

He took her hand and gave it a squeeze. 'Top banana,' he said as he smiled at her across the table.

'One thing,' she said.

'Go on.'

'You have to get Henriksen to wash that bloody hat or I'm on that C-17 in a heartbeat.'

'I promise,' he laughed.

13

It was the sound of the zip that startled her.

The noise was like a trapped, angry wasp and stood out sharply from the constant drone of the wind. Rachael sat up. Through the walls of her tent she could see bright light as the snow reflected the sun's rays, and the shadow of a man with broad shoulders. He was zipping up the outer sheet behind him, then he turned and parted the canvas of the inner layer with the second zip.

'Guy?' she said tentatively.

'Morning!' he replied brightly. 'Is there a coffee on the go?'

She glanced at the stove. On top of it was a pan of water balanced above the flame, next to two tin camping cups, each with a teaspoonful of freeze-dried instant coffee in the bottom. 'Yes,' she said uncertainly. She shook her head. 'What are you doing here? I mean, where have you been?'

He jerked his head towards his left shoulder. 'Out there.'

'But . . . I've been all alone.'

'Well I'm back now,' he smiled.

'No.' She shook her head. 'This isn't right.'

The water in the pan was beginning to come to the boil.

'This isn't right at all.'

'Come on, Rach,' he said. 'It's only me.'

He folded his long frame into the tent and zipped up the flap behind him.

'But you're not supposed to be here,' she continued.

'Where am I supposed to be?'

'Don't do that.'

'Do what?'

'You know what. Don't tease me.'

He grinned. 'I would never do that.'

'But you can't be here.'

'Why not?'

'You know why.'

The water was bubbling in the pot as the flame burned beneath it.

'You can't be here, and I shouldn't be here either,' she added.

'Ah, but you are,' he said knowingly.

'Yes but I shouldn't be. I shouldn't be here at all.'

'Is there a coffee on the go?' he asked again.

She looked at the stove, the water was bubbling violently in the pot, bursting and leaping for freedom.

'You tricked me, Guy.'

He shook his head. 'Nonsense. I just wanted to help. I needed your help.'

'You tricked me,' she said again.

'Is there a coffee on the go?'

'Forget your bloody coffee!' she screamed as she flung the pan of water off the flame, knocking the stove over in the process. It continued to burn and within seconds the canvas base of the tent beneath her burst into flames. Guy seemed completely oblivious to the fire and sat cross-legged, holding one of the coffee mugs with a stupid look on his face as the flames began to lick up around him.

'This is fine,' he said as he took a sip, and for some reason not immediately obvious to her, Rachael wanted to laugh out loud. 'I needed your help,' he repeated, the coffee cup now gone, and replaced with what she somehow knew were satellite photographs. 'I needed your help.'

The flames had now reached the walls of the tent and the fire raged all around her. 'You tricked me,' she shouted at his maddeningly impassive face. 'You tricked me, and now I don't have a chance!'

At that his face changed to a frown of confusion. 'Oh don't be so silly,' he chided her. 'There's always a chance, and while there is, we have to keep fighting. Isn't that right? Don't let the side down. All that.'

Her anger intensified with the flames.

'Top banana,' he said, smiling warmly. 'Top banana.'

Rachael awoke with a start to the tinny beeping of her wrist-watch's alarm. She felt sweaty and disorientated as she blinked her eyes open in the confines of the tent, the heat from the flames and the panic from her dream still feeling all too real as she came to. She pulled her arm out of the sleeping bag and up to her face to see the green display flashing. It was 6.30 a.m. Time to get up. Time to push on. The storm was still raging, pulling and pushing at her tent like it was a little rowing boat being tossed about on the high seas of the Atlantic. She grimaced at the thought of stepping out into that madness once again.

She flicked on her torch and glanced at the entrance to the tent. It was still tightly zipped up. She flashed the light across at the little stove. It was standing upright, next to a single tin mug with a measure of instant coffee in it which she had prepared before going to sleep the night before. She took in a deep breath as she came back to full consciousness and her dream started to come back to her: she remembered Guy, the fire, his madden-ingly passive expression as the flames licked up around him. 'For fuck's sake, Guy,' she said, before leaning over to light the stove.

14

Guy was sipping from his mug as he stood next to the pool table. His map was laid out on the green baize surface and prevented from rolling back in on itself by two pool balls at either end. Rachael, Zak and Henriksen stood opposite.

'Right then, ladies and gentlemen, boys and girls, let's go over it so we're all clear,' he said in his booming voice, before reiterating the nature of their mission. After gathering the data out on the ice, he explained they would have to get their findings to a Senator Morgan in Washington – Guy had been at Oxford with her scientific advisor, David Pilbeam – who would then try to persuade enough of her colleagues to vote against the president's plan to break the Antarctic Treaty and begin commercial drilling.

'How are we collecting the data?' Zak asked.

'We'll be using ground-penetrating-radar,' Guy said. 'I've selected three survey sites at different points on the shelf. The first is just over twenty miles from where we are now, where Mikael and I have been surveying for the past few days. The second is here,' he pointed to a spot on the map. 'On the western side of the Queen Alexandra range, at the foot of Mount Kirkpatrick.'

Rachael peered down at the map. She'd been to the Amundsen–Scott station at the pole once, but had spent most of her time working nearer the coast. She'd never visited these proposed sites. The chance to see some new parts of the continent excited her.

'The Kiwis have a summer base there – Station Z – measuring atmospheric changes. It's ours for the winter and will be our main base of operations for this expedition.'

'Station Z?' Zak said.

'Yes, I know, a bit Alistair MacLean, isn't it?' Guy replied. 'But I'm afraid it's based on nothing more exciting than the fact that they name their research stations alphabetically.'

'It's habitable over winter?' Henriksen asked.

'Oh yes. It's a new station – amazing, actually: accommodation, comms, top-of-the-range labs, everything. And it's fully modular, on stilts, so they can move it if they have to.'

'Like Halley?' Rachael said, referencing the British base that comprised a series of pods on legs and tethered together. It had been designed so it could be dragged to different locations, should the ice shelf on which it was currently based become unstable.

'Exactly like Halley,' Guy replied. 'It was designed as an all-season base, but they haven't got the funds to run it all year yet. So, it's ours for a few months.'

They would be flying out in a BAS Twin Otter aircraft the following day, Guy added.

'And the second survey site is near the base?' Rachael asked.

'Not far, about eighteen miles away.'

'How do we get there?'

'We have vehicles. There at two PistenBully Snowcats at Station Z. They aren't very quick, but they're tracked so they'll go over anything. Perfect for us. We'll use those to access the survey site daily, and return to the base each night.'

Rachael nodded. She'd spent plenty of time clunking along in Snowcats over the years to remote camps. 'And the third site?'

Guy sucked in a deep breath. 'The third site is the most tricky.'

He moved his finger up the map. 'It's here: under Graphite Peak in the Queen Maud Mountain range.'

Rachael squinted at the map. 'Is there a station there, too?'

'No,' Guy said. 'This is proper deep field. But there is an old Apple hut and a generator. The Aussies had it put there for the Mawson Expedition in '89, and Kevin's said we can use it.'

Rachael frowned. 'An Apple hut? In winter? That's not going to be too comfy.' She knew they were little more than tents, with nothing in the way of creature comforts.

'It'll be fine for us,' Guy said. 'We only need to be there for two weeks to collect the data we need.'

'And do we fly in there, too?' Henriksen asked.

Guy shook his head. 'No, for one thing, by the time we're ready to go, we'll be in the no-fly season. And in any case, there's no airstrip there.'

'So how do we get there?'

'The Snowcats. We'll go overground from Station Z. It's about ninety miles away, so should be doable in a day or two. We'll take Scott tents if we need to camp overnight halfway.'

'Sounds simple enough,' Henriksen said.

Guy shook his head again. 'It won't be simple at all. From Station Z, this site is the other side of a shear zone, where two different ice floes meet each other. Miles and miles of crevasses, three or four hundred feet deep – many of them snowed over so you can't even see them.'

'So how do we get across a crevasse field in tracked vehicles that weigh, what, eight tons, without falling to our deaths?' Rachael asked.

Guy explained the Snowcats were mounted with GPR on booms at the front. The lead vehicle would scan the surface as they went, picking a safe route through. The second vehicle would follow in its tracks. And if the first did make a mistake, it would be attached to the other with high-strength cables. 'It'll be pretty slow going, but we'll get there.' He smiled. 'It'll be fun,' he added, his eyes sparkling with excitement.

'Oh yeah, sounds like a walk in the park,' Henriksen replied sarcastically.

'They managed it in 1911 with nothing but dogs and ponies. We'll have it a lot easier than that,' Guy replied.

'Nineteen eleven?'

'Yes. The *Terra Nova* expedition traversed this site on their way to the pole.'

'Scott's crew?' Rachael said.

Guy nodded. 'In fact, One Ton Hut isn't far from where the Apple is now.'

'It's still standing?'

'It was the last time anyone saw it.'

'So you're telling us Scott's team went on this route?' Henriksen asked.

'That's right.'

'Oh well, that's really comforting – they all died on the way back!' The Norwegian started laughing hysterically, but no one else joined in. Rachael shot him a glare – she knew any journey over a shear zone – let alone in winter – was fraught with danger and difficulty. She could do without Henriksen's bizarre amusement at the fate of some of their Antarctic explorer predecessors.

'They were only eleven miles short of One Ton – and in any case,' Guy said firmly, 'we shall be far better prepared than they were.'

'Well that won't be hard,' Henriksen scoffed. 'We won't be taking ponies for one thing.' He shook his head. 'Honestly, Scott was an idiot.'

'I will NOT get into this again with you Mikael,' Guy said, bristling at his colleague's comments. 'He was a very brave leader of men, who did his best in the most extreme of circumstances with the equipment and knowledge available at the time.'

'You know, even if he and his team hadn't all died – *which they did* – they still lost to Amundsen?'

'I know that.'

'Amundsen beat him to the pole by five whole weeks! So as well as being incompetent, Scott was a loser as well.'

Rachael rolled her eyes: she'd seen Henriksen wind Guy up about Scott a dozen times, and he always fell for it.

'You know that Amundsen double-crossed Scott, don't you?' Guy responded. 'He wasn't even supposed to be in the Antarctic. Told everyone – including Scott – that he was going to the *North* Pole. Then turned up in Antarctica instead.'

'Sounds like whining from a loser, to me,' Henriksen smirked. 'Amundsen was better prepared, chose a better route, used dogs instead of bloody ponies, picked better equipment, beat Scott by more than a month AND made it back alive with his whole crew. And don't get me started on Captain Oates.'

'Now look here—'

Rachael had had enough. 'Can we get back to business?' she said curtly. She had no desire to spend the entirety of the expedition playing referee between these two, but clearly someone had to.

Guy shot Henriksen a final, withering look and then returned to his map. 'So, we'll spend two or three weeks at the Apple site here, collecting the data, then we'll head back to Station Z to analyse it and wait out the winter.'

He told them they must get the data to Senator Morgan by 6 August, to give Pilbeam time to have it peer-reviewed, corroborated and then distributed to Morgan's colleagues, so she could persuade enough of them to vote with her. 'The numbers are pretty balanced, apparently, so we only need a couple of her colleagues to see the light. She wins the vote – no more drilling. Job done. Then we'll be on the first plane out in the spring and back home in time for tea and Polar Medals. Easy-peasy, lemon squeezy.'

There were nods all round. Rachael's brain was already whirring – Guy's description made it all sound so simple. She knew it would be anything but. Even just collecting the data they needed in winter was going to be the toughest assignment she'd ever attempted – then they had to hope it would prove Guy's theory *and* be enough to convince a bunch of American politicians.

'Remember, Zak here is designated safety officer, so you do what he says at all times,' Guy said.

'We all know how dangerous it is out here,' Zak began as he assumed the lead of the meeting, 'and it's even more so in winter, especially off base and in deep field. Just because we've all been down here plenty of times before, I will not tolerate any complacency. Your health and safety is my priority at all times. Guy is in charge of the expedition, but I'm in charge of safety. When we're out there, what I say goes.'

The other three nodded. Rachael felt reassured by how seriously he was taking his role. It was a nice contrast to the endlessly joking and apparently nonchalant Henriksen. While she knew that, deep down, the Norwegian took his job as seriously as anyone else, he always seemed to be at pains to make it appear that he didn't care at all. There was something comfortably familiar about Zak as she listened to him – then she realized Adam had given her a similar briefing when they had first met all those years ago.

'Antarctica is the coldest, windiest, driest, most remote, most desolate, most inhospitable place on the entire planet.' Zak walked around the table so he was facing Rachael and Henriksen. 'Human eyes did not even see this continent until 1820, and the pole was only reached a century ago.'

'By a Norwegian,' Henriksen added, to another dirty look from Guy.

'It was the very last place in the world to be discovered,' Zak continued, ignoring Henriksen's interjection. 'This is a place that did not want to be found. It has ice and snow several kilometres deep, and active volcanoes. Where we're going, deep south and far from any other human contact, the environment is so severe that nothing can live. No animals, no plant life, not even insects can survive in these extremes. This is a place that was simply not designed for humans to exist in.'

Rachael, of course, knew all this inside out, but she was not so complacent to think she was above listening. It was rather like the safety briefing the cabin crew gave on a flight – Rachael flew so often she could probably have given it herself, but nonetheless, she listened intently each time she heard it, a firm believer that drumming something like that into your brain again and again would make the information all the easier to access in a hurry should it ever be needed.

'All right, Connelly, we've all been here before,' said Henriksen, who did not share Rachael's patience when it came to such things. 'We don't need your first-timers' lecture.'

'Yes, but none of you have been here with me. And not all of you have done a winter down here, so let me tell you now, it's brutal in a way that you will never have experienced and cannot possibly imagine. You will encounter temperatures lower than you ever thought possible, cold that will attack you like a vicious wild animal at any and every opportunity. Cold that will claim your hands and toes with frostbite. Even the vapour from your breath can freeze your eyes shut so you'll think you've gone blind.'

He paused to make sure they were listening. Rachael absolutely

110

was – she was a vastly experienced polar traveller, but Zak was right: she'd never done a winter trip, and though the prospect excited her, she was humble enough to know she was stepping into the unknown. And she realized she was glad Zak was here to look after them, as he continued explaining the dangers of hypothermia and the physical signs that they must all watch out for, namely the loss of coordination and the power of speech.

'Down here they call it "the umbles",' he said, 'because if it happens to you, you'll lose physical coordination and the power of speech: you'll mumble, fumble and stumble. If any of you notice these symptoms in yourself or others, make it known immediately so we can take action.'

They all nodded.

'The storms down here are brutal. If you're out in the field when one approaches, you must immediately tie down or stow all equipment you have or the gale force winds will blow it all away. Whiteouts are common, and when they happen they are not only painfully cold and physically taxing, but disorienting as well – often you won't be able to see your hand in front of your face, and you won't be able to hear anything other than the roar of the wind.'

That was something Rachael had experienced, when she was out on a survey trip near Halley – in fact, she recalled, it was her first trip with Adam. They'd been caught in a blizzard while trekking between two campsites and the elements had closed her in so completely she was unable to hear or see Adam, despite the fact he was only a few feet in front of her. She'd been very thankful that they were joined together by a climbing rope as she realized just how easy it would have been for them to start walking in different directions and lose each other.

'The perils of polar life are everywhere,' Zak continued, his tone was as serious as his message, 'and any small problem can quickly escalate into a crisis. A small fire in the base could kill us all, if not dealt with. If you were to get lost in the poor visibility of a blizzard, you'd have a few hours at most. After that your body will cool down to the danger point, you'll run out of energy and you'll die. And we cannot risk endangering ourselves to come looking for you. Down here, more than anywhere else on earth, life is delicate and can be snuffed out at any moment. Make no mistake, you will be taxed to your very limits and way beyond every single day you're here. But if you do what I say at all times, you'll be as safe as possible, and we'll all get out alive.'

Henriksen rolled his eyes.

'The standard operating procedures will apply,' Zak continued. 'That means no one goes anywhere alone. Ever. Not even for a moment. In the dark and with these storms, you can get lost before you know it.'

'We all know what we're doing, we don't need babysitting,' Henriksen said.

Rachael wished for once in his life he would shut up.

Zak turned to face him. 'Two years ago, an engineer on this very base went for a walk by himself. In the winter. In the dark. Then a storm blew in. He never came back. Three days later, the search team found his body, just two hundred metres from the base. He was two hundred metres from safety and he couldn't find his way back.'

'All right, you've made your point.'

'The year before that, a research scientist from Chile went for a drive in a Snowcat. He misjudged the snow on a crossing over a crevasse, the Snowcat fell in, taking him with it, straight down, a hundred and eighty feet. He cracked his skull in the fall, and was dead by the time they got down to him.'

Henriksen looked down sheepishly. Zak clearly wasn't going to take any of Henriksen's shit.

'Both of those men were experienced Antarctic travellers, each had more than five seasons under his belt. Both paid the ultimate price for a lack of respect for this environment. They thought they knew it, they thought they could handle it.' Zak looked each of them in the eye, one by one. Was it Rachael's imagination, or did he linger on her for half a beat longer than the others? 'They were wrong. On both counts.'

'Exactly,' Guy said. 'We're here to do a job, but it's no good if we don't do it safely.'

'So, as I said,' Zak continued, 'no one goes anywhere alone. Ever. When out in the field, you two must check in twice daily over radio to us back at Station Z, and when you're out there, you'll be taking extra survival gear with you: tents, sleeping bags, stoves, cooking gas, rations, just in case.'

Rachael nodded.

'Remember, once we're out there, *there is no rescue*. No planes can get in or out until the spring, we'll obviously be unreachable by sea, and we'll be almost a thousand miles from the nearest person. There is no escape. No way out. Once we go in, we're there for the duration.'

Rachael caught his eye again as she let his words sink in. She'd initially been unhappy to learn that a man she'd never met before had been assigned to their team, but after hearing him speak she felt completely reassured and very glad of his presence.

'Right, everybody clear? Good,' Guy said, without waiting for a reply. 'Remember: we've only got one shot at this. If we fail and they drill again next summer, it'll be too late to stop it.'

'I get it,' Henriksen said. 'This is Barcelona, 1999. We're one-nil down in the ninetieth minute, right?' He tapped the Manchester United crest on his hat. 'But don't worry, Solskjær is here. We can still win it.'

Guy shook his head. 'Not everything is a football metaphor, Mikael.'

15

Rachael sat up in her sleeping bag, sipping her coffee and eating a packet of freeze-dried, high-energy porridge as she listened to the storm raging outside the tent. It would soon be time to brave it once again, and she wasn't relishing the prospect.

At two minutes before the hour her wristwatch's alarm went off and, after she'd silenced it, she reached inside her rucksack for her little transistor radio. She clicked it to the 'on' position and waited. A few moments later, the familiar voice arrived.

```
This is the Wartime Broadcasting Service
from the BBC in London . . .
```

As usual she mouthed along to each word as it was spoken, and once it was finished she clicked the radio off and stowed it back in her pack. 'Stay in your own homes,' she repeated as she looked around her tent in the dark, its canvas being attacked by the relentless wind. 'As if.'

She pulled out her journal from her backpack and wrote a short entry, noting the date, her position and her intended destination: Station Z. It was a long way, a very big ask, but she had no other choice. She had to push on for the base. She rolled up her sleeping bag and set about donning her clothes and preparing to face the cold. Once she was ready she removed her gear from the tent, then left the stove in the snow to cool while she packed away her canvas castle – a task she found was even more difficult than erecting it.

Once she was finished, she hauled out the sled from the back of the Snowcat and stowed her tent, stove, sleeping bag and food supplies on it, lashing them down with a bungee cord. She was about ready to set sail when she glanced at the Snowcat. After a second's hesitation she trudged over to the cab to try the engine one last time.

Like double-checking you've turned the stove off or locked the door, even when you *know* you have, Rachael decided it was better to make sure and have peace of mind, than not check and spend all day wondering. Even as the silent machine once again failed to come to life, she was glad she'd made sure. She climbed out of the cab and down the tracks before attaching the sled tow ropes to the carabiners hooked onto her Big Red. Then she checked her heading, and resumed her slow march towards survival.

The fact that the survey site had been the other side of one of the most deadly crevasse fields on the continent had merely seemed to appeal to Guy's obsession with challenges. But when Rachael crested a small hill and was afforded a slightly elevated view of her route, she cursed his name again. Of course he had no control over where the data needed to be collected – that was just how the cookie crumbled – but he needn't have been so fucking gleeful about it, she thought.

For as far as her head torch would let her see in the blizzard and the dark – which admittedly wasn't far – there was line after line of deep crevasses. She had to assume each one to be at least two or three hundred feet deep and certainly fatal if she fell in. To navigate across them meant zig-zagging between each one and crossing where a bridge had formed at the point where two separate crevasses had merged. All she had to do was keep going. At minus fifty-five degrees Celsius, in a force nine snow blizzard, in constant darkness, and dragging a sixty-kilo sled. 'Easy-peasy, lemon squeezy,' she said aloud as she continued to march.

She had more than eighty miles to cover, but she only had rations to last for four days. She knew twenty miles a day was possible – just – in good weather, but she wasn't blessed with any such luxury. She also reckoned that her biggest problem wasn't the isolation, the conditions, the weight of the sled or the toughness of the terrain – it was sweat.

Given she *had* to cover a fairly ambitious mileage each day, Rachael knew it would be all too easy for her to push too hard and, tucked up inside her specially designed polar clothing, work up a sweat inside her jacket or gloves. And that could be lethal. In the minus fifty-degree temperatures she was battling with, that sweat wouldn't take long to ice up – and that meant frostbite. It was counter-intuitive, but Rachael knew she had to prevent herself from getting too warm if she was to avoid freezing to death. She had to tread a very thin line: she must work hard enough to cover sufficient ground before her rations ran out, but she also had to operate under the sweat level or she would succumb to frostbite before she ever made it back to the base.

After eight hours she was satisfied, almost pleased, with her progress. She'd made a steady pace, despite the zig-zag route she had been forced to take, and once she'd settled into a rhythm, even the weight of the sled had become just another part of the fight to stay alive. She thought for a moment that the wind might even be starting to let up a little. She never wanted to stop moving – she knew her best chance was to keep going, even if that meant slowing her pace a little, rather than stopping and starting. If she stopped, she worried she might never start again. But she was in danger of becoming seriously dehydrated if she didn't stop and melt some ice to drink. She was just trying to decide whether to push on for another hour or to stop now when the decision was made for her.

For the first fraction of a second it felt like a hand on her shoulder gently pulling her back, like a friend tapping her on the back to say 'hello'. But the next split second was when she realized she'd made a catastrophic mistake, and even in that infinitesimally small amount of time, she had the brain capacity to reason that her mistake was about to cost her her life.

She must have strayed off track and over a crevasse covered with ice thick enough to support her, but not the heavy weight of the sled behind her. She felt the pull get stronger to the point where it was irresistible, as a feeling of pure panic shot up through her chest. She dug her poles into the snow as hard as she could and desperately leaned forward, but it wasn't enough: the weight of the sled was pulling her down into the crevasse behind her, and she lost her grip on the poles as she was drawn down into the icy abyss.

The whole thing happened in less than a second and then she was gone, falling into the clutches of a would-be icy grave. She let out an involuntary scream as she felt the ground beneath her feet literally swallow her up. She flung her arm behind her, grabbed her ice axe from a hook on her backpack and swung it as hard as she could into the wall of the crevasse as she plummeted down into the black depths. The moment she did, she stopped falling and the sudden stop almost snapped her arm right out of its socket. She howled out in pain, but somehow clung onto the axe, which was now the only thing preventing her from hurtling down to her death. Beneath her, the weight of the sled pulled at her body like a shark trying to drag her beneath the surface. What was once her only chance at survival – her shelter, her warmth, her means of eating and drinking – had now become the very thing that could cause her death. Her new life raft was now trying to kill her.

As she hung precariously halfway down the ice shaft, howling in pain and with her sled dangling down below her, she could feel her hand starting to slip on the handle of the axe.

16

'So was it a big do?' Guy was at the joystick controls of the red Snowcat vehicle as they crunched through the snow. Rachael sat to his right in the passenger seat.

'You'd know if you'd bothered to come.'

'You know I wanted to come.'

'So why didn't you?'

'I was working.'

'You had eight months' notice, Guy.' She turned away and stared out of her window into the white desert. She'd been really upset when he hadn't shown up to her wedding – in a weird way it felt like one of her parents was missing from the most important day of her life. 'You could've made it if you'd really wanted to.'

'I was in the States – trying to get them not to rip up the Paris Agreement.'

She didn't turn round. 'It really hurt me, you know.'

'What, your crusty old boss not turning up to your wedding?'

She gritted her teeth. 'Don't make me say something nice about you when I'm mad at you.'

'What do you mean?'

She knew he was manipulating her. He was infuriating. 'You're more to me than my old boss, and you know it. I really wanted you to be there.'

They continued in silence for a few minutes, with only the noise of the diesel engine and the clanking of the tracks on the ice for company.

'And is it everything you'd hoped for?'

'What?'

'Marriage. Normality.'

She raised one eyebrow. 'I'm not sure what I expected, to be honest.'

'You must have thought about it. I know you, Rachael. You analyse everything.'

'I loved Adam, I wanted to marry him. I didn't think much further than that. I sort of assumed everything else would work itself out.' She shrugged. 'That's what's supposed to happen, right?'

He laughed. 'Two divorces and another one on the way, remember. You're asking the wrong guy.'

He probably had a point there, she thought.

'Still, you've got it all now. Fancy house in the suburbs.'

'It's hardly fancy. It's a Victorian terrace.'

'Yes, but with all the "period features" – isn't that what estate agents say?'

'Yes, it's a nice house. Adam works hard.'

'And all the trappings, too: nice car, antique furniture . . .'

'What are you getting at, Guy?'

'Nothing, nothing,' he said, defensively. 'I've just never been able to pull off that "normal" life thing. I'm interested to know how you do it.'

'It's what you make of it, I guess.' She didn't want to get into this with Guy. She was still trying to work out her feelings about Adam and their marriage, but she daren't show any of that to Guy. He knew her so well that if she showed a crack of doubt, he'd immediately be on to it, teasing more and more out of her. Making her face up to things she wasn't ready to deal with yet.

'I don't buy that. Some people are cut out for it, and some people aren't. And you and I, Rach, we just aren't. It's why we keep coming back to places like this.'

'I'm perfectly happy, thank you very much,' she said, a little more defensively than she'd intended. She really didn't want to say anymore, and she didn't want to lie to him again – he would see right through that anyway.

Guy raised his hands from the controls in a surrender pose, then checked his bearing. It was a full five minutes before either of them spoke again.

'You said, "loved", Guy said quietly.

'I'm sorry?'

'Back there,' he nodded over his shoulder, 'you said you "loved" Adam. Past tense.'

She turned away from him again. He was finding a way in. She had to change the subject. 'I didn't mean that. You know what I meant. Aren't we nearly at the survey site?'

She took a USB drive from her pocket and slotted it into the socket on the Snowcat's stereo. Pink Floyd's 'Nobody Home' filled the cab and prevented further conversation.

After another twenty-five minutes of slow progress across the snow, the GPS tracker mounted on the dashboard emitted a short series of high-pitched beeps, and Guy stopped the vehicle. 'We're here.'

They pulled up their face masks, pulled down their goggles, and braced themselves for the cold that lay in wait for them outside the vehicle. With a final nod at each other across the cab, they both opened their doors and, with some effort against the wind, Rachael pushed hers wide enough to jump down onto the snow. The cold was already trying to find a way in through the layers of her protective clothing. The path of least resistance was around her face – the tiny gap between the bottom of her goggles and the top of her mask. In the summer months the cold was usually tolerable – and occasionally it could even feel almost warm when the wind dropped and the sun was out. But this was a world away from those benign conditions. She busied herself at the back of the Snowcat as she and Guy pulled the ground-penetrating-radar transmitter and antenna device from the storage bay and began to boot it up. Once the machine was ready, he clipped it to the hoops on Rachael's Big Red, then the two of them set off, walking side by side along the survey site, Rachael dragging the device, Guy watching the monitor.

Just short of an hour later Guy tapped his watch. 'We need to warm up. I'll go and grab the thermos, we'll have some coffee and then carry on.'

Rachael nodded.

'Here,' Guy said, handing her the GPR portable screen. 'Finish up this tract and I'll be back in a minute.'

Rachael hooked the strap around her neck and continued on her route, watching the data coming through on the screen as she did so. She thought back to what Guy had been saying in the Snowcat. 'Loved.' Guy was right: she had said 'loved'. It had just slipped out. Was that really how she felt? Had that love she felt for Adam, once so fierce, slipped away? She tried to remember the last time she'd told Adam she loved him, but she couldn't pin it down in her memory. She hadn't been able to say it on the phone when she landed at McMurdo. She thought of their argument in the kitchen when she told him she was coming on the trip. He'd accused her of shutting him out, of running away to Antarctica to escape their troubles rather than face them. Maybe he was right. Maybe it was easier to come to the ends of the earth to save the world than to stay at home and save her marriage. Loved. Was it really past tense? She felt like she was in a fog, as if her true feelings were on the other side of a brick wall that stretched high up into the sky. She knew she didn't want it to be over, but perhaps that was just wishful thinking. And if it was over, why couldn't she work out why? She simply couldn't put her finger on what had changed. It was all so murky.

She reached the end of the survey site and turned around. That was when she saw him: Guy was lying face down on the ice, the snow already beginning to settle on his red polar jacket.

'Guy!' she shouted as she flung the portable screen into the snow and ran back to him, dragging the GPR unit behind her as she went. 'Guy! Are you all right?' She was shouting, but in this wind it was impossible to make herself heard. Once she reached him she knelt down in the snow and pulled his head up. His eyes were closed. She leaned in close to him. He was still breathing. 'Guy!' she shouted again. 'Guy! It's Rachael! Can you hear me?' There was no response. With some difficulty she rolled him onto his side and listened again to his breathing. It seemed steady. Consistent. She remembered her first response training: if the patient was alive, heart beating and breathing, the best thing you can do – the only thing you can do – is go for help as soon as possible. If you stayed to maintain life, you'd be stuck there forever.

'Guy, I'm going to the Snowcat, I'll be back in a minute, OK? Don't worry – I'll be right back.'

She scrambled to her feet and ran to the vehicle, jumped into the driver's seat and turned on the ignition to power the dashboard-mounted VHF radio. 'Station Z, this is mobile survey unit Bravo. Station Z, this is mobile survey unit Bravo, do you receive?'

The machine hissed with static but no response.

'Station Z, this is mobile survey unit Bravo. Request immediate assistance – Guy is unconscious. I need help, now.'

Still nothing. Were they just not listening? Or were they not receiving? She wondered whether the mountains were interfering with the signal. She tried one more time. 'Station Z, this is mobile survey unit Bravo, do you receive? Zak? Mik? Is there anyone there?' she added in an increasingly panicked tone.

Again, nothing. She considered her options: even if they did come to get her, it was over an hour's drive, and then another hour back to the station. Whatever was wrong with Guy, he would be better served back at base. And with Zak and Henriksen apparently ignoring her calls, she made her decision then and there.

She started up the diesel engine, then swung the vehicle around and motored the thirty yards to where Guy lay on the snow. She positioned the Snowcat between Guy and the prevailing wind to give herself a tiny bit of help for the difficult job she knew lay ahead. Then she jumped down and checked his vitals again. Pulse still strong, still breathing, still unconscious. She opened the passenger-side door of the vehicle, and hooked it back so it wouldn't blow shut in the wind.

'OK, I'm going to get you inside now. Stay with me, Guy. Stay with me.'

She pulled his legs up until his feet were directly underneath his knees. She put her left foot on top of his boots and pushed all her weight down. Then she leaned over him and picked up his left hand with her right. She took a deep breath. This was not going to be easy. After steadying herself for half a second, she pulled him towards her. *Jesus Christ he was heavy*. Guy was pretty trim for a man of his age, but he was still more than six feet tall and probably had four or five stone on her at least. She pulled until his torso was upright, then paused to catch her breath.

The next stage was the critical – and most difficult – part of the move. She needed to keep her foot firmly planted on his, then pivot his weight onto his feet until it was past the ninety-degree point, then let his body fall onto her back. She took another breath and pulled. His limp torso got as far as his knees, but she couldn't get it any further than that. She pulled harder, but he just wouldn't budge. She released the pressure for a moment, took another breath and then pulled hard again. Still she couldn't shift his weight. Slowly, she let him drop back to the ice, then took a moment to get her breath back. She looked around her. She was utterly alone. She *had* to get Guy back in the vehicle. If she couldn't, he'd be dead within hours – that was certain in these temperatures. There was simply no other choice.

'Right, Guy,' she said. 'I'm starting to get fed up of this. I know you're a stubborn old bastard, but I need to get you in that bloody Snowcat. I need you to help me. I need you to work with me. You got it?'

He didn't move.

'OK, good,' she said with a nod. She yanked his torso up towards her once again by his hand, and this time, instead of pausing, she pulled with all her might in the one motion to get his weight over the pivot point of his foot. She let out a grunt, as a shot-putter might when going for gold at the Olympics, and with an almighty heave she felt his weight transfer, and bent her own back under his chest to take his weight. Then, knowing she might never summon the strength again, she immediately stood up to her full height with his limp body draped over her shoulders. She took two steps towards the Snowcat, then with her left hand holding his wrist and her right gripping a handle on the vehicle, she hauled the two of them up onto the tracks, and then let his body fall into the passenger seat.

She stood, breathing heavily for a moment as she tried to

slow her heart rate, but there was no time to lose – he was still unconscious and she had absolutely no idea what was wrong with him. She strapped him in with the seat belt, then jumped down, unclipped the door and swung it shut, then raced around to the driver's side and pointed the Snowcat in the direction of Station Z.

'Don't worry, Guy,' she said as they moved off at what now seemed like a painfully slow fifteen miles per hour – the vehicle's top speed. 'We'll be back before you know it. Everything will be fine,' she added doubtfully.

17

She was going to fall. That much was certain. She could feel her hand slipping on the ice axe. Millimetre by millimetre she was losing her grip, being pulled to her death by the very equipment that was supposed to keep her alive.

She tried to think of a way out but any rational thoughts were being trampled and crushed by sheer terror and she was hyperventilating as her body reacted to the adrenaline coursing through her veins. She tried to focus and push the panic aside: there must be *something* she could do, something she could try before it was too late and she plummeted to her death. She felt the weight of the sled pulling her down, clawing at her like a bear trying to drag her down from a tree. She knew she had to cut it loose. As her right hand tightened on the handle of the ice axe, her left swung up behind her back and unclipped one of the carabiners connecting her to the sled. The sudden shift in weight yanked her down as the total mass of the sled and its contents were now hanging from her left-hand side. She let out a cry and her breathing quickened again as another surge of panic shot up through her chest. The movement dislodged her spare gas canister and she just caught a glimpse of it as it tumbled down into the darkness. She listened out but didn't hear it hit the bottom.

Still her hand was slipping. She knew she only had a few more seconds. She swung her arm back and tried to find the other carabiner, but in her panic, her gloved hand slipped over it. She tried again, but she could not move her fingers with sufficient dexterity with her outer gloves on. She was breathing so fast she worried she might simply black out. With her right hand still slipping, she pulled her left around to her mouth, pulled her glove off with her teeth and then swung her hand back round. Her right hand was now at the very end of the aluminium shaft. She tried to tighten her grip, but it was no good. She was losing the fight. The weight was too much to hold. She tried to unbuckle the clasp on the second carabiner but she could not get her fingers around it. Without her outer glove her hand was already freezing up, the fingers becoming stiff, immobile and unresponsive. She willed them to curl around the metal hook but they just wouldn't comply.

Then the ice axe gave way.

With a sudden jerk it came away from the ice in her hand and she was falling again. The breath was forced from her lungs as she slid down into the crevasse, faster and faster and faster.

She let out a terrified scream as she fell, but managed to twist around and with her left hand finally got a hold of the carabiner. She flicked it open to release the weight of the sled. With her other hand she swung a mighty stroke with the axe and with a guttural cry coming right from her belly, she embedded it deep in the wall of ice. And stopped.

She hung in the air, breathing fast. Her right arm burned with pain as it supported her full weight on the axe. Within a split second she heard her sled and all her equipment clatter to the bottom of the icy ravine, hundreds of feet below her. She looked up. Through the blackness, her head torch illuminated the snow swirling around above the crevasse as the storm continued.

She wanted to cry as she hung in the air, her cheek against the icy wall, but she was breathing too fast and too shallow for that. She was stuck, halfway down a crevasse, with no way out, and no equipment to survive even if she did get out. She now had no tent, no sleeping bag, no stove and therefore no way to get water. Exposed, she knew she would be dead in a matter of hours. She would never make it to Station Z, and she could obviously not go back to the Apple now either.

Her prospects were bleak. About as bleak as they could get, and as she held herself up by one hand on her ice axe, the dread and exhaustion and terror consuming her, it occurred to her that all she had to do was gently let go. Even just for a second. It wasn't a big choice. It was a tiny action. It could even happen by accident – it almost just did. She could simply relax her grip – probably one finger would do – and it would all be over. The pain of losing Izzy and Adam would be gone. The cold and the exhaustion and the loneliness and the despair would all be gone. She looked down. The fall was easily big enough. It would all be over quickly. No pain. No waiting to see what would get her first: dehydration or the cold. Game over, simply by loosening her fingers a fraction. *So easy.*

For some reason, her mind went back to that day at McMurdo, when Guy had briefed them all on the expedition. She almost laughed when she thought of Henriksen and his disgusting hat. She remembered Zak's safety briefing. She thought of her current situation, and how she was, in large part, responsible for her own downfall. She hadn't listened to him. God how she wished she had. She thought of Guy: his total certainty about what they were doing. His utter conviction in their cause.

'What's all this carry-on, then?' His big voice boomed inside the cave-like atmosphere of the crevasse. 'You're not feeling sorry for yourself, are you? Come on now, there's no need for all that nonsense.'

He was sitting on a ledge in the wall of ice above her, dangling his legs over the side, and dressed, as usual, in shorts and a rugby shirt, with flip-flops on his feet.

'Fuck off, Guy!' Rachael shouted. 'Just fuck off!'

He smiled. 'Hey now,' he said soothingly, 'there's no need for that. What are you all worked up about anyway?'

'Are you joking? Look at me!'

He shrugged.

'I'm seventy miles from any shelter, down a bloody crevasse, hanging on by my fingertips to an ice axe, and I've just lost all the stuff I'll need to keep me alive, even if I somehow manage to get out of here.'

Guy raised his eyebrows. 'And that's something to get in a tizz over, is it?'

'It's all right for you. You're not even really here. But I am, and this time, I think I'm pretty screwed.'

'Nonsense!' He boomed. 'Take it one step at a time. First job is to get yourself out of here and back up onto terra firma. Or icy firma, at least.'

'And how do you propose I do that?'

'You've done the training. You know what to do.'

She shook her head as she clung onto the axe, hugging the ice. 'And say I do get out, what then? What do I do? With no tent, no stove, no sleeping bag. Where do I go?'

Guy tapped the side of his head with his index finger. 'You'll figure it out. You're a clever one. Top banana. I've always said so.'

'No!' she shouted. 'Help me!'

'You don't need my help, Rach. You've got everything you need to help yourself.'

'Stop it!' she shouted back. 'Just stop it and tell me wh—' She stopped talking and looked up at Guy as a thought hit her. He smiled and nodded slowly. She narrowed her eyes, pulled out her knife from a clasp on her rucksack with her spare hand, then reached up and dug it into the wall of ice as hard as she could. Then she pulled out the ice axe, swung that above the knife and pulled herself up, digging the spikes of her right boot hard into the ice as she did so to help take her weight. She wasn't done yet. There was still a chance. And she knew exactly what she had to do.

18

'Is he doing any better?' Rachael stood in the doorway of the sickbay at Station Z. She looked down at Guy in the bed, his skin was waxy and pale, hair clinging to his glistening forehead. He suddenly looked every inch of his fifty-nine years.

Zak stood up from the plastic chair beside the bed and shook his head as he pulled the door shut behind him. 'It's getting worse. His temperature's gone up again.' He lowered his voice as he took a step closer to her. 'I'm really worried about him. We need to get him out.'

'Get him *out*?'

He nodded. 'His temperature's going up and up, he's in and out of consciousness, and when he's awake he's making no sense.' He took her by the arm and met her gaze. 'And the worst thing is, I don't know why.'

'Yes, but, if he leaves . . .'

'I know, Rachael. But we have to make this decision now. If we're going to get him out, I need to get on the radio to McMurdo in the next two hours. Otherwise it'll be too late. They're flying the last plane out in the morning. If we don't get them to come and pick him up tonight, he'll be stuck here, with no possibility of rescue until the spring. With the way he's going, I'm not at all sure he'll last that long. Do you want to take that chance?'

'But . . . the expedition,' she said forlornly. 'Everything he's worked for.'

'I'm sorry, Rachael. But his life is more important. We can try again in the summer.'

'The summer?'

'Yes. We can have another run at this the other side of winter, when Guy's well again.'

'What are you talking about?'

He frowned. 'Surely you realize we'll have to go as well. We can't do this expedition without Guy.'

She shook her head. 'No,' she said firmly. 'Absolutely not. We stay and finish the job. The summer will be too late, Zak. You know that – the vote is in September.'

'But with one man down, it can't be done.'

'Who says?'

'Me. And I'm in charge of safety on this mission.'

'Yes, but you're not the base commander here, Zak. That's Guy. And in his absence, it falls to me, and I say we stay and get the job done.'

'But you know we need four people at the absolute minimum. I wasn't really happy about doing it with only four of us in the first place – neither were you.'

'I can do the deep field work alone if I have to.'

'No way. Absolutely no way. I wouldn't let you do that in the height of summer. There's no way you can do it alone in this cold, this dark and with these storms.'

'I don't have to though, do I? I'll have you and Henriksen.'

'But that means one of us will be alone in the second Snowcat. I'm not having that – you can't drive and watch the ground radar at the same time.'

'Of course you can – I've done it before.'

'Not in these conditions. Not in winter. I'm sorry, but this is how it has to be.'

She pursed her lips. 'Do you know what's at stake here, Zak?'

'Our lives are at stake: mine, yours. Henriksen's. Guy's. That's what I'm worried about.'

'And that's great. That's what you're supposed to be worried about. And on any normal expedition, I'd agree with you one hundred per cent.' She looked him in the eye. 'But this is not a normal expedition. These are not normal times.'

'I understand that, but that doesn't mean we just say to hell with everything – everything that's designed to keep us all alive.'

'So you're telling me you've never broken the rules to get what you want?'

Zak took a deep breath. 'I'm hungry – let's get a sandwich.' He walked down the corridor.

'We haven't finished,' Rachael called after him. She followed him through to the mess, where she found him removing some frozen bread from the freezer.

'You hungry?' He began pulling out fillings for his sandwich as his bread defrosted in the toaster. 'I'm starving. Really gives you an appetite, working out here, doesn't it?'

Rachael crossed her arms. 'We're not leaving. We came to do a job and that's what we're going to do,' she said firmly.

He took a packet of cheese slices out of the fridge. 'I can't believe we get all this stuff – even out here.'

'It won't be like that when we go deep field, you know. High-energy, freeze-dried packets three times a day then when we're out there.'

He shut the fridge door. 'Do you know what the Swiss cheese model is?'

She shook her head. 'Stop changing the subject.'

'It's a principle used in risk management, the military and

things like the aviation industry,' he said as he buttered his bread. 'Very simply, it states that in something like aviation, or any high-risk pursuit – like Antarctic travel, for instance – there are several layers of cheese which represent the layers of defence against something going wrong.' He pulled three slices of cheese from the packet and held them up together. 'Each layer is like a failsafe. The idea is that each one is protection against catastrophe.'

'What's your point?'

'Every layer of protection has flaws, right? No defence is perfect. And in this model, the flaws in each are represented by the holes in the cheese.' He held up the slices again, pointing at the holes. 'But the beauty is, if there's a weakness at this point in the first layer, the second layer comes into play and stops that issue going any further, or becoming catastrophic. And each layer acts like this for the others.' He put the slices back on the counter and began rearranging them. 'The reason planes crash, or ships sink, or space shuttles explode is very rarely because of one big failure. Very rarely. Almost always it's because a series of tiny issues – that would otherwise be harmless – happen either at the same time, or in an order that means they lead inevitably to disaster.'

'Zak, I—'

'Take the *Titanic*. Why did so many people die in that disaster?'

'Because it hit an iceberg!'

Zak shook his head. 'Wrong. There were a series of critical failures that happened long before that, then plenty more afterwards that caused so many people to die. Not enough lifeboats, a ship nearby with its radio off, the captain ignoring iceberg warnings, the fact that it happened in the middle of the night, the cold weather. Same thing with Chernobyl. Dozens of tiny, seemingly unrelated or insignificant decisions made – each one harmless enough on their own – were made in precisely the order that led to catastrophe.'

'So what are you saying?'

'You think we can send Guy home and still complete the mission, yes?'

'Of course.'

'Because physically we could complete the work with a team of three?'

'I could do it all by myself if I had to.'

'Perhaps. But that's not the only factor here, is it? What if you trip over out on the ice and break your leg? Then you'd need two people to carry you back to base.'

'I'd have two people: you and Henriksen.'

'Sure, but what if you'd hit your head, too? What if you're unconscious? What if only one of us is with you? What if the two of us have got lost or slipped down a crevasse and you're on your own?'

'That would never happen.'

'They thought the *Titanic* would never sink, Rachael.'

She shot him a glare.

'Come on, you're a scientist. Think like one! You're thinking emotionally, not logically. And thinking emotionally in times like this is what gets people hurt. The whole reason we operate by the rules I set out to you back at McMurdo is to stop people acting in a way that could lead to them getting hurt, or worse. You know I'm right. You know I am. You just don't want it to be true.'

She considered his words in silence for a moment. 'You're right,' she said quietly.

'I'm glad you agree,' he smiled. 'I'm only thinking of your safety. Our safety.'

She nodded. 'I know. This is a problem. And problems are there to be solved. And I'm good at solving problems.'

'What do you mean?'

'I agree we need a fourth person to complete the expedition as planned.'

'I'm glad you agree.'

'So what if I can get a fourth person out here to replace Guy?'

Zak raised one eyebrow sceptically. 'Are you serious?'

'Sure. If we've got a plane coming to get Guy, that means we can fly someone in.'

'And you think you're going to find someone qualified, who's already at McMurdo and ready to drop everything to come out here for almost five months – with two hours' notice?'

'I didn't say it would be easy,' she smiled. 'But it's worth a try. McMurdo is full of researchers in transit, waiting for a flight home. One of them might fancy joining us.'

'Fancy joining us?! You're not inviting them to a night at the theatre.'

'I know that, but there are plenty of people who believe in this mission as passionately as we do. And I only need one to say yes. I'll get on the radio now and see if I can twist someone's arm.'

'And how are you going to pay them?'

'We'll think of something. We can always sort that out later. It's only money.'

Zak laughed. 'Fine. If you can find someone and convince them to come out here and join us, we'll stay. Personally, I think you haven't got a hope in hell, but by all means, give it a shot.'

'I will.'

'But if you can't, we're all on that flight out of here tonight.'

Rachael knew Zak was right: the chances of finding a replacement for Guy were slim in the extreme. She needed a backup plan. She shook her head. 'Counter offer: if I can't get someone, we stay here.' Zak shook his head and went to speak but Rachael held up a hand and continued, 'But we only do the research at this site. We forget about the third site at Graphite Peak. That way, we don't have to cross the crevasse field, and we'll never be more than eighteen miles from the base.'

She watched Zak closely as he considered it.

'The three of us can easily manage that, and then we'll just have to hope that's enough to convince Senator Morgan and her colleagues to stop the drilling.'

He shifted his weight as he mulled it over.

'We have to keep fighting, Zak. For Guy, for all of us, for the world – before it's too late.'

'Do you know how corny that sounds?'

She laughed. 'I can do this, I promise you. But I need your help.'

He held her gaze. 'You really care about this, don't you?'

She nodded. 'This is a war, Zak. A war we've been losing for decades. And this is the decisive battle. If we don't win this one – if we don't take our chance now to hit back, then the war could be lost forever. This is the tipping point, right now. If we let this happen, there will be no going back. And the world will never forgive us. Our children will never forgive us. We *have* to fight, and we have to do it now.'

He sighed. 'I want you to know I think this is a mistake.'

She smiled. 'You won't regret this.'

He smiled back. 'Yeah, yeah. Now I gotta get on the radio to McMurdo – and so do you. We better pray for Guy's sake we haven't missed that last plane.'

19

Slowly and purposefully Rachael pulled herself up the inside wall of the crevasse, constantly aware that if she lost her hand- or foothold for even a fraction of a second, or the axe or knife slipped, she would slide to her death and there would be absolutely nothing she could do about it.

Even using her spiked boots as an anchor point to push up from, each pull of her bodyweight was agony on her right arm, which had been yanked so hard when she'd stopped herself falling a few minutes earlier – but she forced herself to block out the pain. The pain can come later, she told herself, as if it was a luxury she would allow only once she was safe.

Her first target was the ledge Guy had been so casually sitting on just moments ago. She didn't even let herself think further than that right now. Reach that – then tackle the next part. With each excruciating pull she got closer and closer, finally pulling herself up and onto the shelf in the wall of ice. She lay in a heap panting, her eyes shut tightly as she let herself rest and recover before the next phase. When she decided she could put it off no longer, she got gingerly to her feet and restarted the process: swinging the axe above her, then ramming her boot spikes into the ice before pushing off from her foot and pulling from her arm. Again and again she repeated the process, slowly getting closer to the edge at the top. With every few feet she ascended, she was rewarded with more wind, more snow and more biting cold as she neared the surface. It felt like she was struggling *towards* danger rather than away from it, but on she pushed, heaving herself up as she clung as close as she could to the wall of ice. Breathing hard and quickly losing the battle to block out the agony, she finally reached the ledge, and with one last push, accompanied by a primal noise originating deep in her lungs that was a mixture of defiance and pain, she hauled herself up and onto the surface of the ice above, then lay there panting, giving herself a few seconds to recover from her climb.

But she couldn't rest for long – she was now out in the open, with no shelter and none of the equipment she would need to survive. She was more than seventy miles from the nearest base at Station Z, and her last base camp was now nothing but a pile of ash and melted fibreglass. She could head back to the Snowcat, but she knew it would be a fruitless pursuit: the vehicle was dead, and even if she sheltered in the cab, without any form of heat she'd be dead within hours. She also knew she was risking frostbite, having sweated profusely in her efforts to climb out of the crevasse. She had had no choice then, but it was now all the more imperative to get some shelter and some way of warming up as soon as possible. She had only one option, and even as she forced her reluctant body to stand up and start marching through the snow, she knew it was a long shot.

She pulled back the sleeve of her Big Red to check her wristwatch. She'd been yomping through the snow for almost seven hours. Her head pounded, her legs ached, her right arm throbbed with pain, and she was terrified frostbite would start to set in soon where she'd sweated inside her clothes, but she daren't sit down to rest, even for a moment. She pushed on.

Hiking through the snow was hard enough – especially in this cold and with the blizzard raging – but doing it in the dark added another layer of difficulty. She could hardly see where she was going, so simply had to trust her compass, and the risk of slipping down another crevasse was never far away. If she did fall in, she didn't think she had the strength to pull herself out again. She tried not to think about that possibility as she marched on through mile after mile of snow, ice, cold and darkness.

She had decided to ration the use of her head torch, since she had no spare batteries and no idea how long the current set might have to last her. She reached up and flicked it on, then looked from left to right to get her bearings. That was when she saw it: the light from her torch bounced back off a man-made surface – the only man-made surface for miles around. A pane of glass. A window.

She had found it.

She quickened her pace as the sense of anticipation and relief grew, pounding through the snow until she was close enough for her head torch to illuminate a small sign that had been etched into an ancient piece of wood and nailed to the door. It read, 'One Ton Camp'.

20

Rachael checked her watch. It wasn't even 3 p.m., yet it was already pitch-black. She bent down and lit the makeshift landing light: one of twenty open kerosene drums which lined the temporary airstrip dug into the ice on a flat plain a few yards from Station Z. Looking down its length and through the blizzard she could just make out the tall figure of Zak walking back towards her, having lit the final beacon at the far end.

'OK – they're only five miles out, should be here in a few minutes,' he shouted through the wind.

Rachael nodded.

'I still can't believe you found someone to come out here,' he said, shaking his head.

It was close to a miracle, Rachael thought. After an hour on the radio and a long list of 'no's, she'd finally found Josh Fraser, an Australian glacial researcher who had just finished a four-month contract at the pole and who was due to fly out of McMurdo the following day. Rachael had met him once or twice on her polar travels. Young, single, and always up for adventure, he didn't have Guy's experience, but he would be a willing and able deputy to Rachael, who knew she would now have to assume the lead of the expedition.

'What did you have to promise him?' Zak asked.

'Not much,' she shouted back. 'I told him he had the chance

to go down in history as part of the team that saved the world. Should be a decent chat-up line for him when he gets back to Oz.'

Zak laughed.

'This storm's getting worse, so they want to be in and out as soon as they can. We need to have Guy ready to go.'

Rachael gave him the thumbs up, cleared her goggles of snow, and started back for the row of conjoined units that made up the Station Z base. Once inside she made for the sick bay, where Henriksen was waiting with Guy. 'How is he?'

The Norwegian shook his head. 'He's in and out, not making much sense. That plane can't come quick enough.'

'They'll be here in a couple of minutes, we need to get him ready.'

'I'll go and get his gear. Can you stay with him?'

She nodded and sat down at his bedside. She took Guy's hand and his eyes blinked open as he registered her presence. She smiled down at him as he lay there, pale and weak. She'd never seen him like this. He was such a big character, so mentally strong, as well as physically. It didn't seem right to see him so lifeless, so vulnerable.

'We'll have you on the plane out soon,' she said soothingly as she rubbed his hand.

'You have to stay,' he wheezed. 'You have to get it done. You know what to do. You're the only one who knows.' He held her gaze through exhausted and bloodshot eyes.

'Don't worry about all that now,' she said quietly as she pulled up his blanket around his neck.

'I know Zak will try to take you all out with me,' he said. 'You can't let him, Rachael. Do you understand?'

'I know.'

'You *must* get the data to Pilbeam by August sixth. He'll do the rest.' He coughed. A deep, hacking, raspy cough that seemed to take all his energy. 'Promise me,' he said as he gripped her hand tightly for a few seconds. 'It's more important than me, or you, or any of us. *Promise me* you'll get it done.'

Tears were forming in her eyes but she tried to hold them back. 'I promise,' she said softly. 'I promise.'

He loosened his grip on her hand and his eyes closed again as he seemed to slip out of consciousness. She let the tears stream down her face as she held onto his hand tightly.

'It's time.' Zak was standing in the doorway.

Rachael stood and picked up Guy's woolly hat from the cabinet next to his bed, then pulled it down over his head.

Zak and Henriksen wheeled the stretcher to the door, then each took an end as Rachael held the door open for them. She followed as they carried him out into the dark, down the steps and loaded him aboard the red Twin Otter, its two engines idling to prevent them freezing up as it stood on the ice airstrip, the whole aircraft screaming impatience as the propellers kicked up even more snow to add to the blizzard.

She stood off to one side, keeping well back from the spinning props. She saw Zak speaking to the pilot but could see no sign of Fraser. Had he already made a dash for the safety of the base? No, she would have seen him. Where was he?

She watched as Zak and Henriksen ran back inside the accommodation block, then emerged again seconds later, each of them carrying two large kitbags. She frowned. Something wasn't right. She made for the plane and felt the wash from the propellers as she approached. The two men handed the bags to the pilot, who stowed them at the rear of the aircraft.

'What are you doing?' she shouted through the wind.

Henriksen glanced at Zak nervously, who waved him away. 'We're leaving, Rachael. We're all leaving. Get your stuff.'

'What are you talking about?' she asked incredulously. 'We're staying.'

Zak shook his head.

'But what about Fraser?'

'He didn't come. The pilot's only just told me. Apparently his bosses in Canberra caught wind of all this, panicked, and ordered him not to come.'

Rachael felt like she'd taken a punch to the gut. 'I can't believe it. How did they even know?'

Zak shrugged. 'I don't know.'

Rachael shook her head. 'But we stay anyway. Do the research here. That's what we agreed. What *you* agreed.'

'I've thought about it since then. It's not safe. I can't let this happen. Even doing this site – we've not got the manpower. It's too dangerous. I know it's not what you wanted, but I just can't let it happen.'

Henriksen arrived back with Rachael's kitbag as the pilot shut the rear door and walked back around to join them. 'The storm's getting worse. I need to get us out of here before this wind gets any stronger,' he shouted.

Zak nodded.

'Put those down,' Rachael said to Henriksen.

'Put them on board,' Zak ordered.

Henriksen looked completely torn, but began to move towards the plane where the pilot was waiting, arms outstretched. Rachael snatched the bags from his hands. 'I said, put them down,' she repeated firmly.

The pilot pulled up his collar against the wind. 'We need to go now,' he shouted. 'Are you lot coming or staying?'

Rachael looked back at Zak, challenging him to defy her.

'Come on, Rachael. It's madness to stay without a full team. You know that.'

She stood stock still. 'You can leave if you like, but I'm staying to get the job done, with or without you.' She stared straight at him. 'It's up to you.'

They locked eyes as the blizzard raged around them, like two poker players on a winner-takes-all million-dollar hand, waiting for the other to blink first.

'It's too dangerous, Rachael, and this is our last chance to get out.' He nodded at the plane. 'You don't turn down a seat on the last chopper out of Saigon.'

'No one wants us here, Zak. No one cares about this. If we don't act now, no one will and it'll be too late. We *have* to stay.'

The wind gusted hard and rocked the plane.

'We need to go NOW,' the pilot repeated.

Still, Rachael was unmoved.

The pilot shook his head. 'I'm taking this aircraft off. If you want to be on it, get on. Now.' He turned and swung the door shut, and double-checked the catch had caught.

Rachael didn't move a muscle.

Finally, Zak blinked. 'Wait!' he shouted. 'Get our bags off.'

The pilot shook his head as he opened the door and passed the kitbags out to Henriksen. 'Good luck,' he said as he climbed aboard and pulled the door shut behind him. Seconds later the whine of the engines increased so it drowned out even the noise of the blizzard, and with an almighty roar, the plane thundered down the ice strip and up into the inky black sky as Rachael, Zak and Henriksen watched it go with their kitbags at their feet and the snow swirling around them, the orange glow of the kerosene fire beacons illuminating the scene.

'Well that's it. We're stuck here till the spring now,' Zak said. He turned to Rachael. 'I hope you know what you're doing.'

21

Rachael had found one of Scott's old huts from the doomed *Terra Nova* expedition. A hut that was more than a century old, had been relentlessly battered by the pitiless cold and wind of the Antarctic, and was wholly lacking in any of the equipment – communication or survival – that would help her. But it was *something*. And right now, in this cold, dark expanse of nothingness, that was enough.

Set at the foot of a mountain, it was no more than fifteen feet in length and half the width. The whole north side was covered in snow, right up to the tip of its sloping, corrugated iron roof. On the south side there was a small lean-to porch, and a single, tiny window peeked out from the western wall.

Even as she approached the little building she felt the weight of history on its ancient timbers. It was built as one of the crucial resupply points for Scott's return journey from the pole in 1912, but he never made it: he and his team perished just eleven miles short, after an eight-hundred-mile journey to the bottom of the earth. It proved too far for Scott, Oates and the rest of the men, but now it would be Rachael's sanctuary.

Exhausted, she staggered up to the door and gingerly tried the handle. It was stuck, welded shut by decades of cold and ice. But she had not come this far to die on the doorstep. She twisted it again and pushed hard against the reluctant wood with her shoulder, and with a groan that could have been the tiny and long-dormant hut waking from its century-long slumber, it gave way. She hauled herself inside and with a final surge of energy she slammed the door shut behind her and slotted the deadbolt into place to keep it from flying open in the gale. With the chaos of the savage wind shut out, for the first time since she'd left her Apple she felt something approaching quiet.

She slumped down on the floor of the tiny lean-to porch and let her head fall back gently against the door, being careful not to aggravate the cut, and closed her eyes. Ever since the moment when she'd felt the sled pulling her backwards down into that crevasse, she'd been striving and straining every sinew to simply keep going and stay alive. Her only thoughts had been about her imminent survival: stop herself from falling to the bottom, find a way out, then find the hut. Each one a new goal she had pursued with single-minded determination. And she had succeeded each time, digging deeper and deeper into her reserves of strength, energy and resolve to get here. She'd come inches from death, yet she had prevailed. She allowed herself a moment to let it all sink in as she sat on the floor of the little hut – something she'd dared not do before she reached the safety of the cabin.

She took in a deep breath, then let it out as her heart rate slowed and returned to something like normal. But even as she congratulated herself on how she had escaped the crevasse and found her way to the hut, a part of her was already asking what the point had been. Yes, she'd cheated death in the Apple, and in the crevasse. But without a VHF radio or much food, she knew she was trapped all over again. In time, she would lose the fight. And there was no way to cheat time.

Her watch began to beep and snapped her out of that train of thought. It was time for The Broadcast, and she was glad of the distraction. She'd already missed several of them today, and she

148

was anxious not to miss another, so desperate was she to hear the voice of another human. She stood up, swung her rucksack off her back, rested it on the floor and thrust her hand inside to find her little transistor radio. She pulled it out and slid the switch to the 'on' position. The message had already started. She was irritated to have missed the start.

```
. . . the number of casualties and the
extent of the damage are not yet known . . .
switch your radios off now to save your
batteries until we come on the air again.
That is the end of this broadcast.
```

She turned off the radio and sat in silence, staring at nothing for a long, long time. Eventually, the creaking and groaning of the roof timbers brought her back to the present. She rapidly assessed her current needs: light, heat, water, food and sleep – in that order. She cast around the hut with her torch. The floor, walls and ceiling were all lined with timbers. There was a double bunk bed with what looked like spring mattresses along one wall, opposite a stack of packing cases that had been repurposed as makeshift shelves. There was an old tin stove against the far wall opposite the bunks, which was mounted on a wooden bench next to the little window. To the left of that was more bench space, with two shelves above, containing a stack of tin plates, a metal bowl, a cast iron kettle, a large black pan and some old tins with long-forgotten logos for Bisto gravy, Spam, Bovril and Bam Margarine. In the middle of the room was a small wooden table with two chairs tucked underneath it.

On the other side, next to the bunks were more shelves, which still had some books stacked neatly on them. She studied the dusty covers: *Moby Dick*, *On the Origin of Species*, *The Story of Bessie Costrell* and of course, a Bible. Aside from the tins, which upon inspection turned out to be empty, there was no sign of any food. She briefly considered the irony: Scott and his team had died because they couldn't quite reach the hut when it was stacked to the roof with food and supplies. Now she *had* made it here, and it was empty.

But there were three boxes of candles and even a box of Cook's matches. She slipped it open but the sticks were damp and after three failed attempts to strike one, she gave up. She went back to her rucksack and retrieved her own tube of emergency matches, then lit three of the candles.

Light taken care of, she turned to the old tin stove for heat. The door opened with a painful screech of metal on metal. There were still ashes in the grate, but there was no firewood. Unperturbed, she took one of the packing cases that had been stacked up as shelves and smashed it down as hard as she could onto the floor. It made a loud bang, but remained intact. She tried again, and a small piece snapped off. A third hit saw more pieces splinter off, and a fourth collapsed it entirely. She had her firewood. She ripped out a couple of unused pages from the back of her journal and twisted them lengthways, then stacked her kindling in a pyramid around the paper in the grate. To save on matches, she used one of the candles to light the paper and within a few seconds the ancient wood was crackling as the fire started to take hold.

With the cabin starting to warm up, she turned her attention to her own supplies. Having lost most of her food and equipment down the crevasse, all she had left was what she'd been carrying in her rucksack. She emptied the contents onto the table: one packet of matches, the radio, her notebook and pencil, twelve high-protein cereal bars, a USB pen drive containing the results of her research, her head torch, her knife, her ice axe, compass and watch. Apart from the clothes she was wearing, that was it.

With the fire now going she could at least melt snow for drinking water, but that was about the only bright spot she could see. She had food for a couple of days at most – if she rationed herself. She had no tent, or any way to reach Station Z, or to attempt to communicate with anyone. She wasn't even sure whether there was anyone at all out there – and even if there was, they would certainly have no idea where she was now.

She ventured back outside into the madness of the storm to collect some fresh ice, then melted that in a pot on the stove while she ate one of the protein bars. She allowed herself a whole one since it was almost sixteen hours since she had last eaten, and she'd burned a huge amount of calories on her journey to the hut. Once she was fed and watered, the urgent need for sleep began to overwhelm her. Since she had no sleeping bag, once she'd loaded up the fire with another broken-down packing case, she simply lay down on the bottom bunk and pulled her Big Red over herself like a blanket. She was about to blow out her candle when she was hit by a sudden panic. She jumped off the bunk and grabbed her journal from the table and flicked through the pages until she found it: the photograph of her with Adam and Izzy, the two of them smiling back at her. She kissed Izzy's face, then clutched it to her chest as she climbed back onto the bunk.

She felt even more alone than she had back at the Apple hut, and at that moment, she missed Izzy and Adam with an intensity she didn't know was possible. As she lay down, with the wind roaring on outside, she once again cursed her own stubbornness. She shouldn't be here at all. Not like this. Not alone.

And then she wasn't.

First she heard the crying. The unmistakable cry of Izzy stirring. A mother gets to know the cries of their child, and this cry didn't mean she needed feeding or changing, this was the cry

151

she used when she just wanted her mother. When all she wanted was company. Rachael looked up from the bunk and saw Izzy through the slats of her little cot.

'Shhh, Izzy. It's OK. Mummy's here,' she said softly. 'Mummy's here.'

22

Rachael lay on her bunk in Station Z, her laptop perched on her knees, her brow furrowed with worry as she went through the eight days' worth of GPR data she'd collected since Guy had been airlifted out. The figures in front of her showed the crack was certainly widening, but she wasn't sure that would be enough. She knew her report had to be iron-clad, her evidence completely bullet-proof if she was going to convince enough senators to vote against further drilling. There could be no room for equivocation – or for a smart-talking lobbyist to explain it all away with some clever-sounding pseudo-science. She couldn't let Guy down. *We need to go to the third site*, she thought as she tapped her pencil against her cheek. *We can't risk* not *going – not after we've come so far. Not when we've only got one shot at this.* She set her laptop to one side and set off in search of Zak. Convincing him wasn't going to be easy, she thought as she walked through the station's interconnected pods, but she had to try.

She found him in the communications room sitting at the long bench on the wall opposite the door, tapping at the keyboard of a computer. 'Can I get you a coffee?' she asked as casually as she could manage.

He swivelled round on his chair. 'Not for me, just had one,' he said, nodding at a mug on the bench.

'So . . . I've been looking at the numbers.'

He swivelled back round to face the screen. 'Uh huh.'

'I'm worried, Zak.'

'About the crack?'

'Well, yes, of course. But more than that, I'm worried we're not getting enough.'

'What do you mean?'

'I mean I'm worried we won't have enough data to prove it to the Americans and win the vote.' She paused but he said nothing. 'Zak, we need to go—'

He swivelled back round to face her and raised his right hand. 'Stop right there, Rachael,' he said firmly. 'We are *not* going to Graphite Peak.'

'But we need more data,' Rachael replied. 'We've come too far not to succeed now. We'll only need to be out there a couple of weeks. You, me and Henriksen can do it.'

Zak shook his head. 'Rachael, we've been over this. Look: you convinced me to stay here against my better judgement. You persuaded me then, but you're asking too much now. You're not going to win this one. We cannot go out there and we won't. It's too dangerous. I won't allow it. End of story.'

Rachael crossed her arms. 'What if we get back and lose the vote? All because we couldn't prove it beyond doubt – because we couldn't get enough data? Guy picked these three sites for a reason, Zak. I'm trying to win this thing here.'

'And I'm trying to keep you alive. We're not going. That's final. I'm sorry, but this is how it has to be. And I don't want to hear this again.' He turned back around to face the computer and began pecking at the keyboard to shut down the conversation.

Rachael stood behind him and clenched her teeth as she felt the frustration boiling up inside her. 'This is *not* over,' she hissed before she turned away and pushed through the door, not bothering to close it behind her. As she climbed into her bunk and tried to get to sleep later that night, her brain whirred, trying to think of a way to convince Zak.

The banging on her door started in the middle of the night.

'Beckett? You need to come quickly!'

It was Henriksen. She blinked her eyes open and peered at the green numbers on her digital watch. It was approaching 1 a.m.

'What's going on?'

'You need to come!' Henriksen replied. 'Zak's sick. I think really sick.'

'What's the matter with him?' She unzipped her sleeping bag and swung her legs off the bunk.

'He's gone a weird colour. He keeps throwing up. He's talking, but I can't understand.'

It sounded exactly like the symptoms Guy had before they had him medevacked out eight days ago.

'Come quick, Rachael, we need to do something!'

She pulled on a pair of gym trousers and zipped her fleece up, then unlocked the door and pulled it open. There was panic in Henriksen's eyes. 'What shall we do?'

'Let's have a look at him,' Rachael said as they set off for the other dorm.

Zak was on his bunk, huddled up inside his sleeping bag as if he couldn't pull it any tighter around him. The room was warm, and Zak's skin was glistening with sweat. His face was so white it looked almost translucent, and as she got closer she could see he was shaking.

'Zak?' she said tentatively. 'How are you feeling?'

He slowly opened his eyes then shut them again tightly. He mumbled something but Rachael couldn't make out what it was. She glanced at Henriksen to see if he'd caught it but he shrugged and shook his head.

'Zak, can you hear me?'

He mumbled again, but she still couldn't understand. She stepped in closer to his bunk, avoiding the bucket at her feet into which he had vomited.

'Zak?' she said again, this time pressing her palm on his forehead and noting how hot he was. The contact seemed to rouse him for a moment and he shuddered, then croaked a single word at her.

'Home.'

In times of stress Rachael drank coffee, a habit she'd picked up from Guy, she supposed. It wasn't just the drink, it was the business of making it that helped: waiting for the kettle to boil gave her a little time to think. The steam was rising from the spout and the electric switch clicked off automatically. She poured the boiling water into the two waiting cups on the counter, then stirred in powdered milk.

'So?' Henriksen asked after she handed him a mug.

She noticed he was still wearing his Manchester United hat, even at one o'clock in the morning. She shook her head and blew on the coffee. 'I don't know. Doesn't look good, does it?'

'He's gone exactly the same as Guy did. Fever, throwing up, in and out of consciousness. What the hell is going on? Something contagious?'

'I don't know. He's not even making any sense – he knows we can't get him home. Not now.'

'Is there any word on Guy?'

'Spoke to Christchurch this morning. He's in hospital but they can't work out what's wrong with him. They've had to quarantine him in case he's infectious.'

'Shit, Beckett, this is bad. I don't like this at all.'

'I know. And it's all my fault – I was the one who insisted we stay. What if he keeps getting worse? What if you and I get ill as well? We're stuck here.'

'Don't do that to yourself,' Henriksen said, taking a gulp of his coffee. 'You couldn't have known Zak would get sick. We'll have to take care of him as best we can and hope he pulls through. That's all we can do. And if either of us comes down with it, we'll deal with that, too.'

'I'll never forgive myself if . . .'

'Hey, come on. He'll be fine. It's probably the flu. And if it is something worse, we've got a medical chest the size of a tank down there – every drug known to man. And we've got the radio. They can tell us what to do.'

She nodded. Henriksen was right, but she still felt responsible.

'We'll just have to stop the research until he gets better.'

Rachael winced. She hated the thought of the mission being further compromised.

'Probably for the best anyway,' Henriksen continued. 'Checked the weather before I went to bed – there's a helluva big storm coming in. We couldn't travel with that going on.'

'When's it due to arrive?'

'In the next twelve to eighteen hours. Twenty-four at the most. Gale force ten. Winds of up to seventy miles per hour.'

'And how long is it supposed to last?'

He shrugged. 'You know how it is down here – could be a day, could be a month.'

'A *month*?'

'Could be even longer. Latest forecast says that once it moves over us it's not going to stop blowing for at least three weeks.'

'If we can't get out there and work for another three weeks, we're not going to have enough time to collect the data and get it to Guy's senator.'

Henriksen shrugged again. 'Nothing we can do about it.'

She thought for a moment. 'Yes there is. Henriksen,' she paused for a moment to make sure he was listening, 'I've been studying the data. We need to go to the third site.' She paused again. '*I* need to go to the third site.'

Henriksen shook his head. 'Zak told me you'd started on this again. We couldn't go now anyway, even if we wanted to. Not with Zak like this.'

'He doesn't have to come. I can do it myself.'

'Alone? Are you mad?'

'It's our only option now.' Her voice was calm, quiet. She felt total clarity about what she was saying and what she had to do. 'You stay here and look after Zak, I'll go out to the Apple hut, collect the data, wait for the storm to die down and I'll be back here in three weeks – four at the most.'

'But on your own? Deep field? Across the shear zone?' He shook his head. 'You just can't. No way. It's too dangerous.'

'I've been out in deep field on my own dozens of times.'

'Not in winter. And in another week or two it will be completely dark, twenty-four hours a day.'

'If I don't do this, the whole trip will be wasted. All Guy's work, everything.' The image of Guy in his sick bed flashed across her mind. His waxy skin, his clammy hand gripping hers tightly. She could almost hear him whispering to her in that rasping voice: *It's more important than me, or you, or any of us. Promise me you'll get it done. Promise me.* She had no intention of breaking her promise now, not when they were so close. 'I'm convinced we don't have enough,' she continued. 'They'll have that vote in September, and that will be it. The ice we're standing on right now won't even be here in a year or two.'

Henriksen gulped down his coffee as he considered this. 'No, I'm sorry. I can't let you do it. First Guy, now Zak? Doing this expedition with four people was crazy enough, but you on your own? That's just stupid. We're in injury time here and we're three-nil down. We're not going to win this one. Sometimes you just have to accept it. We'll have to find another way.'

'But there is no other way, Mik. You know it, and I know it.'

Henriksen shook his head. 'We don't even know what's wrong with Guy and Zak. What if you go out there and you get sick? You'll be all alone. It's suicide.' He drained the rest of his coffee and rinsed out the mug. 'Let's get some sleep. We'll try and work out a plan in the morning.'

She said nothing as he turned and walked out of the kitchen.

Rachael was staring at the little green figures on her watch in the darkness of her room. The moment it ticked over to 3 a.m. it emitted a tiny electronic alarm. But Rachael was wide awake already and instantly silenced it by pressing one of the buttons on the side. She slipped out of her bunk and dressed in her outdoor gear. A few minutes later she placed the note she'd written under the kettle in the mess, then, as quietly as she could, made her way to the main door of the Station Z complex. She pulled her goggles up and her hood down, and stepped outside into the darkness. The wind was picking up, but Rachael fought her way through it to the second of the two Snowcat vehicles parked on the leeward side of the building. She checked the back compartment and found to her satisfaction that all the supplies and equipment that Zak had packed into each one and insisted they carry at all times – tent, sled, sleeping bags, radio, satphone and ration packs – were all present and correct.

She walked around to the front of the vehicle and flung her bag of personal belongings onto the passenger seat as she pulled the door shut behind her, then turned the key in the centre of the dash. The engine started up with a roar that made her wince, but she knew Henriksen was a heavy sleeper, and she hoped the noise of the wind would drown out the sound of the vehicle's motor. She engaged drive, checked her heading, and began cutting her way through the snow.

By the time Henriksen woke the next morning it was gone seven. He shook his head silently as he read the note Rachael had left in the kitchen. It read:

Gone fishing. Look after Zak. See you in a couple of weeks. Beckett

23

Date: 31 July (I think)
Mission day: 144 (I think)
Temperature: Don't know
Windspeed: Don't know
Days since last contact: 52

I haven't written for days, and I'm sorry. I think it's because writing to you always forces me to be honest with myself. And try as I might, I've been having trouble with that over the past few days.

I've been alone for so long and it feels like the thin ice of sanity on which I've been skating is finally starting to crack.

I know this because Izzy is here sometimes. Often she just sits on the floor and plays with her blocks and her racing car. Sometimes she babbles away in that way she was doing before I left – every fifth word something almost recognizable. Sometimes she wants a cuddle ('Mama, up!') and I pick her up and hold her close as I lie on the bunk. I love her so much.

Occasionally Guy comes too, but he never stays for long. He does cheer me up though. But the radio is starting to let me down. The batteries are dying, and each time I listen to The Broadcast, the plummy announcer guy is a little bit quieter. I'm terrified of the day when he finally leaves me altogether. What will I have then?

I was alone at the Apple, but there I had supplies: I had gas, I had food. I have neither now. My meagre rations are gone. I tried to eke them out for as long as possible, but I finished the last protein bar two days ago. Now I have nothing left to eat. Not a scrap. And the fire is a problem too. In this cold, I have to keep it alive round the clock. But I have no firewood, so I've been using anything I can find. I've already burned the books, the shelves, the chairs, the table – I've even ripped apart the bunks and fed them to the fire. I'm now left with just the mattress I'm sitting on.

There's the hut itself, of course. The whole thing is wood-framed and lined with timbers. You'd love them – very rustic, ha ha. They'd go perfectly in the living room once they'd been sanded down and varnished. That was the next project you were planning. The living room floor. Traipsing around those reclamation yards, looking for the perfect wood. That was your plan for the summer. The next distraction. Anything to keep us from focusing too clearly on what was really going wrong between us. And what was going wrong? I spent months trying to ignore the fact that things weren't right. Since I've been here, alone, I've been trying to work it out, but I'm still struggling to find the answer.

I've started to survey the very fabric of the hut as a potential source of heat. You know how in cartoons if they're starving hungry, they look at someone and see them as a piping hot roast dinner with all the trimmings? It feels a bit like that. Problem is, of course, every timber I remove for the fire will weaken the hut. How many could I burn before the whole thing collapses? I have no idea – but you see the dilemma: leave the hut alone and freeze to death once the fire goes out, or rip out planks of wood one by one until the whole thing collapses and freeze to death anyway.

Some choice. <u>Roofs and walls offer substantial protection.</u>
<u>The safest place is indoors.</u>

Not to mention the fact I am slowly, piece by piece, destroying one of the most historic buildings in the whole of Antarctica. Not that it matters anymore, I guess. I shouldn't have expected it to be my salvation. It couldn't save Scott, and now it hasn't saved me.

Date: 1 August (I think)
Mission day: 145 (I think)
Temperature: Don't know
Windspeed: Don't know
Days since last contact: 53

I think the reason I'm feeling so despondent is the lack of a plan. Even after everything that happened – losing radio to Station Z, The Broadcast, being trapped and alone – I had a plan: stay put and wait out the worst of the weather. I had plenty of supplies. I might even have been able to make it back to base when the sun finally came up and the storm blew itself out. That was a good plan. A sensible plan. And it was working until the explosion.

Then I had another plan. Get the tent and supplies from the Snowcat, and head for Station Z. OK, a bit earlier than expected and in worse conditions than I'd hoped, but you gotta roll with the punches. The show must go on.

And even after the crevasse fall, and losing my sled and my tent and my stove – even then I had a plan. Head here, to this hut. It was the only thing I could think to do, but it was a plan. Something to work towards, something to focus on, something to strive for. And I made it. I can hardly believe I did, but I made it.

And here I am.

But now, I'm finally out of ideas. I'm stuck. I have no plan. Nothing to work for. No reason anymore to keep going. What's the point?

What's the point – I have to confess, I had started to wonder that about us, Adam. What was the point? Did you ever think the same? Did you ever allow yourself to wonder?

I was thinking earlier about when it started. With you. I've never felt like that before. I'd never had such . . . <u>certainty</u>. All I wanted was to be with you. All the time. That was it, really. I just needed to be with you. Do you remember those days? The long dinners in cheap restaurants, the lazy days in your flat watching Netflix and listening to Pink Floyd and having sex and drinking Prosecco. God it was so much fun. The happiest days of our lives. And so . . . right. When I was with you, it felt like that was exactly where I was supposed to be. I don't know where that feeling went.

Do you remember our first 'official' date? You took me to that weird bar done up like a wartime tube station that's been commandeered as an air raid shelter. All those wartime posters about 'digging for victory' and 'careless talk costing lives'. 'Loose lips sink ships!' We both got tipsy on gimlets and ended up singing along to Vera Lynn. Remember that? What happened to our sunny day, Adam?

Date: 2 August (I think)
Mission day: 146 (I think)
Guy visited again today. He didn't say much but it was nice to see him, all the same. It's minus fifty degrees here but he was still only wearing his rugby shirt and shorts. He'll never change.

You really must get over that, you know. Have I told you that? I don't know. But me and Guy . . . it's not like that. Of course I love the old bastard, but not like that. I guess it's too late now. In the end, when it came to you and me, that was just another brick in the wall.

And at least he visits me here. Him and Izzy. But you never do. I don't know why not. Maybe you're still mad at me.

Did it ever really go? Between us, I mean. I think maybe I needed . . . something else. I should never have stopped work. That was a mistake. I can see that now. I should have told you. That would have made things better. But I didn't. I pulled away from you. Like I always do. I pulled away and you could sense it. I pulled away because I couldn't look you in the eye. The only way I knew how to look at you was with love, with longing, with need. And when that started to change into something else, I didn't know how to look at you. Every time I caught your gaze I felt like I was lying to you. Was it the stress of having Izzy? Was it boredom? Was it something more fundamental between us – or was I just epically tired? I felt – feel – mad at you. But I don't really know why. I've been searching for an answer for a long time, Adam, but I could never quite put my finger on it. I wish I could have done – then I could have fixed it. I'm good at that. Fixing problems.

The thing is, you're still the person I want to tell all this to. Yours is still the face I want to see. I've just realized – my journal since I've been here, it hasn't been a journal at all. It's been a letter to you. All of it. And in a notebook that you gave me, with that photo and that note, even though I know you were mad at me. But that's love. Doing nice things even when you're mad at the other person.

I wish I'd told you before I left. I should have talked to you. Instead I clammed up, shut down and hoped everything

165

would just work itself out. You were right: I do put up barriers
and hide behind them. <u>Walls offer substantial protection.</u> I
shut it all away and I ran like hell. And now I'm stuck here,
alone, on the dark side of the moon.

Rachael put down her journal next to the mattress and slowly
got to her feet. She knew she'd have to go outside to fetch some
fresh ice for water, but her heart sank at the thought of the energy
she would need for such an act. Physically and emotionally
exhausted, she'd reached the point where the smallest of simple
tasks were now a monumental effort that required a superhuman
resolve.

Izzy was calling for her again, standing up in her cot, little
hands gripping the bars. Rachael looked down at her. 'Mama, up!'
She cried, thrusting her arms up towards Rachael. 'Mama, up!'
But Rachael simply didn't have the energy to pick up her child.

'The fire's getting low,' Guy said over Izzy's cries. He was
leaning against the wall, sipping from a coffee mug. 'Don't let it
go out.'

'Why don't you do it?' she said irritably. 'You never do anything
around here.'

She shuffled over to her tiny wood pile and opened the door
of the stove. The fire had burned right down, the embers barely
glowing in the ash. She threw on the last remaining splintered
sticks of wood from her pile and clanked the door shut. With
the slow, deliberate movements of a woman three times her age,
she donned her coat and hat, and picked up the black pan from
the top of the stove. She made her way to the porch, slid back
the deadbolt and opened the door. Immediately the wind and
the cold overwhelmed the tiny space of the cabin. Injected with
sudden urgency, she staggered out into the dark and the cold,
scooped up a pan full of fresh snow from the drift against the

side of the hut, and hurried back to the door. Once inside, she slid the deadbolt back into place, then set the pan on top of the stove.

Then she sat on the floor and waited for the snow to melt, and then for it to cool. She poured some out into an old tin cup left behind by Scott's people and drank it down. With plenty of water, she knew the human body could last weeks without food. But to what end?

The shrill beeping from her watch stopped her train of thought.

She lay down on the mattress again and turned the radio on. The voice started The Broadcast, but the words were getting quieter and quieter, further and further away. She realized with mounting horror that the batteries were finally running out. She had to hold it right to her ear to hear it as it got fainter and fainter, until finally it disappeared altogether and she felt compelled to finish it herself.

'. . . We shall repeat this broadcast in two hours' time. Stay tuned to this wavelength, but switch your radios off now to save your batteries until we come on the air again. That is the end of this broadcast. That is the end of this broadcast. That is the end. That is the end. That is the end.'

It made no sense, but she clicked the radio off once she'd finished and set it down beside her.

And then she started to cry.

It came from somewhere deep within her, and once she shed the first few tears, the dam burst. Weeks and weeks of pain and misery and loneliness and madness and grief and darkness and terror had built up inside her, and as she lay crying on the mattress in the tiny hut, it poured out of her like a tidal wave. She screamed and howled and cried and shouted as the despair finally engulfed her.

24

She didn't know how long she cried for. It seemed like a long time. Eventually the tears stopped. She wiped her face with the sleeve of her fleece and lay on the mattress. Nothing to do. Nothing that could be done. She tried to remember Guy's words, but the cold and hunger were slowing her brain as much as her body. And now she wanted him here, he was nowhere to be seen. She was light-headed and fuzzy. Unable to think clearly. What did he always say? As long as there's a chance, keep fighting? Was that it? His voice was now so far away. Once so clear, his words were growing fainter and fainter in her mind, just as the radio broadcast had done. *As long as there's a chance* . . . Did she really still have a chance? She picked up her journal and began to write.

> *2 August (I think)*
>
> *I have to face facts, Adam. I'm coming to the end here. I've been out of supplies for five days and I have no means of escape. I've burned so much of the hut's structure, I think taking one more stick will cause the whole thing to cave in on me, and without any more firewood, I'll freeze soon.*
>
> *I lasted a long time – longer than I think either of us would have given me credit for – but I'm finally out of options. I've used up all my bright ideas and the only control I have over my situation now is to choose how exactly I want to die.*

In this cold, I could walk outside, lie down in the snow, and it would all be over in a matter of minutes. I would drift off to sleep. And never wake up.

I've written something for our little Izzy.

My darling Izzy,

Please know that I love you more than anything in the world. When you were born, you looked so tiny and helpless and so cross about it all! Your little red face scrunched up in disgust, screaming at the top of your lungs – you never stopped doing that.

That day, it became my job to look after you. I was your mum. I was supposed to keep you under my wing. Keep you safe and warm and happy and healthy.

And I did my best. I've loved you more than I thought was possible. I've loved you more and more every day. I've watched you grow, watched you start becoming your very own little person. And I'm so completely heartbroken that I'll never see the child and woman you would have become and all the wonderful things you would have done with your life.

I was so excited to share with you all the amazing things there were in our world: books, music, nature, friendship, love – all the things that make life so glorious. I couldn't wait for you to experience all those joys. I wanted you to see everything. Hear everything. Feel everything.

I know you won't understand why I left. But I had to go away. I had to come here and do this. You can't see it now, but one day you might: I did this for you. I did this for you, and for all of us. I wanted to make things better.

But in the end, I couldn't. I tried. I tried so hard.

I love you,

Mummy x

*Adam, I'm sorry. If the two of you made it, for God's sake,
look after Izzy.*

She shut the journal, lay back down on the mattress and
closed her eyes. Then she began speaking in a soft, low voice.
'This is the Wartime Broadcasting Service from the BBC in
London. This country has been attacked with nuclear weapons.
Communications have been severely disrupted, and the number
of casualties and the extent of the damage are not yet known.
We shall bring you further information as soon as possible.
Meanwhile, stay tuned to this wavelength, stay calm and stay in
your own homes.

'Remember there is nothing to be gained by trying to get
away. By leaving your homes you could be exposing yourselves to
greater danger. If you leave, you may find yourself without food,
without water, without accommodation and without protection.
Radioactive fallout, which follows a nuclear explosion, is many
times more dangerous if you are directly exposed to it in the
open. Roofs and walls offer substantial protection. The safest
place is indoors. The safest place is indoors. The safest place is
indoors. The safest—'

And then she heard a noise.

Rachael pricked her ears up like a cat, held herself completely
still, and listened.

Since leaving the Apple, the only sounds she had heard were
the incessant howling of the polar wind, The Broadcast, the
crackling of the fire and the creaking of the hut. This was nothing
like any of them. This was a thumping. It was urgent, deliberate,
and getting more frantic. It didn't make any sense. It simply
wasn't possible. But slowly the truth dawned on her: someone
was knocking at the door.

25

Bang. Bang. Bang.

She scrambled to her feet and staggered into the lean-to porch at the end of the hut. Three more bangs, and she could see the door vibrating with every one. This had to be real. *Didn't it?* She tried to slide the deadbolt open but her hands were shaking and she kept losing her grip. Breathing fast, she stopped and steadied herself, then slid the bolt out of its housing and pulled the door open. There, standing in the doorway, clad in his Big Red, a blue woolly hat and snow goggles, was the tall and unmistakable figure of Zak Connelly.

They stood looking at each other, both at a loss for words. For Rachael, the moment was too big, too impossible to process, for a 'hello' to suffice.

Zak lifted his goggles from his face. Rachael looked into his eyes, so blue, so reassuring. Still she could find no words. Eventually, he said: 'Can I come in?'

His request seemed so absurdly normal she broke into a half laugh, half sob and fell forward into him, clinging to him tightly as she started to let it all out, the cold, the hunger, the wind and the dark. He hugged her back, then lifted her up and carried her inside, and kicked the door closed behind him.

Rachael had thought she'd cried herself out, but now there was someone here to cry to, she found the tears coming again.

She cried and cried and cried into his chest. She had come to think she might have been the very last person alive – or at least that she would never see another person ever again. To discover she wasn't completely alone – even if the rest of her situation remained hopeless – was a relief the like of which she'd never felt before.

But soon the logical part of her brain began to take over from the emotional. 'What are you doing here?' she asked as she tried to compose herself. 'You shouldn't be outside. Stay indoors. By leaving your home you could be exposing yourselves to greater danger.'

'I came to find you,' he said calmly.

She had a thousand questions. 'Is everyone gone? I heard the radio announcement, then, nothing . . .'

He shook his head. 'I don't know.'

'What do you mean, you don't know?'

'Christ, Rachael, you look like shit. When was the last time you ate?'

'Six days ago,' she said. 'What happened? Please, just tell me what happened.'

Zak looked around the spartan room, then went to the stove and opened the door. 'Let me get you some food, get this fire going again, and I'll tell you everything I know.'

'You have supplies?'

'Some, yes. Out in the Snowcat. Food and some briquette wood burner things. Wait here.'

'I'll help you.' She turned to find her boots, but he took her arm.

'No,' he said warmly. 'You stay here inside. I'll do it. Shut the door after me,' he added. 'Keep out as much of this cold as we can.'

She nodded. 'Roofs and walls offer substantial protection.' She walked back into the main room of the hut. She could hear the roof timbers creaking in the wind above her, like the hut itself was grumbling about being disturbed by another visitor. She sat down on the mattress – the only bit of furniture she hadn't already burned – and waited.

She tried to process what Zak's arrival meant. Answers, she hoped. Salvation, perhaps. At the very least it was someone to talk to. But after a few minutes – or rather, what she assumed to be a few minutes, it was so hard to keep track of time in a perpetually dark environment with no other stimuli – she began to wonder if he was really here at all.

Plenty of people had visited her in the tiny hut: Guy and Izzy mostly. Her mum once. Usually they didn't stay for long, but they'd visited. And they'd felt so real. Of course, if she forced herself to confront it, she knew they weren't really there. But mostly she didn't confront it. It was far more comforting to let them be. It was company. She had nothing else left, so why deny herself that by being too rational about things? Maybe she'd brought Zak here too. Was she still behind the wall? Within milliseconds her mind raced ahead to every possible conclusion. She tried to remember back, to what she knew *for sure*. But everything was so fuzzy, so difficult to pin down. Nothing seemed solid or certain.

After being alone for so long, she felt like her brain was the unreliable narrator in the novel of her own life. Was she even really still in the hut? Or had she in fact made that dreadful choice and gone outside into the cold and the dark and the end? Maybe she had wandered out into the raging black void, as far as her exhausted legs could carry her, lest she be tempted to change her mind and turn back for the safety of the hut. Perhaps she'd gone as far as she could in the black nothingness and laid down in the soft snow, letting it wrap itself around her, the icy tentacles of the wind enveloping her like a thousand grasping, frozen fingers.

Perhaps she was already dead, and now in the afterlife – trapped in her personal version of hell: an eternity spent living in this godforsaken hut with no food, no warmth and no hope. Forever alone, forever starving, forever cold to her bones.

She looked around the cabin. Zak wasn't here. There was no sign he'd ever been here. If he'd taken off his hat, his goggles – anything – that would have been enough for her to cling onto. Enough to know she wasn't mad – or dead. But there was nothing.

Of course, she could get up, go to the door and look outside – that would answer her question. But she didn't move. Two things stopped her: first, she was so weak the prospect of even that small movement was like summoning the energy to climb Mount Everest; and second, if he wasn't there, and had never been there, at this point she decided she preferred not to know for sure. For every second she didn't check, didn't confirm, the possibility remained that he *was* there. And right now, that was better than the certainty that he wasn't. So she waited.

She had no idea how much time had passed when the door creaked open and Zak walked back in, carrying a large rucksack and a slab of high-intensity fire briquettes. She felt elation and relief flood over her. He *was* here. He slung the bag on the floor, unclipped the top and drove one of his hands inside. He pulled out a high-protein energy bar, unwrapped it and passed it to her. 'Eat this,' he said, before cranking open the fire door and throwing on a couple of briquettes. She grabbed the energy bar with both hands and took big, fast bites. With Zak back, she was rooted in reality once more. Each mouthful of food further grounded her in the present.

'Slowly,' he cautioned. 'Your body isn't used to food. If you eat too fast you'll throw it back up.'

She was starving, exhausted, freezing cold and full of questions. After she'd devoured two energy bars as slowly as she could manage, she began. 'So what happened? All I've had for a month is the radio broadcast. The VHF radio and the satphone couldn't pick up anything at all. What happened?'

He puffed out his cheeks as he came and sat down on the mattress next to her. The cabin was already starting to warm up as the fire came back to life.

'The truth is we really don't know. We lost all comms too. The last day we had radio contact with you was the last day we heard from anyone at all. We lost the data signal, the radio, even the satphones. Nothing worked.' He clicked his fingers. 'Just like that. We couldn't raise you, we couldn't raise Cambridge. We couldn't even raise McMurdo. Nothing. We tried everything, but no dice. Nothing. For weeks. Just the same recorded announcement you heard, every two hours, over and over.'

'Communications have been severely disrupted,' she said earnestly. 'And the number of casualties and the extent of the damage are not yet known.'

He frowned.

'So you have no idea what happened?'

'We had plenty of news before that. Tensions rising between the US and Russia – and the North Koreans. They were doing nuclear weapons testing – claimed they'd cracked it. The UN sent weapons inspectors in and demanded the keys to the bombs. The North Koreans refused. The president started talking about taking them by force, and Putin came down on the Koreans' side. Stalemate.'

Rachael shook her head.

'Best guess? One side went too far, backed themselves into a corner so they had to take action, the other side responded and . . . bang. Goodnight Vienna.' He sighed. 'But it could have been anything: could be Russia, North Korea, could be Syria, could be Iran, India/Pakistan – there are a hundred potential flashpoints that could escalate.'

'So . . . they're all . . . gone?'

'Far as we can tell. You'd think someone would have been in touch by now. If there was anyone left who knows about us.'

'But what about McMurdo? There's no way they'd be caught up in this, surely?'

'That's what we thought. But we haven't been able to raise them since last month.'

'But that doesn't make sense. They *must* be there.'

'None of this makes any sense,' Zak said.

'And you've heard nothing? From *anyone*?'

He shook his head solemnly. 'Not for six weeks.'

'It's just . . .' Rachael couldn't find the words.

Zak met her gaze. 'I know,' he said quietly.

'Did you ever find out anything about Guy?'

Zak shook his head. 'Last we heard he was still in hospital. Still in quarantine.'

They sat in silence for a long time as Rachael digested the information. For the first time in days she began to feel something other than cold as the fire heated up the small space of the cabin.

'Where's Henriksen?' she asked.

'Back at Station Z.'

'He didn't come with you? What happened to your "no one goes anywhere alone" rule?'

Zak shook his head. 'That rule applies in normal times, Rachael. But as someone once said to me, these are not normal times. And in this case I thought it best one of us stay behind in case someone did try to get in contact.'

'Makes sense. The safest place is indoors. How's he taken it?'

Zak shrugged. 'Hard to tell with him.'

She turned to face him. 'And what about you?'

His eyes darted away from hers. He sighed deeply. 'It just . . . doesn't seem real,' he said. 'It can't be.'

She nodded. 'I know what you mean.' She paused. 'Before, when you went back to the Snowcat, I . . .' She stopped. 'I suddenly panicked. I wasn't sure if you'd ever been here at all, or whether I'd imagined the whole thing. You were gone a few minutes, but it was like you'd never existed at all.' Tears were forming in her eyes again. 'I feel like I'm losing it,' she said quietly.

He smiled warmly, then pulled her close to him. 'That's only natural,' he said as he hugged her. 'You've been alone, in the cold and dark of an Antarctic winter, with no contact from the outside world except a message telling you everything you know and love is gone forever. Your husband, your family, your life, your child. Gone.'

Her mind's eye flashed to Izzy and Adam. She could feel the tears welling up in her eyes, the pain eating away at her heart.

'It's no wonder you've been finding things difficult. But I'm here now.'

She nodded and pulled back from him. Then she frowned in confusion. 'How on earth did you find me?'

He stood up and went back to the fire. 'I wanted to come out for you as soon as we lost comms,' he said as he added two more briquettes. 'I knew you'd be confused, frightened. But the storm was so bad, Henriksen wouldn't let me. He wanted to wait until it blew over.' He checked the pot of melting snow and moved it off the heat to cool down. 'But it didn't stop. It kept blowing and blowing and blowing. Seven times I've come here to Antarctica, but I've never seen a storm last this long.'

She nodded in agreement.

'Eventually, I decided I had to come anyway. Especially after we still couldn't raise McMurdo or Amundsen–Scott, or anywhere else.' He walked to his rucksack, pulled out a blanket and wrapped it around her. 'So I set off for the Apple hut. It took

177

me two days, and when I got there, I found it burned to the ground.'

'I think the gas line cracked in the cold,' she said. 'Best as I can figure, anyway. I nearly didn't get out.'

'At first I thought you'd gone up with it. I was all set to give up and head back. But there was no trace of you, so I knew you must've made it out alive.' He sat back down next to her. 'I sat in the Snowcat for a full hour trying to figure out what to do. Then I remembered this place and thought it was worth a try. After all, this is where I would've come if I'd have been in your snow shoes.'

She smiled.

'Then when I got near enough, I saw the light from the window.'

'I nearly didn't even make it here.'

'Get lost in the storm?'

'I fell down a crevasse. Lost my sled, my tent, my sleeping bag, my stove, my rations. Damn near everything.'

'Bloody hell.'

He sat back down.

She turned to look at him as another thought struck her. 'What about you? Last time I saw you, you were at death's door.'

'Oh God,' he said, shaking his head. 'That was awful. Never felt so sick in all my life. I really thought I was going to die. And then one day, a few weeks back – must have been just after we lost comms with you – it started to clear up. I was up and about within forty-eight hours.' He chuckled. 'Which was a good job, because let me tell you, Henriksen is not much of a nurse.'

She laughed. 'I can imagine.'

The silence returned.

'What have you been doing with yourself for the last two months?'

She shrugged. 'Only thing I could do: I carried on with the research. Carried on recording the data. I lost the laptop, but I've got all the data on a pen drive.' She nodded at her rucksack. 'Even brought it with me. Don't really know why, but seemed a shame to just leave it after all this.'

'And?'

'Guy was right. The crack is definitely growing.'

'You think he was right about the shelf breaking off entirely?'

'Sooner than we thought, too. There's enough in that pen drive to get the drilling stopped forever. Or there would have been, before . . .' she trailed off.

'Christ.' He shook his head.

'So what now?'

He took a deep breath. 'We have some dinner. Then bed down here for the night, and hope the storm dies down a bit. We can make for Station Z in the morning. We'll be back in twenty-four hours, with a following wind.'

She nodded slowly. 'And then what?'

'We can worry about that when we get there,' he said. 'One thing at a time, eh?' He stood up, rummaged in his rucksack and brought out two vacuum-packed silver pouches. 'Now then, mushroom risotto or chicken dhansak?'

After they'd eaten, and Rachael had a bellyful of hot food for the first time in over a week, she lay back down on her mattress with heavy eyes.

He blew out the candles and lay down next to her.

She slid across the mattress and laid her head on his chest. 'Thank you, Zak,' she said softly.

He draped an arm around her and held her tightly. 'All part of the service.'

Within minutes she had drifted off to sleep.

26

Rachael slipped beneath the waves of consciousness, but her mind never stopped whirring. She hopped from one highly vivid dream to the next, each one as real as the last. Guy, dressed like a headmaster for some reason, telling her again and again about the importance of her mission over the top of his half-moon glasses as they sat in a Dickensian schoolhouse, the ticking of a huge grandfather clock marking the time. Adam, begging her repeatedly not to go on the trip at all as he fussed and fiddled with the coffee machine in their perfect kitchen. Henriksen warning her not to go out alone, his six-foot-seven-inch frame looming over her, his red Manchester United woolly hat pulled down over his ears as they stood in the mess at Station Z. The anonymous face of the BBC announcer beneath a bowler hat, reading The Broadcast over and over and over again. Zak, right here in the hut, switching between telling her everything was going to be OK in his calming, reassuring voice, the whole cabin brightly lit by a powerful midday sun, to agitatedly asking her 'Where is it? Where is it?' as he searched her bag by torchlight in the darkness. She wanted to tell him, but she didn't know what 'it' was. 'Everything will be OK,' he smiled as he lay back down on the mattress next to her. 'Everything will be OK.' And Izzy. Izzy crying. Izzy sleeping. Izzy playing on the floor. Izzy sitting in her highchair, munching on a carrot stick. Izzy with her arms thrust out towards Rachael, desperate to be picked up. Izzy. So small. So perfect. So innocent. Izzy.

By the time she woke, she felt exhausted. She realized she was frowning, and her jaw ached from clenching it in her sleep. She blinked her eyes open but that changed little in the darkness of the hut. She was drowsy, groggy. She looked to the mattress on her left. There was no sign of Zak.

Then the door creaked open, and the light from his head torch cut a shaft through the darkness of the hut. 'Just getting some fresh ice,' Zak said. He threw some more briquettes on the fire. 'That's the last of them. We'll have some brekkie, then we should hit the trail,' he smiled.

She still felt groggy. Everything was muffled, like she was underwater, or covered in cotton wool that she couldn't shake off.

'How did you sleep?'

'Badly. Really weird dreams.'

'Oh?'

'I kept seeing people. Mostly people warning me.'

'About what?'

'About coming here. About what would happen if I didn't. Even Henriksen warning me about taking off for the survey site on my own.'

'Well he was right about that one.'

'You were in them, too. Telling me everything was going to be OK.' She frowned. 'But then you were looking for something. Searching the hut. You kept asking me, "Where is it? Where is it?" but I didn't know what you were looking for. What do you think that was about?'

He shrugged. 'Who knows. I've been having weird dreams myself since the day I landed here. Hardly surprising – our brains must be struggling to process our situation.'

'I guess so.' She nodded. 'Then I was back with Izzy.'

'That's your daughter?'

'It was so real. I could hear her calling for me. I . . . I could feel her skin against mine.' She heard her voice crack as she said it.

The water on the stove began bubbling. 'Come on,' he said. 'Let's have some food and then hit the road. Who's for freeze-dried porridge?'

He prepared a packet and a cup of coffee for each of them, and they sat on the mattress eating. The hut continued to creak and groan as it was battered by the storm raging outside.

'You know when you're dreaming,' Rachael began, 'you don't know it's a dream at the time, do you? It seems completely real.'

He nodded.

'The thing is,' she lowered her voice. 'Asleep, awake – I'm having trouble . . .' she paused as she tried to find the words. 'I'm having trouble with what's real and what's not,' she admitted.

'I'm real,' he said soothingly. 'I'm real, I'm here and I'll be by your side from now on.'

'You're not the first person to visit me here, you know,' she said.

'What?'

'Guy, Izzy – they've both been. Plenty of times. And they look as real to me as you do now.' She shrugged. 'It's hard. I mean I know they aren't here. They can't be. But when they are, that logic doesn't seem to matter.' She turned to face him directly. 'And the trouble is, now you're here, I'm having trouble convincing myself that you're real.'

'I promise you I'm real.' He reached out and rubbed her leg tenderly. 'See?'

She closed her eyes and concentrated on his touch, trying to force her mind to believe the sensation.

'I mean, I'm as real as any of us are.'

'What do you mean by that?' she said, blinking her eyes open again.

He spooned in a mouthful of porridge. 'Have you ever heard of something called the Simulation Argument?'

She shook her head.

'Fascinating theory. Read about it a while ago. Some Swedish philosopher at Oxford came up with it a few years ago. Boston? Bosson? Buxton? I can't remember his name.'

'And what, he says we're living in a computer simulation?'

'Not exactly. That idea has been around for decades at least.'

'Yeah – I saw *The Matrix*.'

'Exactly.'

'So what does this Boston guy say?'

'His argument is very simple – and in a way very convincing.'

'How?'

'Well I'm not a philosopher, so I'm sure it's somehow more complicated than this, but as I understand it, he argues that not only is it possible that we're living in a simulated reality, but that it is in fact *much* more likely than this being actual reality.'

'Much more likely? How does he work that out?'

'Think about the immense computing power the human race already possesses – and think about how that has all been achieved in an evolutionary blink of an eye. Now imagine how much computing power will be available to our descendants in a hundred years – or even less. It'll be staggering. And even if only one person in the future had this capability, that one person would have the power to create dozens of simulations of an entire world, hundreds – thousands.' He took a sip of his coffee. 'But soon the technology wouldn't just be in the hands of one person or even a small group. Technology always spreads. So now imagine how many simulations are likely to be running at any one time.' He didn't wait for her to answer. 'Thousands. Millions. Billions.'

'OK, so there are going to be millions of computer versions of the world running in a hundred years in the future. So what?'

'Think about it: it's likely that at least some of those simulations would've been set to start many years before the inventors were born.'

'So you're saying they could have started a simulation in 1900 and we're still living in it? I don't see why that's any more likely than this being reality – we have no evidence this isn't real.'

'No, that's true, but consider this: if there are millions upon millions of inch-perfect simulations, and only *one single reality*, which are we more likely to be in right now?'

She frowned as she thought about it. It did sort of make sense.

'And not just more likely but, by sheer weight of numbers, we're mathematically *vastly* more likely to be in one of the millions or billions of simulated realities than the *only* real one.'

He was smiling as he watched her think about it.

'So what you're saying is . . . none of this is real.'

'I don't know.' He shrugged. 'Maybe. Maybe that's what all this is about. Maybe we're in some simulation to determine how long it would take the human race to destroy itself under certain circumstances. Maybe the human race did nearly destroy itself, and centuries later, the survivors wanted to discover how it happened? Maybe there's another simulation running in the computer next to ours where the earth is destroyed by an asteroid strike? Who knows?'

'But this feels real to me.'

'Of course – but as you said yourself, when you're in a dream – which is itself a kind of simulated reality – that seems real at the time.'

Rachael sat quietly for a few minutes silently contemplating everything Zak had said while they ate. 'If that's true, if all that you're saying is true, then on the one hand, nothing matters. Nothing we do has any real consequence, since none of it's real, and we might be switched off tomorrow anyway. Deleted out of existence, with a single click of a mouse in the year 2597.'

'I guess so.'

'Except that's not quite true, is it?'

'How do you mean?'

'Well, whether this is a simulation or not, we know our actions have consequences – even if they're only within this simulation. If I only eat cakes, I'll get fat. If I go into town and shoot somebody, I'll go to prison. If I don't pay my rent, I'll be chucked out on the street. Now, maybe none of that is *real*, but it's real to me. It's real to you. Maybe we are all electrons and zeros and ones, but I think, I feel. So do you. So does my daughter. Real or not, this world is real to us, so it matters just as much.'

'I suppose,' he said. 'Or maybe it's all a game. Maybe we're supposed to be trying to win.'

'Win what?'

He shrugged. 'Or maybe it's all as pointless as it seems.'

Rachael frowned at his negativity. Perhaps the isolation, the broadcast – maybe it was all getting to him too. 'Is there room for God in your simulation theory?' she asked.

'Dunno. I guess it depends on what you mean by God.'

'Do you believe in God?'

'I was brought up a Catholic. My mother was very devout. Church every Sunday, without fail. I was even an altar boy.'

'You didn't answer the question.'

He finished his food and began rolling up the empty packet. 'I've fought in some truly horrific wars. I've seen things that would give you nightmares for a thousand years.'

'So you do?'

'Have you ever heard that phrase, "there are no atheists on the battlefield"?'

She nodded.

'Well,' he took another sip of his coffee. 'I must be the only one in the world.'

'Why?'

'I've seen death, I've seen evil, right up close in the face.' His tone had changed, his voice was somehow . . . darker. 'I've seen men shot through their eyes, seen them dying in the most agonizing ways possible. I've seen soldiers screaming in sheer pain, only stopping when they finally expire. I was on a ship once that got hit by an Exocet missile. Suddenly, the ship isn't a ship anymore, it's a mobile bomb where every metal surface is as hot as a furnace.'

Rachael listened intently.

'You try to escape,' he continued, 'but every route is blocked by fire or horrible thick, black smoke. It's like . . .' he thought for a moment. 'Imagine a modern version of hell. Imagine if a big industrial engineering company was given the job of building a new hell. "Great news, lads, we've got the Hell contract, now get to work."'

She smiled at the ludicrous notion. He was good at this – making her smile in a desperate situation.

'Imagine they built a mechanical, machine-driven version of hell made out of iron and fire and smoke and screams.' He stopped talking for a moment as he thought back. 'That's what it was like. And even if somehow – *somehow* – you fight your way out, fight your way to the top, to the clean air – even then you haven't escaped. Not really. All you can see is row after row of men screaming in agony and already horribly disfigured. As if part of the "Hell" contract involves torturing enough poor souls to populate it with new demons.' He turned to look at her. 'I've

186

seen men's flesh literally melting off their bones, off their hands, their faces, like their skin was made of butter. Can you imagine that?'

Rachael shook her head. She was surprised he was being so candid. She'd met service veterans before – her father among them – but she'd never encountered one so forthcoming about his war recollections. Usually it was something to be buried in the past. Why was he telling her this now?

'Something like that . . . it changes you. It changed me. All I'll say is this: with everything I've seen, I can't believe there is a god – any kind of god – who would let it happen.'

She nodded. It made sense.

'And once you shake the idea that your actions are somehow being judged, it's incredibly . . .' he paused for a moment and closed his eyes briefly '. . . freeing.'

Rachael looked up at him and frowned again. His cheery demeanour was slipping. Had he been putting on a front just to reassure her? Or was he actually as mentally fragile as she was at this point? As she watched him, all of a sudden he seemed to snap back into a brighter mood, the darkness lifting from his face.

'What about you?' he asked. 'Scientist? *Guardian* reader? Liberal?'

She hated to admit it, but he was bang on. 'You don't know anything about me.'

'Oh yeah? Any of that wrong?'

She made a non-committal movement of her head.

'Thought so. All that, I'm guessing you're a nailed-on atheist. Am I right?'

'You know, I should be. I'm a scientist, a researcher. I work from evidence. Evidence is what it's all about. Evidence is the only way of judging something for sure.'

'Of course.'

'And you know how much evidence there is for the existence of God?'

'Not much,' he shrugged.

'Less than that. There's zero. Nothing. Not a single shred. Anywhere. There is exactly the same amount of evidence for God as there is for the Tooth Fairy or the Easter Bunny.'

'So you don't believe.'

'Well, I don't tell anyone this – I've always been a bit embarrassed about it.'

'What?'

'I don't know about the Bible and Jesus and hymns and all that. I don't see why our book written thousands of years ago by men trumps anyone else's book, or vice versa.'

'But . . . ?'

'But I can't shake the feeling . . . I've always sort of believed . . . that there's *something* out there. Something or someone, kind of, keeping an eye on me every now and then.'

'Really?'

'I know, right?' She rolled her eyes. 'The scientist who doesn't believe anything without peer-reviewed papers and triple-checked data sets. But I dunno, I've just always felt it.' She shrugged, by way of further explanation.

'Don't worry,' he said with a smile. 'I won't tell any of your science buddies and get you thrown out of the Magic Circle.'

She smiled back.

'Come on,' he said as he drained the last of his coffee. 'Let's get moving. I'll pack up and start the Snowcat, get the heater on.'

'I can help you load up.'

He shook his head. 'No, you stay here in the warm and get your things together. I'll come and get you when the cab's warmed up.' He smiled.

She watched him walk to the other end of the hut, into the little porch and then out the door. He slammed it shut behind him. The whole hut seemed to be creaking, groaning and moaning as the wind and the storm pulled and pushed at it from every direction. The slamming of the door shook the entire structure, and as if it had finally had enough, the hut itself seemed to give up at that moment. Battered by decades of extreme polar weather, leaned on by several tons of accumulated snow, and then weakened even further by Rachael removing internal timbers to keep her fire alive, with a huge creak that sounded like a hundred-year-old giant oak being felled, one of the rotten beams holding the roof up gave way to the immense weight of the snow above it.

Rachael heard the beam splinter apart and with a rising sense of dread she quickly realized she had to get out. Now.

As the beam crashed down on top of the stove, bringing sheets of felt-covered tin with it from the roof, she ran towards the door but in her haste she tripped on a corner of the mattress and fell forward, landing hard on the timber floor with a thud. The snow was already pouring in from the hole in the roof and Rachael could hear it sizzling as it hit the iron stove and was instantly vaporized. She scrambled to her knees just as Zak flung open the door. 'Rachael!' he shouted as he ran into the porch and instinctively threw out his hand towards her.

She pulled herself to her feet and took another step but above her, the weight of the snow had moved to the next beam, which snapped even faster than the first. As that one went, so the pressure moved to the next, and the next and the next, and in a matter of seconds half of the roof caved in on itself. Before Rachael could take another step, the snow poured in on top of her like fresh concrete, pinning her down with its immense weight and suffocating her into the bargain.

She barely had time to let out a scream before the sound was muffled by the snow and a split second later sheer terror kicked in as she realized she was now entombed in it – and completely unable to move.

27

Rachael knew she didn't have long before she would black out from lack of oxygen. She also knew that the worst thing she could do was panic, but she simply couldn't help it. Her every limb was rendered immobile, as if she'd been encased from head to toe in quick-dry cement. She felt a terror she'd never known before as she found she could neither move, see, nor breathe.

Battling against the fear that was threatening to engulf her, she concentrated all her strength in her legs and kicked hard to try to push herself up through the snow. She barely moved a millimetre. She drew on every last ounce of strength she had, strained every muscle and sinew, and pushed again as hard as she could, but still nothing happened. She wasn't strong enough, and with the amount of snow now on top of her, she couldn't even move her head. And she was already running out of oxygen. She'd begun to think she would die in this hut, and now it was about to come true in a new and terrifying way she had never imagined.

But then she felt movement. The snow around her was shifting. She could hear Zak's muffled calls as the snow began to move above her. She tried to call out to him but she couldn't suck in any air and when she tried to shout it came out in a breathless and almost silent wheeze. She was terrified that if he couldn't hear her, he would assume he was in the wrong spot, and move along to dig elsewhere while she silently suffocated just feet below him. 'Zak!' she wheezed. 'Zak!'

But her calls were pathetically quiet, and she felt the movement of the snow get weaker. He was leaving her. Leaving her to die in her ice tomb. She felt the panic rising in her anew, and with everything she had she puffed out her chest, sucking in what little oxygen she had left and screamed out 'Zak!' as loudly as she could. 'ZAK!' she cried again.

There was a pause. Nothing happened. She knew she was out of oxygen and out of time. She could not summon enough strength in her lungs to shout again. She could feel her life slipping away, darkness flooding in from every angle as her brain fought in vain against the lack of oxygen.

Then the snow shifted. It seemed like it was getting lighter. Was he . . . digging? And then she felt it: a hand on her shoulder, a big, bear-like paw patting around as if searching for something in the dark, and then another. She had never been so happy to feel the touch of another human being.

'Rachael!' Zak called. 'Hold on!'

She felt the snow shifting around her as he buried his strong arms deep into the snow. There was more movement as he shifted more and more snow away from her and somehow got his hands under her armpits. Then she felt him heave her upwards. Two, three, four pulls, and with each one she kicked and pulled and pushed and fought and struggled. And then with one more huge, joyous, glorious, triumphant yank, she broke free at the surface and gulped the frozen fresh air into her starved lungs. Another pull freed her entirely and she scrambled up out of her snowy grave and embraced Zak as they both fell into an exhausted heap onto the ice, clinging to each other tightly.

'Jesus,' he said between breaths. 'I thought I'd lost you then.'

'It just . . . caved in,' was all she could say. 'I thought that was it.'

She was wearing only a T-shirt, trousers, boots, and her purple fleece. Her Big Red was now buried under several tons of snow, as was her rucksack and all her belongings, including her journal and the photograph of her family. But she'd escaped. And simply being able to breathe and move felt like the most wonderful gift she'd ever received. As the adrenaline began to wear off, the relief at having got out was replaced by the realization that she was freezing and now had no cold-weather gear to protect her from the elements. She shivered in Zak's arms as their breathing returned to normal. He sat up and took off his Big Red, and she gratefully slipped her arms inside and zipped it up.

'Come on,' he said, casting furtive glances left and right as if some great predator might be watching them. 'Let's get out of here.'

They stood up and Rachael could see they were now right above where the north side of the hut had once stood, and were level with the remaining two roof beams that were still standing. She picked up the shovel and immediately began digging back down into the snow.

'What are you doing?'

'My bag,' Rachael said, desperate to recover her photograph of Adam and Izzy. 'I must get my bag.'

Zak shook his head. 'It'll take hours to dig down that far. We don't have time.'

Rachael continued digging. 'My Big Red – my Big Red is down there,' she said, thinking that would sound like a more palatable reason to expend the effort, though she would happily sacrifice that to get her photo back.

'I have a couple of spares in the Snowcat,' Zak said.

She carried on digging, she couldn't bear the thought of losing her photo – it was like losing Adam and Izzy all over again. She was breathing hard as she dug frantically, throwing the snow off the side of the drift that had submerged the hut.

'We have to go,' Zak said.

She ignored him and continued to dig.

'Come on,' he said. 'You're not being rational. Look where we are. You'd need a JCB to get down there now.'

'I have to get my bag,' she repeated as she dug.

'Rachael, stop it,' he shouted as he walked towards her. 'Come on, you know we have to go now,' he added, more softly.

She paused and looked at him. He was already shivering in the bitter cold. She looked at how high they were, how much snow was now packed in on top of her buried possessions. She let out a big breath as she realized he was right: it was hopeless. Adam and Izzy were gone. Again.

She dropped the shovel and stood motionless as she let it sink in. The pain of losing them flooded over her all over again and she felt herself lose her balance and begin to fall forward into the snow, but Zak stepped in and caught her.

She held him close and closed her eyes as she pictured her family and fought back the tears. And all of a sudden she was very aware that Zak was shaking violently from the cold. She pulled back from him. 'Come on, we need to get you in the warm,' she said.

He smiled and nodded, picked up the shovel, then they slipped down the snow drift and seconds later were inside the warm cab of the Snowcat. As they began motoring away, Rachael glanced back at what remained of the hut that had saved her life and had, for almost a fortnight been her home. But in the darkness and the blizzard it had already slipped out of sight.

28

The windscreen wipers on the Snowcat were fighting a losing battle as Zak and Rachael clunked along through the storm. The tracked vehicle only had a top speed of fifteen miles per hour, but in these conditions that was plenty fast enough. Zak sat hunched over the controls, peering through the windscreen as the wiper blades fought to keep it clear of snow. As well as the vehicle's headlights, a high-powered halogen lamp mounted on the roof helped cut an extra shaft of light through the darkness to show them their way through the eerie, deserted landscape.

They approached what looked like two half-finished snowmen, spaced about twelve feet apart.

'What's that?' Rachael asked.

'Every time I found a good crossing point over a crevasse I built these markers for the ice bridge so I'd know where to cross on the way back,' Zak replied.

'Smart.'

He lined the Snowcat up between the markers. The bridge – the remaining ice from where two different crevasses had almost completely merged – was about fourteen feet in length. Rachael watched the small screen that was connected to the ground-penetrating radar device rigged up on a boom that hung out in front of the vehicle. She could see the ice was some twelve feet thick. Below that was more than two hundred feet of nothingness. She found she was holding her breath as they passed over the crevasse below. The last time she had seen one, it had very nearly become her grave. She only breathed out once they were across the bridge. Zak seemed unaffected. His calmness was reassuring.

'I'm sorry,' she blurted out.

He turned to look at her, his brow furrowed in confusion. 'What?'

'I'm sorry,' she said again.

'What for?'

'For not listening to you. Back at Station Z. When Guy was taken out on the plane. We should have gone with him.'

He shrugged. 'I guess it doesn't matter now.'

'Of course it matters. We could have been at home when it . . . happened.'

He didn't respond for nearly a full minute. 'How old's your daughter?'

'Almost twenty months. How about you? You got kids?'

'Two boys. Eleven and thirteen.'

She looked down. 'And if I hadn't been so bloody pig-headed, you could have been with them.' She nearly added 'at the end', but it still seemed too soon – too brutal – to vocalize it.

'I knew the risks when I took the job,' he said.

'Yeah but the risks are falling down a crevasse or getting sick and having no way out. Not being totally cut off from everyone you love because you get caught up in some unimaginable war.'

'Here, there. Ultimately it doesn't make any difference.'

After another hour of driving through the snow, Zak slowed the Snowcat to a stop. 'I need a pee,' he said as he pulled his goggles down over his eyes and zipped up his fleece.

'You can't go out there without a coat.' She began to slip her arms out of his Big Red.

'Don't worry. You keep that one. I'll grab a spare from the back,' he said as he opened the door.

As the cold rushed into the cab before Zak could shut the door behind him, Rachael pulled the collar of his coat up around her neck and plunged her hands into the pockets. She found her left hand brushing against something small and metallic. It felt like a coin, but seemed to be attached to a chain. She pulled it out for a look, and frowned in confusion as soon as she saw what it was: a silver St Christopher pendant. *Guy's St Christopher pendant.* She stared at it for a few seconds.

What the hell? Why does Zak have this? How did he get it?

The door opened and Zak climbed back in and pulled it shut after him, a spare Big Red now zipped up around him.

She held the pendant up for him to see. 'Why have you got this?'

29

Rachael tried to gauge Zak's initial reaction but his face gave nothing away.

'Oh good, you found it,' he said quickly.

'What do you mean, found it? It was in your pocket. Why have you got it?'

'I found it in the sickbay. I figured it was Guy's and he'd taken it off when he was in there, then forgotten to take it with him.'

'He never went anywhere without it,' she said. 'Nancy gave it to him – his first wife.'

Zak shrugged. 'Rachael, he was delirious. Hardly conscious when he left. He barely knew what day it was. Anyway, I found it, and thought you might like to, you know, give it back to him. I wanted to keep it safe, so I decided to keep it on me. Then when I found you, I guess I forgot about it, with everything that's happened.' His face turned to a frown. 'Why? What did you think?'

'I . . . I don't know.'

'You think I *stole it*?' He looked hurt. 'Why would I do that?'

Rachael suddenly felt ridiculous. Of course Guy had taken it off in the sickbay. Of course he had forgotten about it. And Zak had a point – why *would* he have stolen it? That didn't make any sense at all. 'I'm sorry,' she said. 'I'm sorry. I've just . . . I've been on my own for a long time.' She tried to smile. 'I don't think my brain is working properly yet.'

'Well,' he said brightly as he engaged drive and tilted the joystick forward to move the Snowcat, 'you're not on your own now. Now there are two of us.'

'Three.'

'Sorry?'

'You said, "now there are two of us". I mean, Henriksen's a creep but he still counts.'

Zak smiled. 'Of course.'

'I've been thinking about it a lot,' she said suddenly, after almost two hours of silence. 'You know – how it actually happens.'

'How what happens?'

'The . . .' she hesitated to actually say it, 'the bombs. The attack. All that. When the bombs actually hit. I can't picture it at all. I mean, I've seen those old clips of the tests – the big mushroom cloud and all that, but that's from so far away. What do you think it's like if you're in the middle of it?'

'I'd say it's best not to think about that,' he said quietly.

'But I do think about it,' she persisted. 'I haven't had much else to think about.'

'I guess not.'

'I mean, do you hear it? Do you see a big flash of light? What do they aim it at? Just fire it at Big Ben and hope for the best?'

'You're a scientist. Don't you know how it works?'

'I understand the science, the physical reactions that lead to detonation, but I mean what would actually happen? How does it get to that point? How does it all work? What happens . . . to the people?'

'You told me you have a daughter?'

She nodded. 'Izzy.'

'Then believe me, it's best not to think about it.'

'I can't do that – I can't process it if I don't understand it.'

He didn't reply.

'Do they get any warning? Or does it happen out of nowhere?'

'Depends,' he said. 'Someone would've known.'

'Who?'

'There are systems.'

'How do you know?'

'I told you I was ex-Navy, right?'

She nodded.

'For four and a half years I was part of Operation Relentless.'

She looked blankly at him.

'Britain's nuclear deterrent.'

'What does that mean exactly? You were in a bunker some-where with your finger on the trigger?'

He shook his head. 'No, our weapons are carried by subma-rines now. I worked on one of them for a few years, HMS *Vanguard*. I was what they now call a "communications and information systems specialist". We'd sail around the world, undetected, and ready to fire our weapons at any moment, at the command of the prime minister. In the last fifty years, there hasn't been a single day – not one – when there wasn't a Royal Navy submarine out there somewhere, ready and capable of firing, and destroying entire countries.'

'Entire countries? From one submarine?'

'Oh yes. Easily. One sub alone has enough missiles on board to completely destroy forty targets. Each warhead is at least eight times more powerful than the bomb dropped on Hiroshima. Imagine, forty major cities utterly obliterated at the touch of a button.'

Rachael listened in silence as they rumbled along through the endless polar night.

'And remember: that's only a third of the stockpile of warheads.'

'That's terrifying.'

'That's not the half of it. There are eight other countries with nuclear weapons, many of them with more weapons than us. Far more. We have a total of around two hundred. Guess how many the US has.'

'I don't know,' she shrugged. 'Double? Triple that?'

He laughed. 'Not even close.'

'How many, then?'

He turned to look at her. 'Almost seven thousand.'

'Seven *thousand*?'

'And the Russians have about the same.'

She looked back at him wide-eyed and with her mouth open. 'That's insane. All that destructive power.'

'Now I am become death,' he said slowly, turning to face her, 'the destroyer of worlds.'

'What's that?'

'J. Robert Oppenheimer – he was the chief scientist on the first project to build a nuclear weapon. After they successfully detonated the first test bomb, he was plunged into a deep depression, knowing the destructive capacity his genius had unleashed onto the world. He said he was reminded of that line. Apparently it's from Hindu scripture.'

'In a weird way, it's kind of beautiful,' she said quietly.

He shrugged. 'I guess so.'

They carried on through the blizzard. 'You didn't answer my question,' she said after a good ten minutes of silence.

'What question?'

'How does it actually happen? The bomb hits and it all goes dark? What would happen to everyone?'

'I told you: you don't want to know.'

'But I do. I have to. We're talking about my family – my daughter,' she said, her voice cracking with emotion as the pain flooded back into her heart. The black poison. 'I need to

201

understand. I don't know why, but I do,' she sniffed. 'Would they even have had any warning? Did we even have a plan?' She saw her vision of Adam huddled with Izzy in the kitchen, utterly terrified as chaos reigned all around them.

Zak drove with his head pointing straight ahead. He opened his mouth to speak, seemed to think better of it, but then said: 'This is going to sound cruel, but believe me, you should hope they were right in the middle of it. You should hope your house was the first target, absolute ground zero for the first bomb to drop on the country.'

'What do you mean?'

'Look, in a nuclear conflict, you're better off being hit in the first wave. After that, things are only going to get worse. A lot worse. The bomb hitting is only the start.'

'What do you mean, "only the start"?'

'I told you: it's better not to know.'

'But you have to. I need to know.'

'No!' he shouted.

Rachael was shocked. It was the first time she'd heard him raise his voice.

'I'm telling you: you don't want to know. So just leave it.'

She said nothing.

'Nikita Khrushchev,' he said more quietly, 'the Soviet leader during the Cuban Missile Crisis, was once asked about the prospect of nuclear war. Do you know what he said?'

She shook her head.

'He said: "the living will envy the dead".'

His words hung in the air, accompanied by the squeaking of the windscreen wipers and the howl of the wind.

A few minutes later they reached another marker, but this time there was only one. They sat in the Snowcat watching out of the windscreen for a few seconds, both of them trying to spot the second marker, with the sound of the wipers marking time like a metronome. 'I guess I didn't build it properly,' Zak said.

'So what do we do? We don't know which side of this one to drive. Inch forward using the GPR?'

Zak shook his head and pulled his goggles down over his eyes. 'Quicker if I just take a look,' he said. 'It's either to the left or the right of the marker.' He opened the door and the gale whipped into the cab of the truck for a few seconds before he slammed the door shut behind him. Rachael watched as he staggered against the wind towards the lone marker, his Big Red flapping behind him in the wind, its reflective panels flashing as they caught the powerful glare of the roof-mounted spotlight. Their progress had been slow. She looked down at her watch. 11.24 a.m. They weren't making enough ground. If they carried on at this rate, they faced a night in the tent before reaching Station Z.

To counter the blast of frozen air that had infiltrated the cabin when Zak got out, Rachael zipped up the Big Red tighter around her neck and plunged her hands into the side pockets. Once again she felt the tiny metallic disc of Guy's St Christopher in her right hand. As she clutched it tightly she closed her eyes and saw it around Guy's lean neck.

She felt a rush of despair as she pictured him lying in his bunk in the sickbay, the life draining out of him by the minute. She wondered how long he had survived. Even if his mystery illness hadn't got him, he was surely dead now anyway. She opened her eyes and watched Zak testing the ice in front of them by gingerly kicking with his right foot. Had he really found the St Christopher back at Station Z? She tried to remember the last time she'd seen it on Guy, but she couldn't be sure. Zak's explanation had been plausible enough . . . hadn't it? And if he had taken it, why? There was no reason for him to do that. It wasn't worth much. It would be a very odd crime to commit.

And then there was the question of Henriksen. Where was he? Zak had told her he had remained back at Station Z in case anyone tried to make contact. Again, it was entirely plausible. But what happened to Zak's unbreakable 'no one goes anywhere alone' rule? Of course, that was before . . . but still, wouldn't they have stayed together?

She closed her eyes again, leaned back against the headrest and tried to put her suspicious thoughts out of her mind. She was being ridiculous. The isolation was making her paranoid.

She ran her fingers around the edge of the St Christopher in her pocket. She wished Guy was here. 'Why did you have to get sick and leave me here?' she said out loud as she clutched it tightly.

She opened her eyes, half hoping to somehow see Guy's big round face smiling back at her. But he wasn't there. She sighed, glanced out of the windscreen, and realized Zak wasn't there either.

30

She scanned the scene in front of her but there was no sign of him. A moment earlier he'd been ten feet ahead in a bright red polar jacket. He couldn't just disappear. For a split second the thought again flashed across her mind that perhaps he had never been here, but that made no sense at all. How had she got here? Where had the Snowcat come from? No, he *was* here. She scrambled out of the cab and shouted his name through the blizzard. 'Zak!' She ran towards the crevasse and tried again. 'ZAK!' She wondered if he'd be able to hear anything in this storm.

'Rachael!'

She twitched as she heard the muffled cry of her own name. She edged closer to the crevasse. 'Zak?'

'Rachael! Down here! Oh thank Christ!'

Rachael looked down to see Zak dangling in the mouth of the crevasse, some four or five feet down from the edge. He was clinging onto an axe that was embedded in the ice wall.

'Oh my God! Are you OK?'

'I was testing the ice and it just gave way under my feet. Help me!'

She lay flat on the snow and reached down to him. He reached up with his spare hand, both of them straining every sinew, but they were simply too far apart.

'Get the rope!' he cried. 'In the back of the Snowcat there's a climbing rope.'

She nodded and stood up.

'Wait!' he yelled. 'You'll need the key!' He reached down with his left hand and fished a keyring out of his jacket pocket and threw it up to her.

She fumbled but caught it and ran to the storage bay at the back of the vehicle. She unlocked the door, pulled it open and searched the inside with quick, darting eyes. She saw the end of the orange rope under a tarpaulin and yanked it out from underneath the sheet. As she did so, something came out with it and landed in the snow at her feet. A flash of red against the white of the snow – she knew she had seen that colour somewhere before . . . It was a hat. A red Manchester United woolly hat. She stopped dead and stared down at it as it flapped in the wind. *Henriksen's hat.*

'Rachael!' she heard Zak call through the wind.

She didn't move. Henriksen never took that hat off. *Never.*

'Rachael, hurry!'

She bent to pick it up, then slung the rope over her shoulder and ran back to the edge of the crevasse. She stood over Zak as he clung on by his axe and thrust the hat out over the edge. 'What's this?' she demanded.

Zak looked up. 'Throw me the rope!'

'Why have you got Henriksen's hat?'

'Throw me the rope!' he shouted again. 'The axe is slipping!'

'Why have you got Henriksen's hat?' she repeated. 'Where is he?'

'I told you: he's back at Station Z. Throw me the fucking rope, Rachael!'

She shook her head. 'I don't believe you. I've known him for ten years. He never goes anywhere without this hat.'

'He must have dropped it when he was helping me load the Snowcat.'

She didn't buy it. Henriksen would never be so careless with that hat. Something told her Zak was lying. 'Bullshit! What have you done to him?'

'Nothing! I swear! He's back at Station Z now waiting for us! Pull me up and we'll be with him in a few hours.'

There was a cracking sound as the ice began to weaken. Zak tried to hug the wall of the crevasse. 'Rachael please!'

She stood firm. She thought of Guy's St Christopher. She remembered her dream of Zak going through her bag back at One Ton. Was it really a dream? She knew she was in a unique position to get to the truth. This was her chance. 'You said "two of us".'

'What?'

'Earlier, when I said I was all alone, you said "don't worry, now there are two of us".'

'So?'

'So what happened to Henriksen?'

'I meant two of us here, now!'

'Did you?' she asked sceptically.

'Of course!'

'Why was the back door of the Snowcat locked?'

'I don't know. Force of habit. Throw me the rope!'

That didn't ring true either. No one bothered to lock anything. It was pointless out here with no one else around. 'I don't believe you. Tell me where Henriksen is. And don't lie to me again.'

Another crack.

'OK!' he shouted. 'OK. Throw me the rope and I'll tell you. I promise.'

'No. Tell me now.' Her voice was hard. Cold.

'Rachael!'

She didn't move a muscle.

'It's . . . it's not what you think.'

'Then tell me what it is.' Her tone was as cold as the very ice he clung to.

'He's . . . dead.'

She took a sharp intake of breath.

'How?'

'The fever! He caught the fever – the same thing Guy had, the same thing I had. He caught it after you left. But he got worse and worse, and he died. There was nothing I could do.'

Another crack. He was crying now, begging for his life. 'Please, Rachael, please! You have to believe me. Why would I lie?'

'I don't know,' Rachael said. 'But you've already lied to me. Why should I believe you now?'

'I can take you to him. I buried him. I kept his hat – I knew what it meant to him. I was going to take it back to his family.'

It was the same story he'd given her about Guy's pendant. 'If that's true, why didn't you tell me when you found me?'

His breaths were coming in short bursts now, between tears. He seemed small, weak. 'When I found you, you were half dead. You told me yourself you thought you might be losing it. I could see you were close to the edge. You'd been alone for two months . . . you knew your family were dead. I didn't think you could handle another death. So I kept quiet.'

That made some sense, she conceded.

'I was going to tell you when we got back to Station Z.'

It could be true. It could so easily be true. She wanted it to be true. What was the alternative? That Zak killed him? For what? It made no sense. She couldn't think of any possible motive Zak could have had for killing Henriksen. It was absurd to even think it. A murder in the Antarctic? It was ridiculous. And if he had,

208

why would Zak then have risked his own life to drive ninety miles across a crevasse field in the dark, in the dead of winter, alone, to rescue her?

She heard another crack.

'Rachael, please!' Zak shouted. 'The ice . . . it's cracking!'

Still she hesitated. Still something held her back. Was she being paranoid? Something definitely didn't feel right – but . . . she could so easily be wrong. Was she willing to let Zak die because of a bad feeling? She was desperately trying to clear her mind, to think rationally. She saw Adam sitting at their kitchen table, he was speaking but she couldn't hear what he was saying. The roar of the wind and the cries from Zak were drowning him out. 'Shut up!' she shouted. She closed her eyes and turned down the volume of everything except Adam's voice. *I've seen people crack . . . Rothera . . . Brian Collins . . . He flipped out. Lost his marbles. He became paranoid . . . He thought two of the others were trying to kill him, so he set fire to the lab while they were working. The straitjacket.* Was this her Collins moment? Had she strayed that far from sanity?

'RACHAEL!' Zak's shouting brought her back to the present.

She looked down at him. He was openly crying now, and had even given up pleading. He simply clung to his axe. He seemed vulnerable, weak. Helpless. At that moment she realized he was the only other human on the planet she knew for certain was still alive. And she resolved she wasn't going to let him die because she'd found a hat in the cargo bay.

She stuffed the hat into the pocket of her fleece and picked up the rope. She tied one end to the front bumper of the Snowcat, then threw the other down to him. He grabbed it and Rachael began to haul him up. She heaved with all her might as her body, weakened by malnutrition, struggled to pull him up and over the edge. When he was close enough, he swung his axe down hard

209

into the ice to gain purchase and pulled himself over the cliff and onto the snow bank above.

He collapsed onto the ground, gulping in deep breaths of air. 'You were going to let me die!' he shouted. 'Are you fucking mad?'

She shook her head. 'I . . . I found Henriksen's hat. I panicked. It didn't make sense. And after Guy's St Christopher . . . I just thought it was odd. I didn't know what to think.' She sighed deeply, as if composing herself. 'I'm sorry,' she said quietly. 'I'm sorry.'

Zak said nothing as he got to his feet and began looping the rope around his hand and his elbow. When he got to the Snowcat he untied it, finished the loop, then walked around to the back and slung it inside, before slamming the door shut. 'Come on,' he said gruffly. 'We need to get a move on.'

He walked around to the driver's side of the cabin and climbed in. After a brief pause, Rachael followed and they set off once again into the snow.

31

They drove on through the blizzard in silence, the mountain looming over them from the left, the vast white plain of the shear zone to their right, the cabin filled with tension. It was as if they were a couple on a long drive after a particularly hurtful row, and now neither knew what to say to the other to make it OK again, or even if it would ever be OK after this. She kept trying to think of something to say to break the silence, but nothing came to mind that didn't seem ludicrously inadequate after what had happened. She had been moments away from letting Zak die, and they both knew it.

Then the Snowcat stopped moving. She looked at Zak. He was staring dead ahead into the darkness, the windscreen wipers flapping back and forth in the snow.

She followed his gaze and the line the Snowcat's headlights cut through the gloom and saw they were just a few feet away from the next crevasse. It was the biggest they had encountered yet – she estimated at least thirty feet across. She saw the two snow markers that had been left either side of the ice bridge. And then she saw why Zak had stopped: the bridge was gone. They both leaned forward in unison to try to get a better look, both hoping that it would somehow materialize if they got their faces a couple of inches closer to it. Zak revved the engine and inched the Snowcat nearer to the edge, but it only confirmed their first assessment. The bridge wasn't there. Swallowed up by the hungry crevasse it once defied.

'The crevasses are already getting wider,' Rachael whispered. 'Just as Guy predicted.'

Zak reversed the Snowcat, then turned to the right and lined it up alongside the crevasse, pointing the headlights and the roof-mounted lamp along its length. They both narrowed their eyes as they followed the three shafts of light. They illuminated the long crack in the ice and both of them could see the fissure grew wider and wider and wider as it snaked away from them. Zak reached down into the storage box between the two front seats and fished out a set of binoculars. He pulled his hood up over his head and grabbed the release catch on the door. The cabin was instantly flooded with wind, noise and snow as he fought to get out, before he slammed it shut again, leaving Rachael alone. She watched out the window as he stood between the two headlights with the binoculars raised to his face. Then he battled his way through the wind back to the cab and climbed inside.

'It just gets wider and wider,' he said. 'And there's no sign of any bridges.'

'How far can you see with those?' she asked.

He shrugged. 'Maybe two thousand feet? In this visibility probably less than that. But it's our only option: we'll have to drive along until we find a crossing.'

She shook her head. 'No. That's a bad idea,' she said quietly. 'We could be driving for days. Weeks. You said yourself it only gets wider. We'll run out of fuel and freeze before we find a way across.'

'So what do you suggest?'

'The only thing we can do. We'll have to go around the mountain.'

He raised his eyebrows. 'Go *around* the mountain? Seriously?'

'We double back, say fifteen miles, then go around the shoulder of the mountain as low as we can, then swing round it and get back on course on the other side.'

'How long is that gonna take? And will this thing even do it?'

'We'd better hope so – we're stuffed if not.' She spoke mechanically, in a flat tone. She was still unsure how to talk to him after what had happened.

He sighed and swung the Snowcat through one hundred and eighty degrees as they began retracing their tracks.

They drove on in silence. After a couple of hours Zak glanced at his watch. 'It's late. We should make camp here,' he said. 'We can get a good run at the mountain in the morning.'

Rachael nodded.

'I'll go and put the tent up. You stay here in the warm.'

'I can help,' she offered.

'No. You stay here – I'll do it myself.'

Before she could object he zipped up his Big Red, slipped out of the door and slammed it shut behind him.

Alone. Silence. She heard the clank of the cargo bay door being pulled open, then slammed shut a few seconds later. His form cut across the beam of the headlights and she watched him begin work on the tent on his own. He'd shunned her offer of help – clearly he was angry with her, but didn't he have every right to be? After all, she'd come painfully close to letting him die. But then, she'd had her reasons. Hadn't she? She frowned as, ever the scientist, she questioned the validity of her own position. What did she know for *certain*? She'd found Guy's St Christopher. Unexpected? Yes. Suspicious? Perhaps. Conclusive? Not in the least.

But what of Henriksen? Poor Henriksen. She knew he was dead, the question was, did she believe Zak's explanation? It was entirely plausible. She'd seen the effect the mystery illness had had on both Guy and Zak himself. Whatever it was, it was particularly nasty and she had no trouble imagining it could be fatal. But why hadn't he told her about Henriksen earlier? Again, Zak's explanation was entirely plausible. She *had* been mentally unstable when he found her at the hut and it was perfectly reasonable of him to avoid exacerbating that by telling her there and then.

And what was the alternative? That he had somehow killed Henriksen? But how – and more importantly, why? She still couldn't think of any possible motive. It didn't make sense – especially since he'd then risked his own life to come and rescue her. And he'd saved her when she was buried in the snow at One Ton. For a fleeting moment she relived the utter terror of being trapped under it all, unable to move and unable to breathe – until Zak had come to her aid. She would surely be dead by now – one way or another – if it hadn't been for him. She remembered the rush of relief she'd felt wash over her when he'd turned up and she knew for the first time in months that she wasn't entirely alone in the world. His was the first real face she'd seen for weeks on end, other than those of Adam and Izzy staring back at her from her photograph – the photograph she'd lost, along with her rucksack and all her other belongings when the hut had collapsed.

Her mind flashed back to the dream she'd had of Zak frantically searching through the very same bag. But *had* it been a dream? Had reality got mixed up somehow? No matter how much she tried, she just couldn't nail it down in her own head. What she needed was evidence. If he'd been rifling through her bag looking for something, a quick search of it would have told her if anything was missing. But her bag was buried under several tons of snow back at One Ton. A dead end.

What about his bag?

It must be in the cargo bay – the cargo bay he kept locked.

The one he'd insisted on loading himself back at One Ton. Why hadn't he wanted her help with the tent? She'd already found Henriksen's hat, but what else was he hiding from her back there?

She looked out of the windscreen and watched him battling with the tent in the full glare of the headlights and the roof-mounted lamp. She was in darkness. She could see he was making good progress – if she was going to act, she had to do it fast.

She reasoned that with the combination of the glare of the lights and the roar of the wind, she could slip out of the cab and round to the back of the Snowcat without him noticing. And she knew she could access the back compartment: he'd just opened the door to retrieve the tent and anyway, she knew he hadn't locked it again – she still had the key.

She took a deep breath and pulled the release catch on her door. She stepped out onto the tracks then down into the snow, watching him intently. He was still facing away from her, fighting with the canvas in the blizzard. He made no move to indicate he had heard anything. She pushed the door shut as quietly as she could, then crept to the back of the vehicle and swung the door open. A tiny roof light illuminated the loading bay. She saw the climbing rope, a sled, walking poles, two sleeping bags and a rations box. And there, wedged in between a gas canister and a spare tent, was his rucksack. She peered round the corner of the Snowcat but Zak was still working on erecting the tent. She reached out and pulled the bag towards her. Even as she unclipped the clasps and loosened the drawstring at the top she had no idea what she was looking for. Perhaps nothing? Indeed, if she found nothing out of the ordinary it would lend more credence to the notion that she was simply showing signs of paranoia. Going the same way as Professor Collins had at Rothera.

She pulled the top of the bag wide open, reached down inside and felt the contents. A torch. What felt like clothes – a T-shirt probably, and a thick jumper. A wash bag, two pairs of balled-up socks and a spare woolly hat. She felt around until her hand closed around a small plastic object. It felt like a cigarette lighter. She pulled it out and frowned in confusion. It was a USB pen drive. It was *her* USB pen drive. She felt the zip-up inside breast pocket on her fleece and felt the same outline shape of the backup drive she had stashed there back at the Apple hut. So it hadn't been a dream, he *had* been rifling through her belongings that night – and clearly he'd taken her pen drive. *But why?* She placed the USB stick on the floor of the cargo bay and reached back into the bag.

Then she felt something else pressed against the side of the bag. It was flat, with a glossy surface. A photograph. She pulled it out. It was her photograph. Herself, Adam and Izzy smiled back at her. She thought it had been lost along with her other things when the hut had collapsed. Her joy at discovering it was not lost after all was tempered by the realization that Zak must have taken it from her bag the night before.

Why would he take that?

She slipped the photo into her inside fleece pocket and reached back into his bag. What else was he keeping in there? She felt the same items again: torch, jumper, socks, wash bag, T-shirt – she stopped as she felt something new. It was right at the bottom of the bag. L-shaped, cold and metallic to touch. Her breath stopped altogether. It had to be . . . it was. A gun. She pulled it out of the bag and held it up by the end of the barrel, with her other hand pressed against her chest, as if to steady her heart.

'I suppose you wouldn't believe me if I said it was for hunting polar bears.' Zak was standing just two feet away from her. He looked her up and down as a thin smile crossed his lips.

She looked back at him but could find no words. She noticed a change in his face – he had a look of cold, detached determination in his eyes. Then he moved, bringing his muscled arm up above his head, as if ready to strike. She fumbled with the gun and managed to get it turned round and pointed at his chest. 'Don't!' she cried. He was supposed to stop. In the films he would have stopped – she had a gun trained on his chest at point-blank range. She'd won. Hadn't she?

But he didn't stop. He swung his fist down hard. In the same split second she heard a deafening thud, felt a searing pain overtake the whole right side of her head, dropped the gun, and then felt nothing.

32

The pain was the first thing she was aware of. Her head hurt like half her skull had been caved in. She could feel every throb of her pulse as the blood pumped around her brain, each beat bringing with it a new wave of hurt. She slowly opened her eyes and found him staring directly at her, a half smirk on his face as he studied her. She was back in the passenger seat of the Snowcat.

'Rise and shine, sleepy head.'

Between the grogginess and pain, her brain was not fully up to speed, but she knew she had to get away from him. *Get out and get away*. It was her only thought. But even as every atom in her body screamed at her to simply run, the logical part of her brain kicked in and resisted. Get away to where? How? She knew death lay outside the doors of the Snowcat. There was no hope for her outside and alone. She would have to stay where she was, at least for the moment. The self-satisfied look on his face told her he knew it too.

Was he going to hurt her now? Kill her? She tried to think how she could defend herself if he attacked her: she thought of her knife, but that was a dead end – buried along with the rest of her things under several tons of snow at One Ton Camp. She remembered the gun, but she could see it peeking out from the inside of Zak's Big Red. He'd never let it out of his sight now.

If she couldn't escape and she had no weapon, she wanted answers. 'What happened to Henriksen?'

He laughed. 'I didn't lay a hand on him.'

'But he's dead?'

'Yep,' he replied casually.

'You killed him?'

'No. You did that.'

'What?'

'The moment you didn't get on that plane at Station Z. The moment you made your "heroic" last stand. That was the moment you sealed his fate.'

None of this was making sense and the steady drum beat of the pain in her head was making it even more difficult for her to focus and work out what he was talking about. 'I don't understand.'

'Of course you don't.'

'Did you shoot him?'

'No, no. Nothing so crude.'

'But you did kill him?'

'In a manner of speaking,' he conceded.

'How?'

He turned back to face the windscreen as he pushed forward on the joystick and drove on through the snow. Clearly he'd abandoned plans to make camp for the night. 'He killed himself,' he said simply.

'Not Henriksen.' She shook her head. 'He wouldn't. He's never had a suicidal thought in his life.'

He shrugged.

'I don't believe you.'

'Believe what you like,' he said. 'That's what happened.'

It didn't make any sense. Henriksen was an uncomplicated guy, not a man given to much introspection – and he was well seasoned in the particular mental demands of living and working in the Antarctic. There was no way he'd have killed himself. 'But why? Why would he do something like that?'

He turned to face her and smiled again. 'Because I made him.'

She went to speak but something in his eyes, his voice, made her stop momentarily. It was as if she was looking at an entirely different man from the one who had come to rescue her, as if some perfect imposter had come and replaced him while she was unconscious. 'Why would you do that? You're a medic.'

'I have some medical training, but I wouldn't call myself a medic,' he said, his eyes now fixed on the snow ahead as they trundled along.

'What are you then?'

'Something much more . . .' he paused as he considered his words carefully '. . . skilled.' He nodded, apparently pleased with his choice. 'I'm a soldier.'

'So what are you doing here?'

'Money, mostly.'

None of this was making any sense. 'Money? But Guy was doing this whole thing on a shoestring.'

'He wasn't the only one paying me.'

'What do you mean?'

He laughed. 'You still haven't worked out why I was sent here, have you?'

'What are you talking about? You were in charge of safety – you were our security officer.'

'I was security, yes. For *you*, Rachael.'

'For me?'

'You and your boyfriend Guy. I was here to make sure your research never made it out of here before that vote. If you hadn't been so bloody stubborn and insisted we stayed when Guy got sick, we wouldn't be here now, and you never would have known.'

Her mouth dropped open and her eyes narrowed. She was horrified, appalled and terrified all at the same time. Her mind whirred through the implications and she brought her hand to her mouth as a shocking realization hit her. 'Oh my God – Guy's illness. You did that to him?'

'Potassium cyanide. Didn't take much.'

She pictured Guy in the sick bay at Station Z, his skin waxy, his face gaunt and pained. To learn that someone had done that to him – to someone she loved and cared for so deeply – on purpose . . . it was too horrific to process. She felt like she had been punched in the stomach. 'Is he . . . dead?'

Zak shrugged again. 'I guess so. They're all dead now, aren't they?'

'So you came here to kill us?'

He shook his head. 'Not necessarily. I came to stop your research getting out.'

She was reeling from his revelations and a kind of automatic response had kicked in as she struggled to process it all – instead of taking it all in, she began firing questions at him. 'Who sent you?'

'It's complicated. But I don't think it's a surprise to you that a lot of very powerful people did not want you coming down here. People at the very top.'

'The government? The US government?'

'Among others.'

'And you'd go as far as *killing* to stop our research?' She could barely believe what she was saying.

'If I had to.'

She shook her head. 'I don't believe it. That doesn't happen in real life. There's no way anyone would have us killed to stop this research getting out.'

He laughed, louder this time. 'Are you really that naive?'

'Naive? You're talking about . . . about murder! *State sponsored* murder – just to stop some scientific research.'

'It's not just research though, is it? You and Guy told me yourselves – the big speeches about how important it was, the consequences it could have. You think they don't already know what you know? They just don't want to see it proved. Then it becomes harder to ignore.'

'Then why ignore it in the first place, if they already know?'

'They don't care! The oil crisis is real. It's affecting people now. The election is coming up. The president needs this crisis solved now. Worry about the next crisis tomorrow. Or better yet, hope it holds off until this lot are long gone, then you never have to deal with it.'

'That's disgusting.' She couldn't keep the distaste from her voice. 'Let someone else clean it all up? It's their planet too.'

'You're talking about a bunch of rich white guys in their sixties and seventies. This is never going to be their problem. But the oil crisis is.'

'And they're willing to *kill* to solve it? Kill innocent people like us?' She shook her head. 'I just can't believe that actually happens. Not in the real world.'

'Are you joking? I mean, are you actually joking? Wars have been fought over less. *Actual* wars. Countries invaded. Governments toppled. Troops sent into battle. Men and women dying on the battlefield. Children killed in drone strikes. Loved ones lost. You think anyone would bat an eyelid at a couple of researchers getting sick or falling down a crevasse in the Antarctic?'

She had no answer to that.

'Why you? Why do it?'

'I told you: money. Lots of money.'

'And that's enough?' It was utterly abhorrent to her that

anyone could do such things, much less do them simply for money. And to Guy of all people – the most noble man she knew. A man to whom money meant nothing, a man who had sold all his possessions to fund this very trip because he believed in the cause so deeply. And he had been killed by a man who clearly valued nothing more than money – even human life.

'I'm a mercenary. I've spent my life fighting other people's wars. This was just another job. Until we lost all contact, anyway.'

Rachael shook her head. It couldn't be real. This couldn't be real. Guy, Henriksen, and now . . . her? A thousand thoughts raced through her head about what he would do to her, each more terrifying than the last. She couldn't get her head around such casual brutality. She suddenly felt ashamed that she'd been so taken in, so charmed by him when they first met back at McMurdo. She felt so stupid, so used.

'How did you do it? With Henriksen.'

He smiled again. 'I simply made him believe that there was no hope, and that death was the only option left.' He laughed to himself. 'I watched him strip all his clothes off, step out of the base and walk off into the blizzard. The full Captain Oates.'

Her mind raced back to her lowest ebb in the hut, when she had considered doing exactly the same. 'But how did you do that?'

'I have my ways.'

'But why? Why go to the trouble? Why not just push him down a crevasse if you wanted him dead?'

He paused for a moment and smiled. 'For the sport of it. I wanted to see if I could.' His eyes sparkled with glee and self-satisfaction. 'And out here, in this cold, this darkness, this isolation? It didn't take much to push him over the edge.'

Her mouth dropped open in disgust. He seemed not to notice. She remembered Collins. Rothera. The straitjacket. She knew straying from sanity was easy enough down here.

223

'Why are you telling me this now?' she asked in a low voice.

He shrugged. 'No one else left to tell.' He let that hang in the air for a moment. 'And anyway, what are you going to do? Run?' He laughed. 'To where? To who? How? You'll be dead in minutes if you step out of this truck.'

He was right, she realized with a terror that came from deep inside her chest and radiated out through her body in every direction. She knew then she was never getting out of here. It was simply a matter of how and when he killed her too. All her efforts to stay alive, all her struggles against the elements, escaping the fire, climbing out of the crevasse – it would all be for nothing. She wondered why he hadn't done it already – and why he had come to rescue her in the first place. 'Why did you come all the way out here to find me?'

'I had nothing else to do,' he said matter-of-factly.

What the hell did that mean – did he have something worse planned for her? 'So what now?' she asked.

'I told you: we go back to Station Z.'

'And then what?'

'And then,' he looked her up and down in a way that made her shudder with revulsion and fear, 'we find some way to . . . amuse ourselves.'

She felt physically sick and light-headed. She knew she had to get away. Get away from him. Away from this monster. *Somehow*. But even as she had the thought, she ruefully dismissed it as completely impossible. He was right – there was nowhere to run to. She was trapped. She tried to focus on something else, tried to fill her mind with anything other than the terrifying thought of what he would do to her once they reached Station Z.

She saw Izzy. That was her happy place. Izzy and Adam. Izzy, Izzy, Izzy. She couldn't hold back the tears as she thought of her beautiful little daughter. *People will say you're a bad mother.*

That's what Adam had said. She knew he'd said it out of anger and hurt, but was he right? She sniffed and wiped a tear from her eye. She thought of Izzy, tucked up in her cot, clutching her cuddly Tigger. So peaceful. So beautiful.

They drove on through the dark and the snow and the wind. Rachael was trapped in a metal box with a trained killer, thousands of miles from anyone or anywhere. Her husband and daughter were dead, and she would join them soon. She felt hollow. Completely empty, as if her very insides had been scraped out. She watched the twin beams of the Snowcat's headlights as they showed the way along the side of the mountain, which loomed over them like an impassive, sleeping giant. The view ahead was unchanging: snow, darkness, snow, darkness. But then the headlights picked up something . . . else. Rachael frowned as she leaned forward and tried to see what it was. *It can't be.* The Snowcat drove on towards it and it got bigger and bigger in the windscreen. *It is.*

'Izzy,' Rachael said quietly, as she looked at the tiny figure of a small child half buried in the snow.

'What?' Zak asked.

Rachael shook her head. 'Nothing.' She had seen Izzy plenty of times over the last few weeks or so, but she didn't want to let Zak know that she was here now. Her visits – and Guy's – were private and none of his business. She strained her eyes to try to see better. Izzy didn't seem to be moving. She was lying completely motionless in the snow. Rachael was filled with a mounting sense of horror. Was she . . . dead?

Then Zak brought the Snowcat to a stop just yards from the tiny figure in the snow, peered through the windscreen and said, 'What the fuck is that?'

33

Rachael pulled the release catch on her door and jumped out of the Snowcat. Her mind raced in confusion: how could Zak be seeing her, too? It wasn't possible. She ran up to where Izzy lay in the snow, hoping . . . hoping what? She knew it wasn't rational, but at that moment all Rachael hoped was that her little girl was alive.

But as she got closer she realized that, other than the completely impossible discovery of her daughter in deepest Antarctica, something wasn't right. She was too small, too young – not much bigger than a newborn. The skin was too pink, too shiny, the body too unaffected by the ravages the polar cold would inflict after just minutes of exposure. And she didn't recognize the little red babygrow the child was wearing. As Zak arrived on the scene and joined her in the glow of the Snowcat's headlights, Rachael realized she wasn't looking at Izzy. She wasn't looking at a child at all. It was a doll.

Relieving though this revelation was, it was no less confusing. The two of them stood, looking down at the toy with the wind whipping up the snow around them, its plastic lifeless eyes looking back up at theirs, its red outfit in stark contrast to the pure, white snow. Rachael scanned the horizon, but could see no clues as to how this utterly incongruous item had found its way a thousand miles inland in the most inhospitable environment on earth. She picked it up and turned it over in the light cast by the Snowcat's headlights. There were no other clues. 'Get back in the truck,' Zak ordered.

Rachael placed the doll in the gap behind her seat as Zak pushed the joystick forward. The Snowcat jolted into action and they continued in silence. What was there to be said? How to begin to explain the unexplainable? Neither had an answer, and Rachael was determined not to speak any more than was absolutely necessary to the ruthlessly casual killer she now found herself trapped with. Instead she devoted her thoughts to finding some way out, some way to escape before he could kill her too. Although, as she stared out into the black nothingness that surrounded them for hundreds of desolate miles, she knew escape was surely impossible.

It was little over an hour before the yellow beams of the headlights illuminated something else that simply should not have been there: a large, stainless steel teapot.

Zak didn't even stop as they drove on past it. 'Maybe some previous expedition ditched it?' he offered.

Rachael shook her head. 'No chance,' she said coldly. 'This isn't a route any expedition would take. I don't know of a single one that's tried this side of the mountain. It's not on the way to the pole or anywhere else significant.'

'How else could it be here?'

'You know of any expeditions that took a massive teapot with them?'

'Not since Scott's day,' he said.

'Exactly. And why the doll? They must be connected – but why would an expedition team be carrying a doll?'

As the Snowcat lumbered on through the snow the only sounds were the growl of its engine and the howl of the wind. It bumbled and bumped along, its tracks eating up the miles at a steady but relentless pace. Zak was hugging the mountain side as they circled around its base, so the whole vehicle was at a lateral angle that caused Rachael to hold onto the handle above her door. Zak used the controls to swing the Snowcat to the right as they crested a snowdrift that Rachael calculated to be about ten feet high. But as soon as they had cleared it, he stopped dead as the headlights picked out something else that simply should not have been here.

'It can't be,' he began, as he and Rachael stared out through the windscreen at what was before them.

Some twenty feet away, up to her waist in the snow, eyes wide open and staring right at them, was an old woman. She was wearing a light green, floral dress and her grey hair was frozen in place.

'Are you seeing that, too?' Zak asked without looking at Rachael.

She nodded slowly. 'What the hell's going on?' She searched her brain for an explanation. 'Something to do with the war? With the nuclear bombs?'

Zak shook his head. 'I don't know how it could be.'

'How else do you explain the body of an old woman in the middle of Antarctica?'

Zak shrugged.

'I mean the doll? The teapot? It's possible – *possible* – that an expedition could have been carrying those things. I don't know why they would, but it is at least possible. But an old lady? Out here? Wearing only a dress – no arctic gear, not even a coat – it's not possible. It's just *not* possible,' she repeated.

Zak said nothing.

'Maybe we should bury her,' Rachael said as she went to get out.

'No,' Zak replied. 'We carry on.'

'But we can't just leave her there like that.'

'We can and we will. She's long dead. We keep going. If you insist on burying her, I'm not waiting.'

Rachael had no choice in the matter and she knew it. Instead she busied her mind with searching for an explanation for the three baffling finds they had come across, and with finding a way to escape the dreadful monster that sat only inches away from her. Try as she might, she could find answers to neither.

They drove on through the night. It was only when they slowly crested the ridge that swept down from the summit and began the descent down the other side of the mountain that they finally understood. It made sense of everything: the doll, the teapot, the old woman.

'What the hell is that doing here?' Zak said as they looked down.

Half buried in the snow and resting at the bottom of the western side of the mountain was the wrecked fuselage of a large airliner.

'I mean, what the fuck?' Zak said as they peered down at it, the windows glinting with the reflection of the Snowcat's headlights. Rachael could see the whole tail section of the aircraft was missing, as was the starboard wing. The fuselage itself had one green and one blue stripe painted along its length. The cockpit and front section were covered with snow, and it looked as if it was embedded in the mountainside. 'What is that?' he asked. 'A 373. No,' he corrected himself. 'It's a DC-10. A passenger model. What the hell is it doing all the way out here? There are no passenger routes over the Antarctic. At least it explains the old woman, she must have been sucked out when the tail was ripped off,' he said as he drove the Snowcat closer to the wreck. 'But it still makes no sense at all.'

Rachael studied the remains of the jet. 'I know exactly what it's doing here,' she said quietly. 'I can't believe we found it.'

'Found what? You know what this is?'

'Yes,' she nodded. 'I just can't believe we found it.' Rachael, a keen student of the Antarctic and its many tragedies and secrets, was certain she knew what they were looking at. 'That,' she said, 'is Air New Zealand Flight 742.'

Zak was none the wiser. 'Air New Zealand?'

'It's one of the biggest mysteries in the history of aviation. In the seventies, Air New Zealand used to run sightseeing flights of Antarctica out of Auckland. A twelve-hour round trip with a guide on board to point out landmarks, and a low fly over McMurdo Sound, before turning and heading for home.'

'So what happened?'

'One day, I think it was in 1979, one of these planes took off from Auckland, and was never seen again.'

'Until now.'

She nodded. 'Until now.'

'But how come they didn't find it? Was there no rescue operation? No radio communications from the plane?'

'There was no distress call, no SOS, nothing. After a while the US Navy realized they'd lost comms and when the plane wouldn't respond, they launched a search and rescue mission.'

'SAR? Out here? Christ.'

'Six planes set out from McMurdo, flying up and down the flight plan, but nothing was ever found.'

'No wonder – this is miles off course.'

They were now less than two hundred yards from the broken metal hull and Zak brought the Snowcat to a stop. Rachael could see the tube of the remains of one of the jet engines that had been torn off in the crash. It had been ripped open and multicoloured wires and cables sprang out from within.

'The tail must have clipped the mountain behind us, presumably as they tried to pull up to miss it,' Zak said.

'There were more than two hundred and fifty people on board.'

'I wonder if any of them survived the crash, only to find themselves way out here in the freezing cold of the Antarctic, miles and miles from any possible hope of help or rescue. Imagine that.'

'The living will envy the dead,' Rachael said quietly.

As they sat in silence and surveyed the great hulk, torn from the sky and rammed into the mountainside like a toy, Rachael had a sudden flash of inspiration. It was almost certainly a terrible idea but at that very moment, she knew she had nothing to lose. Without allowing herself to think about it much more, she took advantage of the fact that Zak was momentarily distracted by the wreck, leaned over to the centre console, pulled the key from the ignition, and ran.

34

As she ran through the snow as fast as she could in the direction of the wrecked plane, Rachael knew she had three things in her favour: the first was the element of surprise. As Zak had said to her when she first learned the truth, 'Where are you going to run to?' He wouldn't have been expecting this. Secondly, she would have a small, but potentially crucial head start. He would have to get out from his side and then run around the Snowcat before he could begin pursuit. And third: the visibility was terrible. With the dark, the wind and the snow, once she was a few dozen yards away, he would struggle to even know where she was.

She ran and ran and kept running. Her heart was racing as fast as her legs, which she pumped again and again as she gulped in lungfuls of the frozen air. Running through the blizzard and the deep snow in her polar gear and Zak's Big Red was like trying to run through treacle wearing a sleeping bag, but Rachael kept going, fuelled by a massive surge of adrenaline coupled with a fear the like of which she had never known before: fear that a man with a gun was coming after her.

What is my plan? What am I actually going to do?

Right now she didn't know. Her plan did not extend further than simply getting away from him. That evil, ruthless, terrifyingly nonchalant killer. She would have to work out what to do next soon, but for the moment, every ounce of her energy was being used to keep her legs driving on against the wind and through the snow towards the twisted and torn metal of the plane wreck.

In the cabin of the Snowcat, Zak watched as Rachael dived out of her door with the only key to the vehicle, and with it, his only chance of survival. Within a few seconds she'd disappeared entirely from view into the darkness. His first instinct was to follow immediately, chase her down in the snow, retrieve the key, and then punish her. Severely.

But even as his hand reached for the door, he changed his mind. He made a few quick assumptions that he was reasonably certain of, notably that she'd be heading for the crashed plane. It was the only thing that made any sense: it offered shelter, and without that she'd be dead in hours anyway – perhaps sooner. He knew her plan – if she even had one at this stage – depended on him leaving the Snowcat and chasing her. She must be trying to draw him out, away from the vehicle so she could somehow return to it and leave him stranded. Of course, her scheme would only work if he played along. He could simply stay where he was and wait for her to return to the Snowcat. But he quickly ruled that out: waiting was boring. Waiting was no fun. But hunting? That was different.

He smiled, switched on his head torch, then unzipped his coat and pulled the gun from his holster and flicked off the safety catch. *She can have her fun*, he thought, as he pulled down his goggles over his eyes, zipped his coat back up to the neck and slipped out of the Snowcat, *and then I shall have mine*.

He slowly picked his way through the debris from the crash towards the main body of the aircraft, which, despite missing the tail and one wing, seemed otherwise largely intact. At all times he kept his gun cocked and ready to fire, and kept himself in between the wreck and the Snowcat. If Rachael made a run for it back to the vehicle, she would have to get past him first. He moved slowly, but with purpose. He was in no hurry – he had the gun, he had the torch, he had the skills, he had the conviction to do what needed to be done. He had the upper hand.

What did she have? She'd surprised him. That was one for her. But it wouldn't do her any good. Not out here. Not alone like this. She also had the key, of course. He smiled again to himself as he moved through the snow – it *had* been a ballsy move. He liked that. He wondered how he would have responded had the tables been turned, and after a few seconds of contemplation, concluded that, assuming he had the same physical strength and skill deficit to his fictitious captor as she had to him, he might well have done exactly the same thing. Her move had seized back the initiative, if only temporarily. It had also – at least in her mind – inconvenienced him, thrown him off track. Whatever his feelings about the chase, the hunt he was now conducting, he wouldn't be out here in the snow looking for her had she not acted.

It was an entirely futile act, of course. That much was certain, but his training had taught him that when your position is hopeless, you try anything you can to change the odds, upset your enemy's plans, knock him off balance, even for a moment – anything to give yourself a chance, no matter how small. After all, if all was lost and you did nothing, your demise was certain. At least trying something gave you an opportunity. It might come to nothing, but you've lost nothing, so you had to try. As he wiped the fresh snow from his goggles, he approved of her actions – in a strictly hypothetical, tactical sense, at least.

He was now fifty yards from the wreck. He could make out the faded green lines of the airline's logo painted along the length of the fuselage from the glow of his torch. He could see the mass of frozen pipework and wiring from the one remaining engine as it lay in the snow, ripped open and exposed to the brutal polar elements. His boot hit something that wasn't snow. He glanced down momentarily, not wishing to lose focus on the scene in front of him for even a second, lest he miss her. What he saw at his feet would have shocked most people. But the body of the middle-aged man that lay there, almost entirely buried save for the anguished face he had accidentally trodden on, was just another number for him. The expression was difficult to read. It looked pained, scared. But Zak knew the skin tightened around the face after death – especially in this extreme cold – so his instinctive reading of the man's mood before death took hold could not be trusted. There was nothing more to be gained from him. Zak looked back up and scanned through one hundred and eighty degrees. He was certain Rachael could not have got past him – he would have seen the movement of her bright red coat – *his* coat – in the snow, even in this darkness. She must be in the wreck, or hiding behind it. He pressed on towards the huge metal cigar tube that lay before him. The closer he got, the more debris he had to step over: a briefcase, a camera, another body – a woman this time, in a white and green uniform that must have made her a stewardess – a brown leather holdall, and even a trolley used to ferry meals and drinks up and down the aisle of the aircraft. All of them stuck in the snow, sinking beneath the surface as this pitiless landscape claimed them as its own. Once enough snow and ice had built up around the objects they became like barnacles on the bottom of a ship: stuck fast, with even the ferocious southern winds not enough to dislodge them from their final resting places.

He picked his way past them all, mentally assessing each one in a fraction of a second: *is it of any use to me now? No? Then move on.* As he got closer to the wreck he could see for the first time the full violence that must have been inflicted on it to render it into its present state: the whole back end of the aircraft, tail and all, had been ripped off to completely open up the cabin. Rivets pulled right out, and twisted shards of metal which had finally given way after being tested beyond their tolerances, marked the point where the airframe itself had simply given up.

Just a few feet away now, he could see the front of the aircraft was buried in the foot of the next mountain. He walked a couple of steps to the far side of the plane and looked up and down its length. There was no sign of her. He walked back. A flash of his head torch down the length of the liner revealed none of the doors had been opened. The gaping hole at the rear of the plane was the only way in or out. He smiled again. This was almost too easy. He could wait here, he thought. Simply position himself at the opening, out of the worst of the wind, and wait her out.

He thought back to one of his previous assignments: lying in wait in a freezing cold ditch by the side of the road on the outskirts of Belfast. How long had it been? Ten? Twelve hours? And he'd been alert the entire time, ready to strike as soon as it was necessary. His target had made him wait that night. So wait he had, lying in a foot of cold, dank water, his eye to the sight and his finger on the trigger for twelve long hours until the moment came. That had been a long night, but a successful one. He could simply do the same thing here, except this would be much easier. He didn't have to hide, and he was extremely confident that she would give up long before he did.

Yes, it would be easy. But easy wasn't fun, was it? Easy wasn't worthy. Nothing good is ever easy. And where's the challenge in waiting it out? He checked his gun and stepped up into the cabin.

The roar of the wind dulled and it was a relief to have some shelter again. He cast his head torch up the full length of the plane and down the central aisle that ran between the seats – three on each side.

236

Ahead of him was row upon row of passengers, seated peacefully in their seats. The air masks had been deployed at some point, but they hung down from the ceiling of the cabin, untouched. The plane must have suffered a catastrophic pressure loss, Zak surmised, leading to all the passengers suffocating. Not the worst way to go, he thought. Better that than surviving a plane crash only to discover you were trapped in this icy prison with no hope of rescue.

As he slowly picked his way up the central aisle, looking left and right at each passenger, he felt like he'd been transported back to when flares, floral shirts and very wide lapels were the standard fashions. Long sideburns crept their way down the faces of the men, while the women seemed almost universally clad in chintz dresses.

Zak had seen death. He'd seen it more than most, and had learned how to deal with it, how to detach himself from it – to enjoy it, even. But this was, without doubt, the eeriest place he had ever been confronted with in his life. Though the victims had been here for decades, the extreme cold had frozen them in time, perfectly preserving them like a giant morgue. He passed them, one by one, after a while not even seeing their faces – he wasn't here for them. He was here for Rachael. But as he neared the front of the cabin, he began to get a little concerned. Where was she? This was the only place she could be, wasn't it?

He thought back . . . had he made a mistake? Had he over-looked something? He couldn't imagine what. He'd checked outside the aircraft, both sides of it. He'd checked that the hole in the back of the cabin was the only way in or out, and he'd checked every body, every seat, and even every overhead locker as he had made his way down the aisle. And he hadn't found her.

There were six rows to go and as he flashed his head torch up at the next row, his confusion disappeared and a new smile crossed his thin lips. It was only a flash, but he could see his own red coat through a gap between the blue aircraft seats on the left-hand aisle. He flicked the safety catch of the pistol back on and stowed it inside one of the zipped pockets of his coat – he wouldn't be needing it now. As he got nearer he could see she was crouched down in the footwell of an empty seat. She was wedged in between the seat and the pocket of the one in front, hunched right up against the wall of the plane with her head under the window and his coat pulled over her, trying to remain unseen. After her earlier impressive move when she'd surprised him by leaping out with the key for the Snowcat, he was disappointed with the follow-up. Crunching herself up under his Big Red and hoping to avoid detection was a poor effort compared with her seizing of the initiative a few moments ago.

After stowing the gun he stretched out the fingers on both hands as he readied them for action. He'd previously estimated Rachael's weight at between sixty-five and seventy kilos and he knew she was an academic, a scientist, with no combat training or experience at all. He knew she would be no match for him physically.

'I was hoping you would do a little better than that,' he growled as he loomed over her. He placed one hand on the back of the seat to his left for purchase, and reached down with his right, ready to yank her out of her pathetic little hiding place by the shoulder. A couple of swift blows to the head would soon subdue her if she insisted on a futile attempt at struggling.

He reached out and grabbed her by the right shoulder. But instantly he knew something was wrong. His brain worked fast as it went back over the scene like a videotape being rewound and fast-forwarded. The rows and rows of mannequin-like dead bodies, all still in their seats, all buckled in. But what was wrong with this picture? What was amiss with this scene? What didn't make sense? *She was crouched down in the footwell of an empty seat. An* empty *seat.*

The shoulder was cold, dead cold in his gloveless hand. He pulled the figure back and Rachael's red coat slid off to reveal the body of an old man with perfectly white hair, a severely wrinkled face and a thick, bushy beard. *Shit.*

Rachael was fighting to keep her breathing as quiet as possible as she listened to Zak moving down the central aisle of the plane. She sat perfectly still in the opposite aisle seat, one row behind the poor old man she'd used as a decoy. From another deceased accomplice she'd borrowed a floral shawl, and a turquoise clip-on hat favoured by ladies of a certain vintage for Sunday church visits. She held her breath as he passed her, then heard him growl his comment of disappointment as he stood off to her left looking down at her body double. She knew the moment was approaching – he would rumble the deception at any second. She saw his shoulders pivot as he pulled back the coat and she knew she had to move. Now.

She leapt out of the seat and in the same motion raised her right arm high up above her head, clutching the seven-inch-long jagged shard of metal she'd selected from the wreckage in her hand. She swung it down with all the force she could muster and plunged it through the flesh of his left hand and further into the hard plastic that topped the back of the airline seat. She saw him turn to face her just as her makeshift weapon pinned his hand to the chair. His expression was shock more than pain, though it seemed that soon followed as he let out a roar, like a bear who'd caught his foot in a hunter's trap. She didn't wait to see his next move. She ran.

Her heart was racing as she pounded down the centre aisle of the cabin, passing row upon row of disinterested spectators.

Without missing a stride she jumped out of the wreck into the snow and pumped her legs up and down as she raced back towards the Snowcat, her lungs already burning from the cold and the sudden burst of effort. She was nearing the vehicle, gaining a couple of feet with every stride as the wind howled around her. Zak may still have been screaming but she couldn't hear it now as she pushed on through the snow and the wind. Then came a sound she did hear: a deafening crack that pierced even the roar of the polar wind. Then another, and another, the third accompanied by an explosion of snow about two or three feet off to her right. *He's shooting at me.*

He must have shot out the window, she thought as she heard another bullet shoot past her and bury itself deep in the snow just a foot to her right, throwing up snowflakes as it did so. He was shooting at her and he was getting closer. She could either fling herself to the ground and try to make herself an invisible target, or she could push on, run even harder, and hope she reached the Snowcat before he could hit her. She opted for the latter and summoned every last ounce of energy in her body and directed it towards her legs. She was closing in on the Snowcat – it couldn't be more than a hundred feet away. Another crack rang out, only this one was accompanied by a metallic 'ping'. He'd hit the Snowcat. She prayed his shot hadn't damaged anything critical as she instinctively ducked her head – a useless gesture.

Her heart was pounding as fast as her legs now, the lactic acid building up in her muscles was beginning to burn and the icy-cold air her lungs were sucking in by the bucketful felt like raw ethanol washing its way through her insides. Another crack, another ping. She ducked her head again, but then, gloriously, unbelievably, she was there.

She ran around the back of the vehicle. She was now out of his line of sight as she made her way along to the driver's side door of the cab. She yanked the handle, hauled herself inside and pulled the door shut behind her. The worst of the howling wind was shut out and suddenly she could hear herself breathing heavily and quickly. She placed her hand on the controls as she tried to steady herself for a moment. Then a sudden panic overtook her as she tried to remember where she'd put the key – had she left it in his Big Red, draped over her decoy's body in the plane? She ran her right hand down to her trouser pocket and felt a surge of relief to find the small metal key resting there. She took one deep breath to calm herself, pulled the key out and looked to her right to insert it in the ignition. As she did so she heard yet another crack, and saw a puff of snow burst up in front of the Snowcat. She instinctively glanced to her right to the source of the shot, and froze. A flash of high-vis red was visible and moving through the snow squall. *He's coming.*

He must have pulled out the metal shard and freed himself, she thought as she slotted in the key. She had to get the Snowcat moving. Now. Its top speed was not much more than fifteen miles per hour, but in this cold, and with snow and wind like this, he wouldn't be able to keep up if she had any kind of head start on him. She turned the key. Nothing. She glanced at the instrument panel in front of her. It was dead. She frowned and turned the key again. Nothing. She shook her head. *Why won't these bloody things ever start?* The flash of red was getting closer. She turned the key left, then right again as she willed the machine into life, but it remained completely silent and unresponsive. She glanced around the cabin, looking for something she might have missed. But what? She'd driven one of these Snowcats a thousand times. They were simple machines – key in ignition, turn key = power. She tried it again. Come on, she begged silently, *come on.*

The flash of red was now much more than a flash – it was a full figure coming towards her steadily through the snow, getting closer and closer and closer. *This is the moment where it all roars into life*, she told herself as she turned the key left, waited a split second, then tried once more to coax the engine into action. Zak was now looming large in the passenger-side window, he was almost upon her, only a few feet away.

'Come on!' she shouted in desperation as she turned the key again, every fibre of her being willing the Snowcat to wake from its slumber and carry her triumphantly away from the ruthless killer pursuing her.

Nothing.

The passenger door flew open. 'You fucking bitch,' Zak snarled as he hauled himself inside the cab, lifted his arm and smashed her in the face as hard as he could with the butt of his gun.

35

She knew he was there. Even before she opened her eyes. Even before she registered the pounding pain in her head and wrists. She knew he was there, watching her. Again, her primal urge was to get away. *Escape*. She didn't care anymore about the cold, the storm, the snow. Rather face all that – rather die – than face him. She would run. Run and run and run as fast as she could. Run until he gave up the chase. Run to her own death rather than submit to him.

She tried to pull her arms up as she recoiled away from him. But they wouldn't comply. She tried again, but nothing. She looked down as she blinked her eyes open and immediately saw why: he had tied her up. He'd looped an orange climbing rope around her, tying her arms tightly to her torso. The very rope she'd used to save his life, she noted ruefully. She looked down at her feet and discovered he'd strung another rope around each ankle to bind her legs together. She pulled at them but she couldn't get the rope to move at all. She was trapped. She heard him laugh as he watched her struggling. She ignored him and continued to squirm and wriggle, desperately trying to loosen her shackles. He sat and watched her, never making a move to restrain her further, as if he knew it was pointless.

Eventually she gave up and sat still.

'No, no, keep going,' he said with something halfway between a leer and a sneer. 'I like it when they struggle.'

'You're sick,' she spat. She noticed his left hand was wrapped in a white bandage that already had a deep scarlet patch in the middle. She also realized he had draped a Big Red over her shoulders. She wondered if it was Henriksen's.

'Sick?'

'You heard me.'

He pushed forward on the joystick to continue the journey. 'I'm plenty more than that. I know how to disconnect the battery on one of these things, for starters.' Another smirk.

'You disgust me.'

'And why is that?'

'You're a killer.'

'And that makes me "sick", does it?'

'Of course. I could never kill someone.'

He laughed. 'Of course you could. What a ridiculous thing to say. You could kill in a heartbeat. And you'd be shocked at how little you'd feel.'

Rachael stared at him. 'I don't care what you say,' she said. 'I could never kill. Never.'

He shook his head and laughed again. 'You're wrong about that. Believe me.'

They continued in silence as the snow drove hard against the windows of the vehicle. Rachael didn't move any more than was necessary. She didn't want to give him the satisfaction of seeing her struggle against the ropes that bound her.

Zak eased off the throttle and slowed the Snowcat as they approached another crevasse. They must be getting close to the edge of the shear zone, Rachael thought, as she realized they'd cleared the mountain and were now back on their original course towards Station Z. She wondered how long she'd been out cold as the vehicle came to a halt.

She peered through the windscreen as the wipers tried to keep it clear of snow. The headlights cut a shaft of light through the darkness ahead, but she had to squint to work out what she was looking at.

Zak eased the Snowcat a little closer and it soon became clear: the snow had been falling so heavily, it had built up a drift covering the ice bridge between the two snow markers he'd left to point the way across. It must have been two or three feet deep, with the bridge itself probably thirty to forty feet long.

Rachael eyed Zak, waiting for him to make a move. He sat for a moment, hunched over the joystick, staring dead ahead through the windscreen, the wipers flapping back and forth, squeaking across the glass with each swipe.

'For fuck's sake,' he muttered, before pulling on his goggles and slipping his hood over his head. Then he pushed open his door and she heard a clunk as he slammed the door of the cargo bay at the back of the cab. A few seconds later his shadow cut across the headlights and she watched as he began shovelling the snow clear.

She burned with fury at everything he had done. Guy, Henriksen, and now her. She felt physically sick at what she knew he planned to do to her once they reached the base. There was no hope now. Everything she relied on had gone. Her husband, her daughter, her friends, family. All the constructs of society had gone with them: the law, consequences. The rules had changed. Now there were no rules. She watched him shovelling snow like nothing had happened.

'You bastard!' she screamed in the silence of the cab. He didn't turn around. 'You fucking bastard!' she screamed again at the top of her voice. He didn't even flinch.

With the blizzard and the snow and the wind swirling around him, he clearly couldn't hear anything else. 'You fucking bastard BASTARD!' she screamed again with more anger than she ever thought could exist inside her as tears ran down her face. And when she stopped shouting, she was left sitting in the cab, the engine idling, the snow falling, the wipers still flapping back and forth.

She glanced at the controls, and then back at Zak. He was still working, still facing away from her. She looked again at the joystick that controlled the vehicle. She tried to pull herself free of her ropes, but he'd done a good job with the knots. She wondered how many others he'd tied up in the past, and what their fates had been.

She focused instead on the knot he'd tied to lash her feet to the seat, using the handle that pulled it back and forth on its runners. He'd clearly done that one in something of a hurry and she found that by gently lifting her legs up and down at an angle, she was able to generate some force and enough friction for the rope to catch against itself. It was just enough. Peering down with her arms tied to her sides, she gingerly moved her bound feet up and down, forwards and backwards. As she worked she looked back up through the windscreen. She could see he was nearly finished – the ice bridge was almost clear of snow. She was running out of time. She looked back down and kept up the movement, and with one more glorious slip, the rope loosened and the knot came undone. She immediately swung her feet up and across the central console between the driver's seat and hers so she was almost lying flat across the cab. As soon as she was in position she kicked her feet forward until they hit the joystick controller, then she kicked again.

The Snowcat began to move.

She couldn't see out of the windscreen from her stretched-out position, but she knew the vehicle had been pointing directly at the ice bridge when Zak stopped it, so all she needed to do was keep pushing the joystick directly forward to keep it moving dead straight. One slip to the left or right, and the Snowcat would slide off the ice bridge and plummet to the bottom of the crevasse, taking her with it. To put pressure on the joystick meant contorting her body into a terribly painful position, but at that moment she didn't care. She pushed harder with her feet and heard the note of the engine get a little louder as the speed increased.

Zak was getting hotter and hotter as he shovelled. It was heavy, difficult work. Doing physical labour while wearing polar clothing was always hard: the size of it restricted movement, and it was so brilliantly designed to keep as much heat in as possible that it soon got extremely hot, despite the freezing air temperature. He was starting to sweat inside his polar gear as the blizzard raged around him, but he knew he couldn't stop working – he had to push on. They were nearing the edge of the crevasse field, which meant they were getting close to Station Z. As he carried on shovelling he thought of the hot shower and the warm meal he would enjoy when they arrived. He thought of Rachael and her soft, pale skin. Her curves, her scent. He smiled to himself as he worked, knowing he would have his reward soon, whether she liked it or not. Preferably not, he thought with another smile.

The snow continued to fall as he worked – or rather the snow hit him, apparently from every angle as the ceaseless wind howled around him. In his long career he'd spent time in the most inhospitable places on earth, each one a war zone, each one a place he would never wish to return to, each one more like hell than the last. But this? This wasn't his first polar trip, but he'd never known conditions like this. The wind never seemed to let up, never seemed to run out of energy. It was unrelenting, and with the snow added into the mix, it closed him in, visually and aurally in a way he'd never experienced before. The only sight was the white of the snow, occasionally interrupted by the orange flash of his shovel, the only sound the howling gale. Still he worked.

He looked up. He was almost done – the path to the other side of the crevasse was nearly clear. He paused for a moment to catch his breath before one final push. After that he could take refuge back in the cabin of the Snowcat.

It was at that moment that he thought he heard something. He tilted his head up like a fox trying to pinpoint the sound of a mouse a hundred yards away, but the wind picked up again and overwhelmed his senses. Then he felt a vibration beneath his feet, but even as he began to turn around he knew it was too late: the Snowcat was bearing down on him and he realized with horror that his left boot was already caught under the left-hand track. He tried to yank it away but as the excruciating pain began to register, he realized the Snowcat's tracks were already gripping him like a crocodile's teeth and there was no escape. He screamed as the clanking metal machine remorselessly pulled him under, but the noise was lost in the roar of the wind.

36

Rachael kept her feet on the joystick as the Snowcat continued across the ice bridge. For a split second she thought she heard a terrified cry from Zak, but she couldn't be sure – it could just as easily have been the wind whistling through a bad join in the cabin. She kept going. She knew he might well have heard or seen her coming and simply stepped out of the way. If that was the case he would surely kill her there and then. Then again, what did she have to lose at this point?

She estimated she must have been at least halfway across the ice bridge, but she dare not lift off the joystick and look so she pressed on, hoping she'd managed to surprise him.

She expected him to rip open her door, drag her out into the snow and make lethal use of his gun. Instead, she suddenly felt the Snowcat lurch violently down with a thud on its right-hand side. The jolt knocked her feet away from the joystick and the vehicle stopped dead. She was now almost on her head in the footwell, but with some more painful gymnastics she managed to right herself. She looked out of the windscreen, the wipers still flapping away. She was about halfway across, the rear end of the tracks just having cleared the bank, the whole weight of the Snowcat now pushing down on the bridge. The vehicle was tilted at a twenty-degree angle, its right side now facing down into the emptiness of the crevasse. She realized that the right-hand set of tracks must have slipped off the ice bridge and were now hanging in thin air.

She could see no sign of Zak. She must have got him – or knocked him over the side, perhaps? With the immediate danger gone, she slumped back in her seat for a moment to think. She was still trapped, still tied up, and now she couldn't move the Snowcat at all, for fear of driving off the bridge completely. But first she needed to get free. She managed to stand up and hook the ropes at her back onto the plastic headrest of her seat. She found that the more she pulled and strained, the more they loosened. She wriggled and shimmied, pulled and slid and then with one final yank, they came loose from around her arms. She shrugged herself free and then set to work on the ropes binding her feet together, making short work of those.

Just as she freed herself from the final loops of rope, the driver's door was flung open and there he was: his head covered in streaks of blood, his cracked goggles on his forehead, his face a contorted picture of agony and rage.

He let out a noise that contained no words, just concentrated fury distilled into audible form as he moved into the cabin towards her. She felt pure terror rush through her veins. She looked back over her shoulder and could see only the black of the deep crevasse. She was trapped. Her only options: death by falling down the crevasse, or death at the hands of this snarling, bloody monster. He pulled himself into the cab of the Snowcat. She could see his left leg was a mangled mess of blood and ripped flesh. He was putting no weight on it as he dragged himself inside and closer towards her. She kicked the passenger door and watched as it flapped open with the pull of gravity down into the crevasse. The Snowcat was leaning into its dark depths, inviting her in. As the door swung open out into nothingness, every cell in her body screamed at her to retreat back into the cab, but with

Zak now crawling his way over the centre console she had no time to think about it. With two hands on the frozen door frame she went to pull herself out of the cab. But as she lunged forward she felt herself somehow moving backwards instead.

Shit. He's got me.

She was jerked back inside the cab violently as he let out another growl. She scrambled to find something, anything, to hold onto, to get purchase on and get out of his clutches but her frozen hands slipped on the plastic seats and dashboard. Even in his bloodied and weakened state he was too strong for her. As he pulled her back with one hand, he raised the other high above himself and then smashed it down on the back of her head. The pain was instant and intense. She felt as if she'd been struck by a timber plank, and before she could even process what had happened, he swiped his arm sideways with full force, hitting her in the side of the head and causing her to cry out in pain.

She swung an arm wildly behind her in a desperate act of self-defence, but he simply grabbed it, and twisted her arm around in one quick movement so hard she thought he would actually break it. Then with another yank, he used her own arm to spin her round in the cab so she was now facing him. The tears rolled down her face from the pain in her head and shooting up her arm, but she barely got a single cry out before he caught her on the cheek with the back of his fist, his knuckle connecting with her cheekbone with a crack.

Then BANG, another hit, this time on the other side of her face. He was no longer even holding her – he no longer needed to – she was being beaten into compliant submission as the pain reverberated through her body with each blow.

And then for a moment, for a blissful moment, it was over. He stopped. She squinted across at him as she tried to work out what was happening but as she did he lunged at her across the centre console and wrapped his hands tightly around her neck. He pushed her so she was lying down across her seat as he bent over her, his jaw clenched in rage, his eyes ablaze with fury. And then he squeezed.

'Die, you fucking bitch,' he spat, his hot saliva dripping down from his mouth onto her face.

She was by now barely conscious from the beating he'd given her and she felt a curious mix of pain and anger, but also an increasing urge to give up the fight. As he starved her brain of oxygen, it began telling her to simply go with what was happening. That was far easier than resisting now. Just go to sleep, go to sleep, go to sleep . . .

'You fucking BITCH!' he growled again as he intensified his grip on her neck, and as he did so, she was suddenly filled with an overwhelming sense of rage and a surge of adrenaline. *No*, she thought. *Not like this*. She pulled her hands up and grabbed at his wrists, but he was too strong and she couldn't move them an inch. She dug her nails into his flesh, but all that did was renew his vigour. She beat her fists against his chest and clawed and scratched at his face as her desperation grew, but he was unmoved. She was starting to lose her ability to think and reason as the oxygen flow slowed to her brain. She looked up at the rage in his bloodied face. He was utterly and completely focused on snuffing out her life right at that moment. Wild horses couldn't have stopped him.

She swivelled her eyes as she looked around the cab for something, *anything* she could do. As his grip on her throat tightened, she could feel her own grip on consciousness getting weaker and weaker. Her vision was being clouded in by dark spots, the noise of his fury was getting quieter and quieter. The world was closing in around her.

Then she saw his leg. His Gore-Tex trousers had been ripped

open and she could see the bloodied limb beneath which had been chewed on by the tracks of the Snowcat. The mess of flesh, blood and visible bone was stomach-churning – it looked like his leg had been gnawed on by some giant ravenous animal. She marvelled that he was even conscious, given how much pain he must be in. She looked down further and saw her own legs were free, and then with the last ounce of strength she possessed before she passed out entirely, she raised her right leg, aimed it at his open wound and kicked as hard as she could.

The instant she made contact he let out a roar of pain, and loosened his grip on her neck. Before he could regain his composure, she bent her knee back and then kicked him again even harder, and this time she heard a sickening crack as she connected directly with the exposed bone. He let go of her neck entirely as he reeled backwards in response to the pain surging through his body. As her vision began to return to normal she scrambled back from him towards the passenger door, still flapping violently in the gale. She was struggling to think coherently as her mind fought against the battering her head had taken, but as she hauled herself out of the cab the extreme cold hit her like a slap in the face from an icy hand – and it had the same effect: at once she was alert, with extreme clarity of purpose. And her purpose was to survive.

She pulled herself out into the blizzard and allowed herself a split second to look down into the abyss: she couldn't see where it ended – she could barely see two feet in front of her thanks to the dark and the snow – but she knew one slip and she would be hurtling to the bottom of a crater probably two or three hundred feet deep. If that happened she only prayed the fall would kill her instantly.

She stepped out onto the vehicle's tracks, and as she did so she felt the Snowcat jolt down on her side again – perhaps only by an inch, but the movement caused her to lose her balance and a sudden and instinctive burst of panic shot up from deep within her chest. She flung an arm at a handle to the side of the passenger door and steadied herself. She was outside now, away from Zak, but hanging onto the side of an eight-ton vehicle that was perched precariously on an ice shelf over a three-hundred-foot-deep crevasse.

The wind was gusting harder and harder, flinging snow in her face one moment, and threatening to tear her from the side of the vehicle the next. Her back to the Snowcat, she looked left. That side of the edge of the crevasse was closer, but it meant climbing back past the open door. It was too risky.

Instead she began inching her way along the tracks towards the opposite side, back where they had come from, when she felt the vehicle shudder again. She glanced back and there he was: climbing out of the door in cold pursuit, fuelled by rage and pure adrenaline. But his face was no longer contorted in fury, it was rearranging itself into something else altogether. Something like . . . smugness? Yes, that was it. He was even smiling as he looked at her. Through the whirling blizzard of snow she saw a flash of black in his hand and she instantly understood. *The gun*.

He was leaning against the cab, all his weight on his uninjured leg as he balanced on the tracks, just a few feet away from her with a loaded pistol. He had won. It was over. He raised it and aimed it right at her: she knew he was a trained killer – he would not miss. Even she wouldn't miss at this range.

She looked up at his hateful, smug face and remembered his veiled threat from a few hours earlier. *We'll find some way to amuse ourselves.* She shuddered again and as she glanced back down at the weapon she thought she would rather die than have to suffer further at the hands of this deranged animal.

'Why couldn't you just do as you were told?' he shouted over the roar of the blizzard.

'Because I had to do what was necessary,' she shouted back. 'Someone had to.'

'Funny isn't it,' he said with a sneer. 'You came all the way here to save the world. And now it turns out there's no world left to save.'

She didn't reply, she simply closed her eyes and waited. It would all be over soon. She heard the shot ring out, a sharp crack that pierced the incessant roar of the wind like a whip slicing through flesh. She felt a jolt, but no pain. She wondered if she might escape that completely. Perhaps she would die before her brain had the chance to register it. She opened her eyes to take one last look at her surroundings, the landscape she had done so much to try to save. Instead she saw Zak pulling the gun back up into a firing position. Something was wrong. Suddenly, she understood. The jolt had been the Snowcat slipping on the ice bridge, not the bullet. *He'd missed.* He must have lost his balance as he took the shot. No matter, he wouldn't miss a second time, and he was already aiming directly at her. But as he shifted his weight to counter the kickback from the gun, there was a creaking sound that echoed down the crevasse as the ice bridge began to struggle under the great weight of the vehicle. A chunk of ice sheared away and dropped into the darkness and the Snowcat jerked another few inches down on one side. Rachael lost her footing but clung onto the handle and managed to steady herself. But it caught Zak by surprise and she watched as he slipped, and with a look of sheer panic in his eyes, was forced to drop the gun and lunge at the door handle to prevent himself from falling over the side. She watched the pistol clatter onto the tracks, before it slipped off and was lost into the abyss.

Like a death row prisoner getting a pardon at one minute to

midnight, she'd been granted a last-second reprieve. She looked back at Zak; his rage had instantly returned at this reversal of fortune, and in between gusts of wind he began inching his way along the tracks towards her.

Pressing herself as flat against the side of the vehicle as she could, Rachael moved towards the edge of the bridge, but every step was fraught with danger on the tracks that had become slippery with fresh snow and ice since they'd been stationary.

Zak, driven by fury and blood lust, seemed to be somehow fighting through the pain of his horribly mangled leg and was still coming for her, pulling himself along through a combination of hand grips and his one good leg. In her hurry to escape him she slipped on the icy tracks and felt a shot of panic come rocketing up from her stomach as she clung onto the side of the truck. After she'd been slowed momentarily by her near-fall, Zak had managed to gain on her and began to swipe his left arm towards her, trying to get a grip on her Big Red, but she remained just out of reach each time he swung.

The ice bridge creaked and cracked again under the weight of the Snowcat and more ice fell away into the darkness below, shaking the big vehicle. Zak slammed his body against the metal side of it, crouched down, then unzipped the bottom of his right trouser leg to reveal a six-inch knife he had in a sheath, strapped to his shin. He drew the blade, pulled himself back up to his full height and leapt after her, swiping the knife at her wildly as she inched along the tracks, his eyes wide with fury, his face a perfect depiction of distilled rage. Then he lunged forward and extended his arm as far as he could, the end of the knife catching on the arm of her jacket and tearing open the red material. In trying to miss the thrust, she'd shifted her weight too far forward and her foot slipped on the icy tracks. Too late, she knew she was going over the edge and her hands scratched at the cold metal surface of the Snowcat as she tried to find something to grip. As she felt her momentum carrying her over, she managed to hook her finger into a handle mounted on the rear of the vehicle.

The sense of overwhelming panic subsided momentarily, but the relief didn't last long. Zak was still coming for her, and with an animalistic roar he thrust towards her again with his knife. This time she was too slow, too off balance after his previous effort, and she felt the steely blade pierce her skin, the very tip cutting through her Big Red, her fleece and her jumper and burrowing itself into the soft flesh of her left arm. She howled in pain and yanked her arm out of range as he withdrew, ready to make a second, killer blow. Rachael instinctively pulled her right hand to the wound as the blood began seeping out, but the wind gusted again and she had to remove it to steady herself. She looked back at Zak as he pulled his knife back, his eyes sparkling with excitement and anticipation. She looked across at the bank, and down into the black mouth of the crevasse, its walls spiralling down beneath her. He was too close now. She had to jump. It was perhaps eight or nine feet to the bank, but she was out of time.

Emboldened by catching her with his previous effort, Zak steadied himself, drew the knife back behind him and with a deep bellow he thrust it at her with all the force he could muster, determined to finish the job.

Rachael launched herself off the slippery tracks, leaving nothing but snow and wind for the blade to cut through, and landed with a soft thud on the snowy bank of the crevasse. As she turned to face him she heard the ice bridge creaking again as the Snowcat sank another few inches. Zak halted his progress as he was forced to cling on tightly. She watched as more ice sheared off and fell down into the crevasse below, then she spotted the shovel Zak had been using to clear the snow. It must have been swallowed up and spat out by the tracks of the Snowcat.

She swiped it up and began hacking as quickly and as hard as she could at the edge of the crevasse, where the ice bridge met the bank. She chipped, chipped, chipped away and chunk after chunk of ice fell into the snowy ravine below as the blood flowed from the wound in her arm, weakening her with every drop that left her body.

In a break in the wind, she saw Zak look up and see her. She could tell he instantly realized what she was doing as he limped towards her across the tracks, dragging his mangled leg behind him.

With each pang of the sharp shovel edge against the ice he was getting closer and closer, her arm was getting weaker and weaker, the pain worse and worse. Her instinct told her to run, to ditch the shovel and run as fast as she could away from this madman, but the logical part of her brain knew that this was her only chance to survive. She had to fight the panic and the intense pain, and do what was necessary. She hacked and hacked with the same fury Zak had summoned when he was beating her inside the Snowcat just a few minutes earlier. Another great chunk of ice fell away and the Snowcat jolted down even further. *Come on*, she silently pleaded. *Come on!*

She looked up to see Zak within a few feet of her. Another few seconds and she would be within reach of his knife. She saw him raise it again, this time high above his head, ready to strike. She mirrored his movement with her shovel and for a split second she caught his eye as, like two gunslingers standing a hundred feet apart on the dusty main street of a frontier town, they both prepared to make their move.

He swiped down with this knife, but before the blade could complete its arc, she rammed the sharp edge of her shovel into the ice, and with a crack that was loud enough to penetrate through the noise of the blizzard just for a moment, the ice bridge gave way. Rachael caught his eye again in the fraction of a second before it began to fall. She could see the raging fury give way to sheer panic. By the time the blade of his knife had finished its journey, it cut through nothing but thin air as it, the ice bridge, the Snowcat and Zak himself fell away into nothingness.

In a final act of desperation he hurled the knife in her direction as he fell. It seemed to be coming at her in slow motion and Rachael felt like she had all the time in the world to move her head to the left to dodge the flying weapon as he plummeted into the icy cavern below.

And then he was gone.

37

Rachael collapsed back on the snow as her heart pounded in her chest and her lungs fought to keep up with her breathing. The blizzard swirled all around her and as she lay there, having just battled to the last for her life, the thought crossed her mind once more that she could simply stay where she was, wait for the snow to cover her and for her consciousness to slip away.

Zak may be dead at the bottom of the crevasse, but her wounds, the elements, the weather, the cold, the dark – Antarctica herself – were still trying to kill her at every turn. Should she simply accept this was a battle she could not win?

No, she would *not* give in now. Not after everything she had overcome. She felt the full extent of the intense pain she was in. Her arm screamed as the blood continued to seep from the wound. Her head throbbed with every beat of her pulse as the blood pumping round it reminded her of the fierce beating Zak had given her in the Snowcat. Her neck was sore and bruised where he'd tried to throttle her, and the rest of her body ached from a combination of the cold and the physical effort she'd exerted to escape him.

She was now without any supplies whatsoever. She had only the clothes she was lying down in. She had no food, no water, no fuel and no shelter. And she was losing blood. They'd been driving the best part of twenty-four hours and there was no going back to One Ton. Even if it had still been standing, she would freeze long before she got there. She knew she must be closer to Station Z – Zak had said as much before they stopped. That was her only hope: push on towards the camp, and hope she got there before the cold got her. She had to try – there was nothing else left to do.

She hauled herself up into a sitting position and then gingerly stood up, feeling the pain in each of her joints as she did so. She slipped off the Big Red and trapped it between her knees, then she ripped off the sleeve of her fleece at the point Zak's knife had cut it, and using her other hand and her teeth, managed to tie a makeshift bandage around the wound on her arm. Then she pulled her outer coat back on and zipped it up tightly.

With the ice bridge now collapsed entirely, she knew she would have to walk down the length of the crevasse until she found another place to cross, and so, reasoning that there was no time to waste, she set off, heading north through the blizzard.

She had no idea how long she'd been walking when she came to the spot where the crevasse closed up on itself into a point, like the source of a river. She had overcome another opponent, but she didn't stop to dwell on it as she checked her compass and changed direction, heading straight for Station Z. As she walked she began singing to herself to help keep her pace, repeating over and over again the refrain sung by the children's choir from Pink Floyd's 'Another Brick in the Wall'. She pictured Adam singing it to himself as she marched.

Adam.

She tried to block out thoughts of him and Izzy – it was too painful. But that's the problem with the mind: it just won't do as it's told. She saw his face, she felt his hand on hers as she walked, side by side with him. She smiled and tears formed in her eyes at the same time. 'Adam,' she said out loud.

On she walked, through the snow, through the wind, through

the cold, through the dark. As she marched her mind began to wander along with her. Walking out here in the eternal nothingness of the Antarctic, she found she struggled to reconcile her current predicament with the fact that only a few months earlier she'd been drinking fair-trade coffee in her tasteful and well-appointed kitchen in a London suburb. All so sickeningly normal. How she'd hated it: the mundanity, the routine, the *normality*. She knew she lived in a world where millions strove to be 'normal' – whatever that meant. She'd been the same: buy a house and an Ikea sofa, get married, have a baby, a pension plan, a juicer, an environmentally friendly car. That bloody coffee machine.

She could see it now. She'd just been frustrated. Unfulfilled. *That life should have been enough. Why wasn't it enough for me?* She had thought something was wrong with her, so she'd walled herself off from Adam and hoped the feeling would simply go away. But it hadn't. That, she could see now, had been her mistake. *I should have talked to you, Adam. And I should have gone back to work. I didn't know I needed it. But I did. I do. I need that. Why did you make me give it up – why did you make me do that?*

She cocked her head to one side as she walked through the snow and narrowed her eyes as she tried to think back. *Except . . . you didn't, did you?* She leaned forward to counter a powerful gust of wind. *I did it myself. I assumed you would want me to – you have to admit you are a bit of a traditionalist – so I did it. But you never asked me to.* She shook her head. *All this time I've been blaming you for that, but it wasn't your fault. I closed myself off and never spoke to you about it. I just silently seethed. About something you hadn't done.* 'I'm sorry, Adam,' she said out loud into the white abyss. 'I'm so sorry.'

And then there was Izzy. Her beautiful Izzy. Yes, she hated the lifestyle, the trappings, the bourgeoisie bullshit – but how she *loved* that girl. She longed to hold her in her arms, to feel her warm skin against hers. 'Mama, up,' she said to herself. She longed to hear that call, just one more time. If she really strained her ears, she could almost convince herself she *could* hear Izzy calling for her through the incessant roar of the wind. It was as if the noise was just out of reach, and if the howling of the gale would only pause for a second she'd be able to hear it clearly. But it never did. She walked on as the tears rolled down her face and froze against her cheek.

She felt as weak as a kitten. The blood loss from her arm was making her woozy and she felt more nauseous with every step. Her body had been battered and bruised, as had her mind, and however tough someone is, there's only so much they can take. Everyone has a breaking point. Rachael wondered when hers would come. It wouldn't be long. Not here. And she knew the moment she did succumb, the cold and unfeeling Antarctic would swallow her whole without even blinking. The driven snow would soon cover her, and she wouldn't even be a speck in this endless, barren desert. Lost forever, like a grain of salt dropped on a beach.

She walked on.

With no change in the light she lost all track of time. Had she been walking for minutes? Hours? Days even? Now she was out of the crevasse field the landscape stretched out before her in all directions, vast and featureless, like she was the size of a microscopically small amoeba planted right in the middle of a great big sheet of white paper. She had no sense of time or progress. And with the storm still blowing hard all around her, waiting to gobble her up should she stumble, she started to lose any sense of motion. Was she really even walking forward? She looked behind her, but it all looked the same. She felt like one of those pilots she'd read about who lose all sense of direction and end up crashing because they don't realize which way is up. Was she actually just standing still and walking up and down on the spot? She had no way of knowing anymore – not for certain. Her mind told her she was moving forward, but she had started to mistrust what her mind was telling her over the last few weeks. And even if she *was* moving forward, was she really achieving anything more than picking a different spot in which to die?

Her mind returned to Adam. Her love. She had not known love like that was possible. Had it slipped away? Had it got lost in a sea of domestic frustrations? No, she thought. *No*, she still loved him. It was there, she just hadn't been able to see it. As if it had been moved, somehow – been hidden out of sight. Bricked up behind a wall. But she could see it now. Now he had been taken away from her, now he was gone, it was like a bottle had been uncorked – her love and her need for him was pouring out of her heart like a tidal wave. Now it was all too late, the wall between them came tumbling down and for the first time in months she could see it so clearly: she was bursting with love for Izzy and Adam. For both of them. At that moment, more than anything in the world, she wanted him to know that. 'I love you, Adam,' she shouted into the wind. 'I ran away so easily, so cheaply, and I'm so sorry. I love you.'

Her heart was breaking all over again as she thought he might have died not knowing that she loved him. She unzipped the top of her Big Red and then her fleece, and pulled out the photograph of her family that she had kept pressed against her chest ever since she'd found it in Zak's bag. She pulled up her goggles so she could see their faces more clearly, but the snow made it virtually impossible and her tears froze on her face.

She felt herself stumble, and a haziness descended upon her. The wind was still howling but it began to get quieter and quieter, as if someone had shut a door to keep it out. Was it getting darker?

That didn't make any sense – at this time of year it should start getting lighter any day now. Before she could register what was happening on any conscious level, she realized she was kneeling on the snow, her legs had given way. Her torso followed and she found herself lying on the ice. She rolled over onto her back and looked up at the snowflakes dancing around her. She felt like she was in the middle of a snow globe. It was beautiful, she thought, as she felt her heavy lids pulling themselves down over her eyes and her fingers lose their grip on the photograph.

38

'Rachael.'

Someone was calling her name.

'Rachael.'

There he was: standing just a few feet away and smiling down at her. Adam. The sun shone brightly around him. He was wearing an old Pink Floyd T-shirt, with the prism from the *Dark Side of the Moon* album cover on the front. She recognized it as one he used to wear around the flat when they were first together.

'You came,' she smiled.

'Of course I did.'

'I love you, Adam.'

He smiled back. 'I know. I love you too.'

'What are you doing here?'

'I came to tell you something.'

'What is it?'

'You have to get up,' he said softly. 'You have to keep going.' He looked up at the sky as the sun's glow began to penetrate the darkness. 'It's going to be a sunny day.'

She nodded, and he looked back at her, smiled one last time, then turned and began to walk off into the snow.

She blinked her eyes open as she came to. Then she rolled over onto her front and pulled herself up onto her knees. 'Get up,' she ordered, and her battered body somehow complied. It wasn't over yet.

She reached inside her coat but the photograph wasn't there. She remembered holding it, staring at her family before she'd collapsed. It was gone now, whipped away by the ceaseless, punishing wind. But there was no time to ponder her loss, she needed to keep going. 'Start walking,' she said. Again, her legs followed their orders. She didn't know how she still had the energy, but she decided that as long as she could find the will to put one foot in front of the other, she would keep going. There would be no giving up.

She didn't know how long she had been walking when she slowly became aware something was different. No, that wasn't right – two things were different. The first was apparent both audibly and visibly: the storm was passing. With each step she took she seemed to leave it further and further behind. The howling, baying, incessant wind that had roared on and on for weeks now was finally blowing itself out. She carried on walking and soon the blizzard was over. She could hear . . . silence.

An overwhelming sense of relief washed over her. It was suddenly peaceful. The snow was no longer dancing about, being driven into her face at an ever-changing but always painful angle. Instead it sat softly on the surface of the ice. She knelt down and grabbed a handful. In that state it seemed so benign and friendly. So innocent, as if butter wouldn't melt. She stood back up and looked around her. White, as far as she could see. Soft, white snow, and complete silence. It seemed impossible that this was the same landscape she'd been battling with ever since she'd embarked on this trip, that this was the same environment that had been mercilessly and remorselessly trying to kill her every single day for months.

But something else was different as well.

She could see further – and more clearly. It was starting to get light. After months of having nothing but total darkness enveloping her like an inescapable prison, the sun was finally and ever so slowly coming back. The Antarctic dawn was breaking.

Something was unnerving her as she made her way across the ice, and she eventually realized it was the fact she could hear her own footsteps crunching in the fresh snow, now the wind was not howling in her ears.

She walked and she walked and she walked. On and on, mile after mile of snow and ice. Until she saw it. She didn't believe it at first – or at least didn't trust her brain enough to fully believe it, but she quickened her step nonetheless as she got closer. Only when it was in plain view above the horizon did she finally allow herself to believe it was possible: a forty-gallon oil drum, set into the snow. She must be at the very far end of the airstrip – Station Z should be just over the next rise.

She picked up her pace again and was almost running when she reached the drum. She reached out to touch it with some trepidation, as if it might vanish in a puff of smoke and reveal itself as another product of her fevered imagination. But it was real, she could feel it in her hands. She made her way to the next one, and the next. With each one her heart rate rose a little. Until she saw something that drained all the excitement out of her in a millisecond, and made her stop dead in her tracks.

A body. A naked body.

Henriksen. She remembered Zak's chilling words.

I simply made him believe that there was no hope, and that death was the only option left. I watched him strip all his clothes off, step out of the base and walk off into the blizzard. The full Captain Oates.

He was curled up in the fetal position, the snow had built up around him and he was clearly long dead. She couldn't see a single mark on him and his lifeless eyes stared out at her. She tried to close them but they were frozen in place.

So Zak hadn't been lying about that, she thought as she looked down at him.

Poor Henriksen. He didn't deserve that. From her pocket she pulled out the Manchester United hat she'd found in the back of the Snowcat and pulled it down over his head. 'Rest in peace, Mika,' she said quietly as she crouched down next to her fallen colleague.

After a moment of silence, she stood up and continued towards the base. As soon as she crested the small rise she could see the top of the red and blue interconnected pods that made up Station Z. She headed straight for it, almost falling through the snow in her haste to reach it. She felt like it would disappear at any moment – like the mirage of a fantastic oasis in the middle of a desert which Donald Duck or Bugs Bunny would dive into, only to come up spitting sand.

But as she got closer she started to believe. She flung herself against the cold steel of one of the giant feet that held up the pods and for a few moments there she stayed, flattened against the side of the structure, as if she needed to have as much of her body in contact with it as possible. *I've made it.*

Once she was sure of herself, she peeled herself off the metal and made her way up the steps to the main door. She turned the handle and pushed it open, then shut it firmly behind her, and stopped. Her whole body relaxed. The building was quiet. More than quiet: it was completely silent, and completely dark – which somehow made it seem even quieter.

She felt along the wall to her left in the dark – all doorways had battery-powered torches kept on a hook on the wall in case of a power outage. She felt the cylindrical tube and slid her hand down the top until she found the switch.

Now she had shelter and light. Sustenance was the next item on her agenda. Lighting the way with the torch, she walked through the interconnected pods until she reached the storeroom. She pushed the door open and shone the torch inside. She flashed it up and down the metal racks, each one was stacked high with crate after crate of freeze-dried pouches of food. She estimated there was enough to get through three seasons at least. *If I'm going to die here, it won't be from hunger,* she thought as she swung the big metal door shut.

She pondered her next move. Her wounds would need looking at. She was also starving, and she realized how dirty she must be. She hadn't had a proper shower for months, and suddenly she was very aware of it. She decided to assess her arm injury, do her best to stitch herself up and apply a proper bandage, then make a quick meal, have a hot shower, and then sleep. But before she could do any of that, she needed to get the power back on.

She walked purposefully back through the pods, one by one, past the mess, past the glass-walled labs, past the dorms and the comms room, past the medical bay where Guy had pleaded with her to finish the work they'd started before he had been medevacked out. God, can that really only have been two months ago?

She made her way into the pod at the very end of the chain: the engine room. It contained the generator for the whole base – a ten-foot-long mass of orange pipes, cylinders and fans – as well as the boilers for heating and hot water.

She turned the fuel pump switch to the 'on' position, checked the fuel level, then pressed the starter button. With a few coughs, it suddenly roared into life and she could feel the hum of it reverberating through the floor. She allowed herself a small smile of satisfaction as the lights blinked on throughout the pods, and she could feel warm air coming through the vents. She let her eyes close for a moment as she stood closer to a vent, letting the warmth waft over her like a blanket.

From somewhere down the chain of pods a hissing sound of radio static made its way towards her as another system came back online. Then an almost forgotten reminder from what seemed like another existence entirely suddenly filled the previously silent base.

```
This is the Wartime Broadcasting Service
from the BBC in London. This country has
been attacked with nuclear weapons. Com-
munications have been severely disrupted,
and the number of casualties and the extent
of the damage are not yet known. We shall
bring you further information as soon as
possible. Meanwhile, stay tuned to this
wavelength, stay calm and stay in your own
homes.
```

That voice. That almost-plummy-but-not-quite, middle class, Radio 4, supposedly calming and reassuring bloody voice. How she hated it. She was suddenly filled with rage: rage that this bastard, whoever he was, had sat in a nice cosy radio studio and read out this script, probably before walking off to have a lovely cup of tea. Rage that now she was the one, here, alone, at the ends of the earth having to listen to it. Rage that with every word, he reminded her that she was alone, that Adam was dead, so too her little Izzy, everyone she loved or had ever loved, everyone she had ever known. That she had left them all to come and do this. Left them to die in unimaginable pain and misery, while she had flown away to try to save the world. And this was her punishment for that endeavour: to sit alone for as long as she would survive, listening to this message over and over and over

271

again, knowing it was all gone, like she was trapped forever in an all too real purgatory.

Remember there is nothing to be gained by trying to get away. By leaving your homes you could be exposing yourselves to greater danger. If you leave, you may find yourself without food, without water, without accommodation and without protection.

She slammed the torch down with such force that it snapped open, its batteries clattering onto the floor and rolling away under the generator. But Rachael didn't notice: she was already marching back through the interconnected pods, searching for the source of her tormentor.

Radioactive fallout, which follows a nuclear explosion, is many times more dangerous if you are directly exposed to it in the open. Roofs and walls offer sub- stantial protection. The safest place is indoors.

It was coming from the communications room.

Make sure gas and other fuel supplies are turned off and that all fires are extinguished. If mains water is available, this can be used for fire-fighting. You should also refill all your containers for drinking water after the fires have been put out, because the mains water supply may not be available for very long.

She flung open the door so hard it slammed back against the wall. The room was no more than eight feet by six, with a wooden workbench running along the length of the wall opposite the door. Up above the bench were racks of radio equipment, next to shelves stacked end to end with ring binders. There was a desktop computer on the bench which was blinking into life as she walked in. Next to that on a smaller shelf was a VHF radio, the mic hung on a little hook, its black, coiled cable connecting it to the base unit, its dial glowing a dark yellow. Her eyes darted left and right as she tried to discover the source of the wretched voice.

```
Water must not be used for flushing
lavatories: until you are told that lav-
atories may be used again, other toilet
arrangements must be made. Use your water
only for essential drinking and cooking
purposes. Water means life. Don't waste
it.
```

The computer screen showed a log-in prompt, but Rachael was distracted by movement coming from one of the racks of radio equipment on the wall. She narrowed her eyes in confusion as she got closer. It was a tape cassette, its tiny wheels turning round and round as the voice droned on in its painfully familiar way.

```
Make your food stocks last: ration your
supply, because it may have to last for
fourteen days or more. If you have fresh
food in the house, use this first to avoid
wasting it: food in tins will keep. If you
live in an area where a fallout warning
```

```
has been given, stay in your fallout room
until you are told it is safe to come
out. When the immediate danger has passed
the sirens will sound a steady note.
```

She was sick to death of the voice and what it meant. She spied the radio with a hatred she'd only ever felt once before in her life, and cried out in almost physical pain as she tried to work out how to stop it. She searched the array of knobs, dials and buttons on the equipment, looking for a way to shut it up. In her fury she pressed anything she could see, any button that was available, she tried. She just wanted it to stop.

```
The 'all-clear' message will also be
given on this wavelength. Do not, in
any circumstances, go outside the house.
Radioactive fallout can kill. You cannot
see it or feel it, but it is there. If
you go outside, you will bring danger to
your family and you may die. Stay in your
fallout room until you are told it is safe
to come out or you hear the 'all-clear' on
the sirens.
```

She hit a spring-loaded button underneath the tape deck, and the cassette stopped dead.

And so did the voice.

Silence.

She frowned and took a step closer to the radio unit. There was a piece of masking tape stuck to the cassette with four words scrawled on it in bad handwriting. The writing was upside down. Rachael cocked her head to one side to try and read it, squinting as she brought her face as close to it as she could.

She read the words aloud slowly and deliberately: 'BBC NUCLEAR BROADCAST TAPE'.

Her mind raced. A tape? Of The Broadcast? But why? What did it mean? Wait . . . She frowned as the possibility began to dawn on her.

She saw Zak.

Now I am become death, the destroyer of worlds.

He was grinning at her from across the cockpit of the Snowcat.

I simply made him believe that there was no hope . . .

He couldn't have . . . could he?

. . . and that death was the only option left.

Her brain rushed over the details: *Zak* had packed the Snowcat before she'd set out for the Apple.

You're living in a simulated reality.

Zak had packed the VHF radio in the Snowcat. *Zak* had packed the satphone.

I was security for you, Rachael.

Her mind flashed to the image of Zak furiously rifling through her bag in the hut in the dead of night. She remembered the USB drive containing her research data. She patted her fleece pocket and felt its familiar shape safely stowed away.

I came to stop your research getting out.

She checked the log-in screen of the computer for the date: 4 August. She was surprised it wasn't later than that – she must have lost track of the date when she was alone at the hut. Though that was hardly surprising given there was no sunrise or sunset to mark the passing of the days – and she wasn't at full mental sharpness either. She remembered Guy's imperative to her: 'You must get the data to Pilbeam by August sixth. He'll do the rest.'

I was here to make sure your findings never made it to that vote.

She saw Henriksen's naked body in the snow, the lifeless blue eyes.

Suicide is cleaner.

She saw faces: Guy's, Izzy's and Adam's. She remembered how close she'd come to walking out of One Ton Hut and to her death.

Out here? In this cold? This darkness? This isolation? Anyone could lose their marbles and do themselves in.

Oh my God.

Now I am become death, the destroyer of worlds.

Could he really have pulled this off? Had he really done it? Had he taken away everything she cared about – taken away her whole life, destroyed her world? Had he taken away every reason she had to live? Isolated her and then played her that message over and over and over again to drive her to her death?

I was security for you, Rachael.

Could it be true? Could Adam and Izzy still be out there?

Now I am become death, the destroyer of worlds.

The VHF radio unit on the shelf hummed with static. As she reached out for the mic, her hand was shaking. She lifted it to her mouth, pressed the transmit button and spoke into it, her voice trembling. 'McMurdo, this is Station Z, do you read, over?'

The radio fuzzed and crackled. And then she heard a voice. 'This is McMurdo. Go ahead Station Z. We read you.'

Acknowledgements

I can't remember exactly when I first seriously attempted to write a novel, but I know it's well over a decade ago and that my first few efforts were predictably well wide of the mark.

It was in the middle yet another attempt at redrafting my first book when I was struck with the idea for *Whiteout*, after I came across the text – now declassified – of the actual radio announcement that would have been broadcast to the UK population in the event of a nuclear attack during the Cold War.

The business-like 'keep calm and carry on' tone of it fascinated me, given the terror and devastation those listening to it would be experiencing.

The focus of most post-apocalyptic novels and films I'd come across was usually what happens in the big cities – it's more visually impactful, I guess, to show these usually teeming places in panic mode and then deserted. But I started to think what it would be like to hear that emergency broadcast when you were already entirely cut off from the rest of the world.

I'd always thought the Antarctic was the perfect place to set a thriller – and suddenly the two things came together in my head, and the genesis for *Whiteout* was born.

I began jotting down a plot in my notebook – it was one of

those joyful and all-too rare moments when you're scribbling frantically because the ideas are coming so fast that you're terrified they will disappear before you can get them all down.

Over the course of actually writing the book much has changed from that first scribbled outline – but a surprising amount has remained, and the plot is essentially the same. And I still haven't got around to reworking the novel I put on hold to write this one.

My thanks go to my wonderful agent Jemima Forrester who took a chance on me and was a huge champion of the book from the get-go. Thanks also to everyone at David Higham who has been involved since Jemima signed me up.

I will be forever grateful to my editor Morgan Springett for believing in the book and working so hard to knock it into shape, along with everyone else at HarperCollins who has been integral to taking *Whiteout* from draft to the finished article.

I must also thank Eve Seymour for her excellent and always brutally honest writing advice over the years – and for her encouragement on *Whiteout* in particular.

Thanks also to Veronica for introducing me to a book that helped inspire this one (I only wish you had had the chance to read *Whiteout*), to my sister Emma for some invaluable advice about parenting and young children, and my brother Jib for the Pink Floyd.

Finally, I must make an apology to any readers who have lived and worked in the Antarctic. I did as much research as I could, but I know I will have got plenty of things wrong about the experience. The errors are all mine – which I hope one day to correct if I ever get the chance to visit the frozen continent myself.